HOSTILE WATERS

WILLIAM NIKKEL

SUSPENSE PUBLISHING

HOSTILE WATERS
By
William Nikkel

PAPERBACK EDITION
* * * * *
PUBLISHED BY:
Suspense Publishing

COPYRIGHT
2019 by William Nikkel

Cover Design: Shannon Raab
Cover Photographer: iStockphoto.com/Biletskiy_Evgeniy

PUBLISHING HISTORY:
Suspense Publishing, Print and Digital Copy, December 2019

ISBN: 978-0-578-57447-9

OTHER BOOKS BY WILLIAM NIKKEL

Jack Ferrell Series
GLIMMER OF GOLD
NIGHT MARCHERS
CAVE DWELLER
MURRIETTA GOLD
BLOOD GOLD
SHIPWRECK
SAILOR TAKE WARNING
SEA OF HEARTBREAK

Max Traver Series
DEVIL WIND
DANCE WITH THE DEVIL

Novellas
TIBETAN GOLD

AUTHOR'S DISCLAIMER

Hostile Waters contains the actual names of people and places. The same is true for certain businesses and bars frequented by Jack Ferrell, Robert, Cherise, and Lindsey.

In all other respects, this novel is a work of fiction. Names (unless used by permission), characters, places, and incidents in the story are either the product of the author's imagination or are used fictitiously. Any resemblance to actual persons, events, or locals is unintentional and coincidental.

To my wife, always.

ACKNOWLEDGEMENTS

While my imagination inspired this novel, the contributions of people around me brought the story to life. First and foremost, a big thank you goes to my wife Karen for her invaluable suggestions. And especially for her support and understanding during the writing of the story and the many hours I spent at the computer. Also to my brother Ray for his colorful story ideas, Jim Jackson for his input, and Ruth Horne for her editorial advice. And a special note of appreciation to Kathy Takushi, the owner of Captivating Journeys, for her time and advice. Of course, no novel would be read without a publisher bringing the story to light. A big thank you to Shannon Raab, her husband John, and her team at Suspense Publishing for the wonderful work they do. As always, all errors in the book, of which I hope there are few, rest solely with me.

PRAISE FOR
HOSTILE WATERS

"Adventure, mystery, and solidly written characters—*Hostile Waters* has it all. Willie Nikkel's experience with law enforcement and human conflict shines through. Terrific stuff."
 —Marc Cameron, *New York Times* Bestselling Author

"I've been a fan of William Nikkel since his first *Jack Ferrell* story—but *Hostile Waters* was pure dynamite, a blast of big-fisted action, a rollicking treasure hunt involving Mayan treasures and lost rare manuscripts. If you're looking for adventure with a capital A, pick this up, batten down those hatches, and get ready for a great read!"
 —James Rollins, #1 *New York Times* Bestselling Author of
Crucible

"A tantalizing premise, engaging characters, and a plot to savor. It's a wonderful piece of pure entertainment."
 —Steve Berry, International Bestselling Author of *The Malta Exchange*

"A wave-tossed wild ride. Warm up your page-turning fingers. You're going to need them."
 —Grant Blackwood, #1 *New York Times* Bestselling Author

"There is no friend as loyal as a book."
—Ernest Hemingway

HOSTILE WATERS

WILLIAM NIKKEL

Spring Into Danger

A Paula Savard Mystery

Susan Calder

Print ISBNs
BWL Print 9780228625568
LSI Print 9780228625582
Amazon Print 9780228625575

BWL Publishing Inc.

Books we love to write ...
Authors around the world.

http://bwlpublishing.ca

PROLOGUE

Sam King kept to the rutted path, thick foliage closing in on him from both sides. The remoteness of the location gave him pause, as though he had been led into a trap. An absence of bird sounds added to his tension. He never should have agreed to come along.

But Corey insisted they had nothing to worry about. Sam knew better. There were always dangers to be concerned about. In the city or in the jungle. Still, he couldn't ignore the curiosity that brought him to the fringes of what had once been a center of Mayan culture.

Even if it meant risking his life.

He swiped away the sweat streaking his face. "You sure you have your directions, right?"

Corey peered over his shoulder at Sam and said, "Relax. Belize is a tourist mecca. It's developed into one of the premier dive locations in the world."

"That doesn't mean where we're going is safe."

"Lighten up. We're here."

Sam stopped and studied the peeling exterior of the whitewashed structure, little more than a board shack, sitting in a small clearing carved out of what appeared to be an impenetrable tropical forest. He had ventured through the remotest parts of Africa and never once experienced the dread he sensed in this place. Possibly because of the nature of their business here. Or perhaps the presence of ghosts from an ancient civilization.

He held back a moment longer. But his nerves refused to settle. Even with calming reassurances.

The hut glared at him as though daring him to step closer. The one window visible from the path had been draped with a swatch of filthy cloth. Movement of the curtain drew his attention.

The hair on his neck and arms bristled.

"Not what I'd call hospitable looking."

Corey tossed a glance over his shoulder. "You worry too much. Come on."

"I still think I was foolish allowing you to talk me into this." Sam fell in stride and followed Corey to the door.

"Your tune will change in a minute," Corey said.

Sam kept an eye on the window. "I'm not so sure."

Corey knocked on the weathered entryway. His chuckle didn't help ease the tension.

The door creaked opened in mid-knock, held in place by a beefy man maybe in his mid-thirties dressed in denim pants and a t-shirt that could have been white at one time. The man at the window, Sam guessed. He'd had a feeling he and Corey were being watched from the moment they were within sight of the shack.

Now, he was certain they had.

"Juan is expecting me," Corey said.

The man scanned them up and down, then stepped back permitting them to enter.

Sam took a deep breath and followed Corey inside. Nothing more had been said by the two men. A couple of steps beyond the doorway, Corey paused.

In for a penny, in for a pound.

Sam needed no further encouragement. He had come too far to turn back now. Having been momentarily blinded by the bright sunlight outside, he let his eyes adjust to the dimly lit interior. The room came into view.

And with it an increased sense of dread.

A simply-dressed man seated behind a wooden table not much larger than a student's school desk, studied him from the center of the floor. An armed thug stood in the gloom a half dozen steps behind him. The rail-thin man sitting at the table looked to be about forty. He had leather brown skin, cold dark eyes, and thick, curly black hair. A low-wattage light bulb screwed into the top of a simple bare table lamp illuminated his face and the object in front of him.

"This is Juan Perez," Corey said to Sam when Juan rose to his feet. "He's the guy I brought you here to meet."

Confusion furrowed Sam's brow. He hadn't realized he'd actually been brought there to *meet* someone in the way Corey had put it. Merely to accompany him while he made a purchase.

Sam offered his hand out of politeness. "Nice to meet you, Mr. Perez. I'm Corey's friend Sam King."

"I also am pleased to meet you." Juan gripped Sam's hand with surprising strength. "Now let us get on with our business."

"The gold idols," Corey said. "You brought them?"

Juan unfolded a stained coarse-weave muslin cloth sitting on the tabletop in front of him. "They are everything I said they were, are they not?"

Corey leaned close and smiled at the antiquities lying before him.

Sam felt himself drawn in by the crude attractiveness of the three graven images staring up from the table. His hand trembled as he fought the urge to run his fingertips over the ancient craftsmanship.

"Magnificent, indeed," Corey said. He looked at Sam. "What do you think?"

Sam stared at the gold figurines. All distinctly male. Not the beautiful, soft flowing lines of voluptuous love goddesses. They were squat, round-bellied effigies with wide-open clown-like mouths, looped ear lobes, and a fringed cap or crown. Each one similar but not identical. Quite ugly in his opinion. But the idols were Pre-Columbian and over four inches tall. That made the artifacts unique and valuable far beyond their gold content, regardless of purity.

That's what Corey told him. And he had no reason not to believe his friend.

If the guy knew the truth.

He leaned close to Corey and spoke in hushed tones. "You're sure these are authentic? I mean, even if they're gold, they could be fake."

Corey whispered back, "The pieces are authentic. Guaranteed.

And solid gold worth at least sixty thousand apiece to the right buyer in the States."

"But how can you be sure?"

"I've bought antiquities from Juan before. And they've always proved genuine and brought top dollar."

Sam couldn't quell his apprehension. The heat inside the shack, heavy and thick with humidity, only added to his discomfort. Overhead, the slow moving fan circulated the hot air but did little to bring even a hint of freshness to the stale room. Beads of sweat trickled down his neck.

Once again, he studied the idols.

And again, he felt them stare back at him through empty eyes.

"If that's the case"—he looked at Corey—"why is he offering the set to you for fifty thousand?"

"Do you have to ask?"

"I'd kind of like to know. Are they stolen?"

"Let me put it to you this way. We don't ask and Juan doesn't say."

"What about US Customs? You have to declare items you bring into the States. And I'm sure even a small country like this has strict laws against this sort of thing. You could be locked away in prison for a long time."

"Not if a person knows what he's doing."

"You sound convinced." Sam studied the artifacts. "So you're going through with the deal?"

"I want to in the worst way." Corey sighed. "Unfortunately, I don't have that kind of cash readily available. I'd have to move some investments around—probably be a month or more before I'd be in a position to buy the set."

"Didn't you know that coming here?"

"Artifacts like these don't come along often. The way each piece was described to me, I had to see the set for myself. Call it curiosity."

The same thing that brought me here.

Sam understood completely. But he wasn't fooled.

He searched Corey's eyes for answers. "Surely you're not thinking I could loan the money to you?"

"Actually. I thought *you* might be interested in purchasing them. Trust me. Pieces like this are an exceptional find. Someone will snatch them up in a hurry."

Sam struggled with the belief the artifacts would be secreted away and locked inside the vault of a collector of rare and unusual antiquities. One man's obsession robbing the world of precious pieces of ancient Mayan culture.

He suppressed a shudder of disgust.

Relics this unique belonged in a museum.

"I do have another buyer," Juan Perez said. His dark eyes flicked back and forth betraying an eagerness to conclude the sale. His gaze settled on Corey. "Since you and I have done business before, I offered these superb pieces to you first. But if you are not interested, and your friend isn't—"

"I didn't say that." Sam looked at Corey and saw him smiling.

Juan nodded. "Then we have a deal?"

CHAPTER 1

Jack Ferrell lay sprawled on his back on the forward bunk. Beyond the portholes along the hull, the sky glowed orange with the setting sun. His thoughts wandered with the last rays of the day.

He had rented his colleague's fifty foot sloop with the intent of spending a week with Cherise Venetta—the woman who had saved his life more than once—sailing the Northwest Hawaiian Islands. And it had already been three.

No bullets. No one's life on the line.

Time to mend the soul.

They both deserved the break.

Cherise stepped into the open hatchway beyond the foot of the bed, the setting sun in full glory bathed her naked body in a golden glow that rendered him speechless. Her black hair, slick with moisture, hung limp below her shoulders. Droplets of seawater dappled her bronzed skin and ran in rivulets around her bare breasts and across her flat stomach. A single tattoo of an anchor and chain no more than an inch square, adorned the curvature of her waist near the left hip. A subtle souvenir from the years she spent in the Navy.

He had no such memento from his work as a marine biologist. Only a deep tan and a handful of scars.

Propping himself up on his elbow, he asked, "Did you enjoy your swim?"

She stepped toward him with a mischievous grin he had seen a hundred times during their trip. It usually resulted in him being the loser.

She said, "You should have joined me."

"Why is that?"

"Then I wouldn't have had to do this."

"Don't—"

He reached, but not fast enough to stop her from shaking her head and peppering him with cold drops of water.

"You're a she-devil," he said. "Do you know that?"

"Couldn't resist. Besides, you bring out the best in me."

"So I noticed."

He fell back on the bed and laced his fingers behind his head and watched her sit cross-legged next to him without drying herself or showing a hint of self-consciousness. Her smile slipped, and he noticed her glance at her hands fidgeting in her lap before settling her gaze on him.

He peered into her dark eyes waiting to hear what she had on her mind. What she found difficult to say. He had a feeling he knew what it was.

Thinking back on the past few days, he had noticed a vague tension building, causing her to become moody and less content to while away the hours lounging on the beach. It was as though she felt their time together had come to an end.

Something he had sensed as well.

The danger he and Cherise faced on Oahu two months earlier when they took down the drug dealer Yang Li, had brought them to the solitude of these uninhabited islands. That same devotion to her work drew her back to the real world.

"I'm a good listener," he said. "If you need to talk about something that's bothering you."

He gave her time.

"I guess it shows," she said after a moment. "You and I here in paradise these past weeks, it's all been very wonderful. But I'm anxious to get back to work."

"What you're saying is you're ready to raise anchor and set sail?"

She laid her cool hand on his bare leg. Her eyes searched his in a silent plea for understanding. "It's not you, you know that?"

He smiled. "I'm sure I would've known if that was the case."

"Then you're okay with heading back?"

He had his own reality waiting for him. Buying a boat to replace *Pono* that lay in pieces on the bottom of Ala Wai Boat Harbor in Waikiki. His research with NOAA. The director of The National Oceanic and Atmospheric Administration had been gracious in allowing him time away from his work.

Meg Roberts would be glad to once again have him at the agency's disposal.

"Absolutely," he said. "This atoll we're on now is only a couple hundred miles northwest of Oahu. We'll leave first thing in the morning. Given a favorable wind, a following sea, and a touch of good fortune, we'll be in around midnight. And it's not because I haven't enjoyed every minute with you. Is that okay?"

"That will work fine."

Work fine . . .

That wasn't the response he expected. "You talk like you already have a job waiting for you."

She turned a sheepish eye on him. "This afternoon when you went for a swim, I talked to Susan on the satellite phone. She told me a friend of mine, Lindsey Taylor, left a message for me."

"You called your answering service."

"Susan does more for me than take messages."

"No surprise there," he said. "To work for you, she'd have to have a multitude of talents. What did Susan have to say?"

"Lindsey has a problem and, according to her, I'm the only person left she can turn to for help."

"Did she say what the problem is?"

"Susan asked, but Lindsey wouldn't tell her, saying she'd wait and talk to me. That's Lindsey."

She had his attention. "Just how close of a friend is this Lindsey person?"

"I met her while working for Black Water. She was Army, a Spc. 4, drove trucks at Bagram Air Base in Afghanistan. At the time, there weren't a lot of women at the base so we naturally gravitated together—spent a lot of time in the gym. You can imagine how it was for us there. We still keep in touch, mainly on holidays."

"Makes sense why you want to help her."

"There's more to it. She took a sniper's bullet in the thigh that was intended for me."

"Serious?"

"Enough to get her sent home."

"So this is personal?"

"Very. I owe her."

"She as pretty as you are?"

"No shortage of men chasing her, if that's what you mean."

"How about a husband? She married?"

"She was . . . to a real abusive sonofabitch. I offered to kick his ass but she chose divorce instead. The offer still stands if he ever fucks with her."

He could see her doing that. "Does the asshole know what he's in store for?"

She smiled. "Of course he does. I told him in no uncertain terms."

"You don't suppose he's the problem Lindsey wants to talk about, do you?"

"Doubtful."

"I have to agree. Especially with your threat hanging over his head." He shrugged. "Guess you'll find out soon enough."

CHAPTER 2

Jack raised anchor and scanned the sky. A pale blue swath in the east showed the first hint of sunrise that lay an hour away. The full moon still large and bright hung low on the western horizon. He felt good getting the boat underway. Cherise felt good about returning to Oahu as well. That was obvious from the jaunty tune she whistled. They both had lives to get back to.

She emerged from below carrying an earthen mug in each hand. "Coffee for the road?" she asked, handing him one. "Or should I say waves?"

He grinned. "Why not."

Nineteen hours later, he motored *Sun Dancer* into Honolulu Harbor at eleven forty-five. A favorable wind and a surprisingly smooth sea allowed them to make good time. He glanced toward where he last saw *The Sea Nymph*. Yang Li's hundred and five foot yacht was no longer moored there. Gone, along with the corpses he and Cherise left behind.

The vessel had been seized by the feds, he was sure. The bodies long buried.

He carried no guilt for the men's deaths.

No regrets.

The choice had been theirs.

"Looks better without that pretentious pig's boat sitting there," Cherise said, nodding toward the empty dock. "I wonder what the

DEA did with it?"

"Cleaned her up and auctioned her off, I imagine."

"A few million more for the war chest against drugs. Too bad you weren't part of the bidding. Would have made a nice boat to conduct your research from."

He shot her a sideways glance. "I liked my old boat."

She scoffed. "The one sitting on the bottom of the Ala Wai Boat Harbor."

He had tried without success to not think about Ali or *Pono*. Or Anna. Cherise's comment rubbed salt into the wound. But he couldn't hold what she had said against her. She had been the right kind of medicine when he needed it most.

As he had been for her.

An escape from everything and everyone.

And now reality ushered them back to the lives they had briefly left behind.

He cut the power to *Sun Dancer*'s engine and let the fifty foot sloop drift the last few feet into her slip.

"Tie us off," he called out as he hurried forward.

Cherise hopped onto the pier and held out her hands. "Ready when you are."

He tossed her the bow line and he rushed astern to secure the aft mooring line. The bumpers he'd draped over the side of the hull fore and aft gently nudged the edge of the dock.

"We made good time," he said, adding a final cinch onto the turn cleat. "It's not even midnight yet."

She joined him, fatigue showing in her expression. "In case you forgot, we got an early start."

He sighed, giving way to the weariness threatening to drag him down. "You still plan on flying out in the morning?"

"I talked to Admiral Casey. I'll be hitching a ride on a C-17 to Travis Air Force Base in California. From there, I'll fly commercial to New York and find out what has Lindsey all worked up."

He raked his fingers through his windblown hair. The time they spent together had passed in a blur with few bad moments. He wouldn't kid himself thinking he was perfect. Far from it. Neither was she. But they were good for each other. He felt it. And the uncertainty of a future with her left him saddened.

A melancholy he couldn't keep out of his voice.

"You know I'll be there for you like a shot if you need my help."

"I realize that. And I'll certainly keep it in mind."

He took a deep breath, accepting the inevitable, and let it out. "Then this is our last night together."

She smiled, but her eyes betrayed a similar sadness. "Until next time, sailor."

* * *

At five the following morning, Jack hugged and kissed Cherise in a farewell embrace he didn't want to have end. When finally she pulled away, he helped her into the taxi taking her to Hickam Air Force Base at Pearl Harbor. The driver sped away with her, his hand inches from the door.

He stepped back and watched her go. He'd seen her at her best, strong-willed and confident. But there also existed a chink in her armor that exposed a soft underbelly of vulnerability that oftentimes left her emotional, craving reassurance. A backward glance from her through the rear window of the fleeting cab tugged at his heart more than he could have imagined.

She had been there for him. Now it was his turn.

He held her gaze until her eyes were no longer visible, and stared a few seconds longer. For now, he'd have to be content to hold onto the memory of the three glorious weeks they'd spent together. She had her life to get back to, and he had his.

Vacation was over.

He spent the better part of the next hour tidying up *Sun Dancer*. Cherise had completed most of the cleaning and straightening on the way into port, which simplified the process for him. When he felt the boat had been transformed back into its pristine condition, he placed a phone call to Robert. No doubt he would be surprised. They hadn't talked in nearly a month.

"The wayward travelers return," Robert answered.

"Midnight last night," Jack said. "How's the gut doing?"

"Good as new."

"Do you miss your appendix? Any separation anxiety?"

"We were never that close. Where are you?"

"Honolulu Harbor getting things squared away with *Sun Dancer*. I'll grab a cab and see you at the house in an hour."

"Don't bother. I'll pick you up."

"There's no need for you to make a special trip."

"Forget it. I'm on my way. Kazuko is off island and I'm bored. You can buy me breakfast."

"She working?"

"A NOAA conference in Monterey. You were invited but you were off with Cherise playing patty-cake. And speaking of Cherise, I take it she's off doing whatever it is she does?"

"You know what she does."

"If you ask me, that pretty much remains a mystery."

"Are you going to be this cranky all day?"

"Breakfast will help."

"Then get your ass over here. I'll get us a table at Tiny's. You know the place. Or have you forgotten?"

"Asshole. I'll see you there in driving time."

Jack punched off and smiled. It felt good to be back.

He checked the time. Made a call to *Sun Dancer*'s owner and settled up with him. Then he walked in the direction of the diner, taking his time.

Cherise was on a military transport five miles high over the Pacific, speeding back to her world. He thought about her friend Lindsey's phone call and wondered what that was all about.

Whatever the problem, Cherise could handle it.

That's what she does.

CHAPTER 3

The early-morning crowd had thinned inside Tiny's restaurant. Jack took a seat at a table and ordered coffee. He'd eat when Robert got there. He had taken his first sip when Robert walked in.

"Cup of Joe," Robert said to the waiter.

"No breakfast?" Jack asked. "On the phone you said you were hungry."

"Thought I might be. I ate early." Robert took a seat. "You go ahead."

The waiter set Robert's cup in front of him and filled it from a glass pot. "Anything else?"

"The three-egg special," Jack said. "Over easy. Hash browns and sausage cooked crisp. Gravy on the side."

"Since he's buying," Robert added, "I'll have the same. Only scrambled, no gravy."

Jack raised a brow. "Thought you already had your breakfast?"

"More of a pre-breakfast, actually. And that was a couple of hours ago. And a man *can* change his mind."

"You seem to be in a mood."

"Boredom does that to me."

"So this is about you being bored?"

"Something like that." He handed Jack an envelope. "That arrived a couple of weeks ago. You're settlement check for *Pono*, I imagine. Have you given any thought to a new boat?"

"A little." Jack folded the envelope and slid it into his back pocket.

"Well, I've been doing a lot of thinking for you."

"That's what friends are for."

Jack couldn't get Cherise out of his mind. By now she was well out over the Pacific. Flying five miles up. A cold, hard sea below her. An uncertain future ahead. Her friend Lindsey.

What's that all about?

He had to wonder.

"Are you hearing me?" Robert's voice brought him back.

"Sorry. My mind wandered."

"Cherise. You really like her, don't you?"

He didn't have to think about his answer. Not even for a second. He felt good having spent time alone with her . . . extremely good. And relaxed. She proved to be excellent medicine.

"There's chemistry," he answered. "You were talking about me finding a new boat. That means you've been on the internet."

"So what if I have?"

Still surly.

Jack hoped the food arrived soon. "So what did you find?"

"You remember Hurricane Irma?"

"Puerto Rico is still recovering from that one."

"So are the Keys. There's a fifty-eight-foot power cat in Key West that I think you ought to take a look at. I found out about it through a friend, not the internet."

"A friend, you say?"

"No one you know. More of a business associate, really. His company is helping with the reconstruction effort in the Keys."

"And you think I should set aside my plans and fly to Key West and check out this boat you were told about?"

"Not just you," Robert met his gaze and held it. "Us."

Jack chuckled. "You really are bored."

Robert straightened in his seat. "This has nothing to do with me being bored. I just think this might be an opportunity too good for you to pass up. And knowing you, it'd be good if I tagged along to offer a second opinion."

"Your two-cent's worth?"

"That's right."

Their food arrived and Robert asked, "What do you think?"

Jack spooned gravy onto his hash browns and set the bowl aside. "I'm thinking this could work out in more ways than one. It would also give me a chance to talk to Doctor Goddard at the aquarium there. I sent him data I compiled on reef deterioration and its effect on apex predators, but haven't had an opportunity to discuss my findings with him. Tell me about this boat you think so highly of."

Robert pulled a folded sheet of paper from his pocket, and handed it to Jack. "That's a picture of her. You can tell by the scratches on her hull she took some minor hits in the storm, but she's sound."

Jack studied the printout. "Nice power cat. Reminds me of *Pono* in a way."

"She's better than nice. And she's every bit the boat *Pono* was, and more. The *Adeona* is fifty-eight feet long and built for global exploration. A thirty-foot beam that makes her ultra-stable, two queen master staterooms, one queen aft stateroom, guest quarters with bunkbeds, four heads. She has a twenty-three knot top speed, seventeen knot fast cruise, and a ten knot trawler cruise with a range of eleven thousand miles. Exactly what you need."

"That's a lot of fuel."

"Thirty-eight hundred gallons." Robert grinned. "But that's the best part. You won't have to fill the tank more than once a year."

"What's the asking price?"

"Eight hundred and twenty-five thousand. A real steal."

"If she's everything you claim she is, that's cheap for a boat like her."

"That's what makes this such a sweet deal. The *Adeona* underwent a survey six months ago. Her value is listed at a million three-hundred thousand with a replacement cost of three million seven-hundred and fifty thousand."

"So why is she for sale?"

"The *Adeona*—named after the pre-Roman Goddess of safe and speedy returns—belongs to a former Italian model, Violetta Faggini. Her husband Antonio had the yacht custom built for her. They'd been visiting in Cuba and made the crossing to Key West. Which is where they were when Hurricane Irma hit. Antonio suffered a stroke at the height of the storm. Too much for him, I guess. Left him pretty bad off. He had been living in a medical rehabilitation center in Miami until a couple of weeks ago when the poor man suffered a second stroke and died. Now Violetta can't bring herself to step back aboard the *Adeona*. The memories are just too painful for her to bear."

"I suppose you were up on your Roman mythology and knew all about the goddess Adeona?"

Robert leaned back in his chair. "To tell you the truth, I had to look it up."

"Thought so." Jack gave serious consideration to Robert's opinion of the deal. "And Ms. Faggini will let her go for eight hundred and twenty-five thousand?"

"Only we can't waste time getting there. Not counting today, we have a two-day window to pull the deal together—no later than the twelfth. Hemingway Days officially kick off on the fifteenth. Ms. Faggini wants to have her business concluded and be out of town by this weekend, before the place is overrun with partygoers and drunks. If you're not interested, she'll list it through a broker and the price will go up significantly."

"Will you allow me time to shower and change clothes?"

"You can even finish your breakfast."

"You're a kind man, Robert." Jack forked up a large bite of hash browns.

"You might want to rethink that being kind part," Robert said. "Our flight leaves in three hours."

CHAPTER 4

Cherise crossed her arms, leaned against the bulkhead, and closed her eyes in a mental attempt to block out the annoying vibration and tedious drone of the jet engines. Mind over matter for the next five and a half hours.

Piece of cake.

Short of being in the air and speeding toward her destination, traveling by military transport did not compare, even remotely, to a flight on a commercial airliner. None of the amenities civilian travelers take for granted aboard a plane were available. No smiling flight attendant to see to a passenger's needs. No in-flight cocktails. No movie. Only an uncomfortable web seat and a noisy fuselage.

Not her first time.

And the flight could be worse.

The C-17, though loud in its own right, was far quieter than the C-130s she had flown in during her tour in Afghanistan. She also appreciated having the use of a flush toilet instead of a honey bucket sitting behind a curtain on the cargo ramp.

Whoever adopted that modification deserved a medal.

Perhaps Admiral Casey could make that happen.

He made a lot happen.

The arm of the uniformed soldier sitting in the seat next to hers, brushed against her in a shudder of turbulence that jolted the C-17 as though the plane had been struck by Thor's hammer.

She glanced at the man out of the corner of her eye. Army. Large framed. His big hands rested in his lap, a paperback novel spread open between them. Two other uniformed personnel sat next to him. Air Force. One male. One female. Young stoic expressions. Their thoughts directed inward.

Not unlike herself at that age.

A time when her entire military career lay ahead of her.

She closed her eyes and relaxed against the nylon webbing of the seatback. In spite of the discomfort, she harbored no complaints about her flight accommodations. It had been enough that the admiral had gotten her aboard the transport at such short notice.

A courtesy that saved her from sitting idle at the airport on standby waiting for a seat to open up on a commercial flight.

Wasted hours she needed to avoid.

Time, she felt, was of the essence.

She thought about the conversation she had with Lindsey when they last spoke on the phone to each other. How was she then? Living in New York and working at the United Nations. Still single. And happy she had connected with her biological father. She and Lindsey had warmed to each other immediately as though they had never been apart.

But how long ago was that?

Too many months.

No, years.

Cherise felt bad for having allowed so much time to slip by. Her regret made worse by Lindsey's phone call for help.

A plea Cherise wasn't taking lightly.

The last communication she had with Susan was an exchange of texts prior to take off. Susan sounded glad to have her back. There had been no further contact on Lindsey's part.

Cherise could only wonder why.

The phone call she'd made to Lindsey from Hickam had gone unanswered. So had the text message she sent. She tried not to read anything into the failed attempts to reach her. There could have been a multitude of reasons for her not answering the call. Not all of them bad. Only now Cherise would have to wait until she touched down at Travis before she could try again. Until then, she had plenty of time to wonder what had happened to cause her friend to reach out to her for help.

And why am I her last *resort?*

CHAPTER 5

Jack settled into a first-class window seat aboard Delta's eleven-fifteen flight to Orlando. A relaxing first leg of the trip, though he remained skeptical of its outcome.

"You really think this deal is that good?"

Robert buckled himself into the aisle seat. "Too good not to at least take a look at her. And if the boat doesn't work out, we'll get to spend a few days in Key West. Perhaps this time around, we'll be able to take in the Hemingway Days celebration."

The aisle filled with passengers inching their way to coach.

Jack tugged his seatbelt tight across his lap, relieved to be sitting up front. "Something tells me you had these seats reserved."

"For a couple of weeks," Robert said. "I scheduled the flight hoping you'd return in time. After tomorrow, it would have been a moot point. We'd never have made it by the twelfth."

"So we hit the decks running, so to speak?"

"Allowing for the time change, we arrive tomorrow morning at five-twenty. We'll grab our bags, catch an Air Taxi, and be in Key West by nine."

"Gee, an entire day to make up my mind."

"Don't forget. I'll be along to help."

"That's what worries me. Seems your mind is already made up."

"It's still your money."

Jack leaned his head back and closed his eyes. "And my decision to make."

* * *

At eight-fifty the next morning, seated inside the Cirrus SR22 Air Taxi on approach to Key West International, Jack peered out the window at an endless expanse of deep-blue Gulf water. Boats powered and under sail left a frothy white 'V' of foam in a wake behind them as they cut a path through the water.

"Seems like we were just here."

Robert kept his face turned to his window. "Doesn't feel like it's been five years. But it has."

The plane touched down smoothly with a minor shriek of its tires and settled onto the runway. Jack climbed out of the plane and waited for their bags to be unloaded while Robert headed for the car rental counter.

Fifteen minutes later, Robert led the way to a red and white Mini Cooper with a roof rack. Jack shook his head. "Talk about déjà vu."

"Be glad there's only two of us this time."

"Still, you could have picked a car with more leg room." Jack slid the seat all the way back and wedged himself in.

Robert grinned. "Small town, small car."

Jack forced a chuckle. "Heard that before."

On the way to One Duval Street, Robert said, "I reserved us a suite at the Pier House. Ms. Faggini has a room there as well and is expecting us. We'll dump our bags and let her know we've arrived."

"She'll be conducting the tour?"

"A cousin is in town to help reconcile her affairs. He'll take us aboard the *Adeona*. But any questions we have, will be answered by Ms. Faggini or a Mr. Noel A. Wilson, AMS—Wilson Marine Surveying & Consulting—who surveyed the boat."

"AMS—Accredited Marine Surveyors. So we'll be getting a reputable report?"

"That would be my guess."

"Then there's no reason to wait," Jack said. "We flew a long way to have a look at her. Let's get it done."

They met Ms. Faggini's cousin in the bar at ten. Ms. Faggini had given them his name, Salvatore Vincente, and described him as tall, fit, and handsome, with short dark hair. Jack had no trouble picking him out of the dozen or so customers. Robert made the introductions and they shook hands.

"We understand you will be taking us aboard the boat," Jack said.

Salvatore handed them each a bound sheaf of papers as thick and heavy as a major department store catalogue. "If you look at the specs, you'll see the *Adeona* is more than just an ordinary boat."

Jack thumbed through the pages which consisted of the recent survey report, a comprehensive maintenance history, and a complete set of operator's manuals. More reading than he could do in a week.

He scanned the general-information page of the survey report: 2008 Tennant New Yorker; twin four hundred and fifty horsepower Volvo Penta six-cylinder in-line diesel engines, with two hundred and thirty-five original hours on each; length fifty eight and a half feet; beam thirty feet. Nodding his approval, he noted the additional convenience of oversized fresh water tanks. A must in his mind. He finished the list with a feeling the prior owner had spared no expense. On paper the *Adeona* was everything Robert made her out to be and more.

"Impressive," he said. "Shall we take a look at her?"

"If you'll follow me."

They stepped aboard a Boston Whaler dinghy. Salvatore started the twenty-five horsepower Mercury outboard and put them on a course for Key West Bight. A short ride of two or three minutes. There were a lot of large and small boats sitting at anchor. Even so, having seen the photo of *Adeona*, Jack had no trouble spotting her.

He had been around enough yachts to not be easily impressed. Still, he liked the look of this one . . . even from a distance.

They boarded by way of the stern. Steps molded into the fiberglass hulls. Not unlike *Pono*. But she had a wider beam by several feet. Jack liked that feature.

"My kind of boat," Robert said, peering in through a window.

Jack wasn't sold on her yet. "We'll see."

They entered the richly equipped salon through the rear hatchway. A large dining booth with plenty of seating to starboard.

A more than adequate galley to port. Granite countertops. A lot of polished hardwood. He made a careful inspection of the aft compartment before continuing on. Robert followed close behind him, refraining from comment.

A hatchway with three steps leading up, separated the salon from the forward cabin. A corner sofa sat to port with the main control console located to starboard. Directly next to the helm, a watertight door provided access to the outside deck. He examined the controls, gauges, and the ship's electronics. So far *Adeona* appeared every bit a fine vessel. He wanted to see below.

He moved quickly through the staterooms and the adjoining heads to port and starboard. Everything spotless. He led them back into the forward cabin.

"Is she not beautiful?" Salvatore asked.

"She is that," Jack said. "I'd like to see up top."

They climbed the steps to a hatch that opened up onto a spacious upper deck with patio furniture and a swing-out winch for stowing the dinghy. Forward of that sat the topside controls. He walked directly to the panel, unsnapped the waterproof cover, and examined the levers and instruments. Pleased when he found them polished and free of corrosion. The closed and open radar arrays and weather antenna were mounted on an arch over his head. A ladder led up to an observation platform forward the arch.

He turned to Salvatore. "The *Adeona* is quite nice. And I'm extremely interested in purchasing her if everything checks out. I'd like to speak with Ms. Faggini and arrange for a test run."

"You have the survey report." Salvatore pointed to the packet in Jack's hands. "I assure you everything is in perfect working order."

Jack shot a glance at Robert, got a nod in return, and looked at Salvatore. "It's still an eleven-year-old boat. If something is going to go wrong with her, it'll go wrong at sea."

"I understand."

"It's almost noon. Perhaps we can talk over lunch."

Salvatore motioned aft. "I suggest we go."

CHAPTER 6

Cherise fought fatigue as she approached the baggage carousel inside New York's La Guardia Airport. Too many hours in the air, with too little sleep.

Half her adult life had been spent that way.

She checked her phone for the time. Nine-thirty. Fifteen minutes ahead of schedule. She scrolled through her messages and found a missed call and two texts from Lindsey. The first text had been sent four hours earlier and read:

Sorry I missed your call. I've been so busy. Got your messages. Glad you're on your way. My father is missing and I'm hoping you can help me find him. I'll fill you in when you get here.

The second message sent an hour later read:

Arranged for a driver to pick you up and take you to the Grand Hyatt Hotel. I've booked a room in your name. I'll meet you at the hotel restaurant at noon. Can't wait to see you.

She took a deep breath and tapped a text back that she had arrived.

Finally.

She scanned the crowd and saw a thick-chested man in a black suit holding a card with her name printed in bold black letters. Her bags arrived and she wheeled them over to him.

"I'm Cherise. We can go any time."

"My name is Daniel," he replied. "My car is right across the street."

He took hold of her bags and rolled them outside to a parked black Lincoln Town Car with tinted windows. She slid onto the rear seat, looking forward to seeing Lindsey.

And hearing the entire story.

Daniel jockeyed their way to Grand Central Station and the second level entrance to the Grand Hyatt Hotel at 109 East 42nd Street. She didn't count on an early arrival check-in, but hoped to get into her room in time to freshen up before meeting Lindsey for lunch.

A bellman loaded her luggage onto a wheeled cart, and she took the escalator down to the front desk. When a guest ahead of her finished checking in, she took her turn at the counter.

"Cherise Venetta," she said. "I believe you have a reservation for me."

The agent tapped his keyboard and consulted his computer screen. "The room has been on hold for you since late last night. A Ms. Lindsey Taylor checked in for you, with a note you'd be arriving today."

"So I'll be able to go right up?"

"Just as soon as I get your information."

"Excellent." She held out her passport and her black Visa card.

He took the passport and opened it. "I won't need your credit card, Ms. Venetta. Ms. Taylor requested to have the room and all charges billed to her. Her card is already on file."

"That was nice of her, but would you please bill my stay to this card? I'd rather she not be charged."

"But of course."

Fifteen minutes later, she stepped into a corner room on the thirty-fourth floor overlooking the roof of Grand Central Station. She slipped the bellman a twenty, closed the door, and engaged the dead bolt.

Silence at last.

She walked to the window and took in the wedge of Manhattan skyline visible from her room. It amazed her how in only a couple of days she had gone from hours of solitude on a deserted stretch of sandy beach on a getaway in the Northwest Hawaiian Islands to skyscrapers and a city of over a million and a half people.

She turned and scanned the room. Enormous compared to the cramped quarters aboard the *Sun Dancer*.

And nice by New York standards.

She still didn't know why Lindsey had sought her assistance instead of turning to law enforcement for help, if that's what was needed. Or why Lindsey insisted she had no one else to turn to.

Not that it made a difference.

That Lindsey had asked her to come was enough.

Cherise believed that a band of sisters brought together in a time of war is every bit as strong as a band of brothers.

Even if it's only two sisters.

CHAPTER 7

On the short ride back to shore, Jack mentally calculated the numbers. The amount of the insurance check he received for *Pono* and what he would have to pay for *Adeona*. Not a hug difference. They arrived back at the Pier House and stood for a moment outside the beach bar.

"We'll wait in the Chart Room Bar," Jack said. "We can have lunch there."

"Very well." Salvatore glanced at his watch. "I'll let Ms. Faggini know you wish to speak to her."

Salvatore walked away and Robert said, "That's a hell of a boat."

An understatement, Jack thought. *If she checked out.*

"You were awfully quiet about her during the tour."

"I think it's obvious I was impressed."

"But you kept your opinions to yourself."

"I didn't want you to think I was trying to pressure you into a decision one way or the other."

Jack slapped Robert on the back. "I'll buy us a beer and you give me your opinion of her."

They took seats at a table inside the bar. Decorating the walls, an abundance of memorabilia reminded them that Jimmy Buffett began his career here. And that the Chart Room had been a local favorite where Mel Fisher often ended days of treasure hunting.

"A couple of cold draft lagers, please," Jack said to their busty server who sported a parrot tattoo on her left breast. Kathy, according to her plastic nameplate.

For the next few minutes, Jack listened to Robert talk about the positives and the negatives *Adeona* offered. The biggest drawback being Ms. Faggini's husband had clearly custom-fitted the interior with a woman in mind. Jack assured Robert minor modifications would need to be made.

They were still working on their first glass of beer when Salvatore Vincente and a beautiful dark-haired woman stepped into the room. Jack had tried to picture what Ms. Faggini would look like. The woman's appearance, he was sure, deceived her true age. Elegance, grace, beauty. A certain familiarity about her looks suggested she could pass for Sophia Loren's sister. Twins born a couple dozen years apart.

He and Robert pushed away from the table and stood at her approach.

"Mr. Ferrell. Mr. Foster," Salvatore said. "This is Ms. Violetta Faggini."

"Nice to meet you." Jack offered his hand. "Please call me Jack."

"And please call me Robert." He extended his hand as well. "I'm sorry for your loss. Brian Fitzgerald is a business associate of mine. I understand he and your husband were good friends."

She smiled. "Since before Antonio and I were married."

Introductions made, they sat down. Ms. Faggini sat across from Jack. Salvatore sat to her left, across from Robert.

"I'd like to talk a bit before we eat, if that's all right?" Jack directed the question at Ms. Faggini.

She nodded. "I'm anxious to hear what you have to say."

"Can I get you something to drink?"

"Glass of red wine would be nice."

He turned to her cousin. "Salvatore?"

"The same."

Jack waved Kathy over and placed the order.

She walked away and he said, "You have a very nice boat, Ms. Faggini. And I believe the price you're offering it to me for is more than fair. Are you sure you want to sell the *Adeona*?"

The wine arrived and Ms. Faggini took a sip. "As you know,

Antonio had the *Adeona* custom-refitted for me. It was his dream for us to sail the world together. Now that he is gone, I have no desire to sail the *Adeona* anywhere. If you are concerned about the price being low, don't be. It in no way reflects the condition of the boat."

Jack looked at Salvatore. Nothing in his eyes betrayed concern beyond that of seeing to Ms. Faggini's well-being. The dutiful cousin. If he had a problem with the sale, he didn't show it.

To Ms. Faggini, "You understand why I had to ask?"

"I assure you I'm not offended in any way. My cousin tells me that you wish to take the *Adeona* out to make sure everything is in working order."

"That's correct. However, there is more to it than making sure the engines and electronic equipment work properly. I need to satisfy myself that the boat will serve my needs."

"Am I to assume you are serious about purchasing the *Adeona*?"

"I assure you, I'm extremely interested. My former boat, *Pono*, was very similar to the *Adeona*. So I shouldn't have any problem handling her."

"*Pono*." She offered a curt nod. "When I last spoke to Mr. Fitzgerald, he told me what happened. I'm sorry."

Her comment caught Jack off-guard. Only one way she could have known about the explosion that ripped *Pono* apart and sent her to the bottom. He glanced at Robert and got a sheepish shrug in return.

"Thank you, Ms. Faggini. Since time is of the essence for you and for me, I'd like to take the *Adeona* out for a test run this afternoon."

She gave a slight nod. "Salvatore will be happy to accompany you. First, let's have lunch."

CHAPTER 8

At twelve fifteen, Cherise stood at the bottom of the stairs leading up to the restaurant inside the hotel. Lunch chatter drifted down and mixed with the hustle of activity in the lobby.

Exhausted but wound tight with anticipation, she thought about the phone conversation she had with Lindsey a few minutes earlier.

Her father, missing.

She smiled when she saw her step onto the escalator and ride it up from street level. Her friend's dark, shoulder length hair hung in a gentle curl below the shoulders of her dark pinstriped suit. Her skin, the color of raw honey, looked as smooth and ageless as it had when they last saw each other. She had the same broad friendly smile, but her expression showed weariness and concern uncharacteristic of her.

She obviously hadn't been sleeping well.

Apparently, for good reason.

"I'm so glad you made it," Lindsey said as she stepped toward her.

"Me too." Cherise looked her up and down. "How is your leg? It's not giving you problems, is it?"

"Other than the scar. I'm fine. I was never going to be a beauty contestant, anyway."

Cherise wrapped her arms around her friend and squeezed. "I'm just sorry it took so long for me to get here."

"You're here," Lindsey said, easing herself from Cherise's grasp. "That's all that matters."

"You're living in New York, now?"

"A couple of weeks each year, in a room at the Waldorf. The State Department rents an entire floor when the UN delegation is in town. That's why I asked you to meet me here in the City. My home is actually in D.C., a small place near the Capitol."

"You're doing well, then?"

"My position with the UN delegation keeps me busy."

"Let's have lunch. And you can tell me about your father."

They climbed the steps to the restaurant. Lindsey informed the maître d' she had a reservation. They were seated at a table overlooking 42nd Street. Their waiter appeared almost immediately and asked if they were ready to order.

"Would you like a drink?" Lindsey asked Cherise. "Vodka martini, if I remember correctly."

Cherise smiled. "Am I going to need it?"

"You might."

"Perhaps later," she said.

Lindsey turned to the waiter. "I'll have the cobb salad and iced tea."

Cherise didn't bother with her menu. "I'll have the same."

The young lady walked away, and they turned their attention on each other.

"So tell me everything," Cherise said.

She watched Lindsey peer into her glass of water as though reliving recent events. Putting them in order. Trying her best to hold onto hope.

The way she had in Afghanistan.

Only not doing a good job of it.

"Basically," Lindsey said, "it's what I told you on the phone. My father's missing and the authorities show little or no interest in finding him."

"But they investigated?"

"I guess."

She heard the hopelessness in Lindsey's tone. "You said he took a cruise and never returned home."

Lindsey faced the window, and Cherise followed her friend's gaze. A man strolled the sidewalk on the opposite side of Lexington Avenue carrying a monkey on his shoulder. "Dad should have returned home two weeks ago. Blue Water Cruise Line maintains he got off the *Caribbean Star* in Miami along with all the other passengers."

"And you haven't heard from him?"

She met Cherise's gaze. "Not a word."

"What did the police have to say?"

"It's their opinion he met a woman and ran off with her. They're confident he'll show up once the romance wears off."

"You don't agree?"

"I'm sure Dad's capable of doing most anything, but not that . . . not without telling me."

"You're positive?"

"As much as I can be under the circumstances. You have to understand how it is between us. I'm the only family he has left."

"So what do you think happened?"

"Knowing you, probably the same thing you're thinking." Resolve hardened Lindsey's expression. "The representative for the cruise line lied. I don't believe my father left the ship . . . not in Miami, anyway."

Cherise nodded.

And not under his own power.

CHAPTER 9

Cherise noticed a man and a woman hurry out of the restaurant and take the escalator down. A multitude of scenarios whirled in her mind. If Lindsey's father left the cruise ship in Miami and was on the run, he had a good reason for doing so. If something happened to him at sea, a representative of the cruise line could very well have covered it up to protect the integrity of the company.

"It's not inconceivable the representative of the cruise line lied," she said, peering across the table at Lindsey. "A cruise is supposed to be an opportunity to relax and have fun at sea. But all too often, it doesn't turn out that way. You're probably aware there have been a ton of cruise ship passenger disappearances. Some fall overboard by accident or otherwise and wind up being rescued. Some are never seen again. Others disappear more mysteriously."

"Like my father."

"That's what I'm thinking. The problem with investigations is they're frequently inconclusive, primarily because in many cases missing passengers are never found . . . dead or alive. Either way the reputation of the cruise line is damaged. Oftentimes, quite severely. Especially now that victims' family members flood social media with their stories. So it's entirely possible for Blue Water Cruise Line to be motivated to cover up a suspicious disappearance. No matter what's involved."

Lindsey laid her hand on Cherise's. "So you agree with me?"

Cherise tried to smile convincingly. "I'm saying it's possible. Suppose you start from the beginning. Tell me everything you know or have been told about what happened."

"Are you sure you wouldn't like that martini?"

"Afterward."

Lindsey removed her phone from her purse and set it on the table. "I have several texts to show you. One of which I didn't share with the police."

Cherise hadn't expected to hear the last part. She suspected there was more to the situation than a missing father.

But what?

"You had a good reason for keeping the text from the cops, I'm sure," she said. She'd let Lindsey explain in her own time.

Lindsey nodded. "You'll understand when you see it."

"No worries, Linds. We've been friends a long time."

Their gazes met and held. "You're the only one who calls me that."

Cherise smiled. "Because you mean a lot to me."

Lindsey dabbed at the corners of her eyes with her napkin. "Honestly, I don't know what I would have done without you there with me in Afghanistan."

But I didn't keep you from being shot.

Cherise appreciated what her friend was saying, remembering how alone and vulnerable she felt the day she entered the largely male world of Special Ops. She learned to persevere, and became one of the proud few. But the scars remained.

Pain and loneliness are more bearable if shared.

"I'm sure you would have been fine," she said. "But having another woman to talk to . . . that meant a lot to me, as well."

Lindsey faced the window. After a long moment of silence, it appeared to Cherise her friend was having a difficult time staying focused.

"We were talking about your father," she said. "Tell me about him."

"I know I must sound like I'm procrastinating, but I'm not."

"Take your time. I understand this is difficult for you."

Lindsey turned from the window and offered a narrow smile.

"Can you believe it? I didn't even know who my father was until a couple of years ago."

"I wasn't aware of that."

"Not many people are."

"Do you have a picture of him?"

She pulled a snapshot from her purse and handed it to Cherise. "It's only right that I tell you everything. My mom and dad met in D.C. when she worked for the State Department. He'd just returned from Africa and was there organizing a fundraiser after having spent a year in the bush drilling wells to pipe clean drinking water to several remote villages. According to my mom, they had a whirlwind romance that ended when he returned to Africa to continue his cause. Growing up, I often wondered about my father. Why he had abandoned me. Mom never would tell me who he was. She passed away from cancer two and a half years ago. Near the end, she told me my father never knew about the pregnancy. Which is what she wanted. She claimed he was off saving the world and she didn't want to interfere with his work."

"How sad. Your mother never married?"

"She came close once, but the relationship didn't work out. I think she still loved Dad."

Listening to Lindsey talk, and knowing the mental torment she had been going through, Cherise recalled her own version of hell. Two days following her sixth birthday, watching a dark-haired man gun down her mother in a marketplace in France. And then her father dying in a single car accident in the middle of summer on a rural road outside of Suitland, Maryland. In spite of the suspicious nature of the crash, the Navy ruled his death accidental and closed the file. The years afterward spent searching for answers to the truth behind his death. Her parents, like Lindsey's parents, had never married, even after her mother got pregnant. She had wanted it that way.

Just as Lindsey's mother had.

"We've known each other what, six or seven years?" Cherise said. "And you never shared that story with me. Me, of all people . . . your friend."

Lindsey shrugged. "There was enough prejudice among the

troops. My mother being black and my father white, I didn't want my mixed heritage to add to what already existed."

"And you thought that would make a difference to me?" Cherise reached out and gripped Lindsey's arm. "Linds, we were two women in a man's world—friends to the end. You could have told me."

Lindsey's gaze dropped. "I realize that. But after a while, it just didn't matter anymore."

"Till now?"

Lindsey's lips spread into a shaky smile. "Till now."

Cherise sympathized with her friend. She'd come to help, not criticize. She asked, "How'd you and your father finally connect?"

The question brought another smile. Tears welled in Lindsey's eyes. In them, Cherise saw pride. Understanding.

Love for her father.

"That," Lindsey said after a moment, "is another story."

CHAPTER 10

Cherise didn't push. She saw no reason to.

"My father's name is Sam King," Lindsey began. "On her deathbed, Mom gave me a sealed envelope and told me to look my father up and give it to him. I didn't know the contents of the letter at the time. But I learned later it explained my birth, growing up, everything. It took a few months but I found Dad in D.C. at a fundraiser for his non-profit charity, Safe Water for the World. You can imagine the surprise when he learned he had a daughter. But he warmed to me right away."

"And you've kept in contact with each other?"

"When he's not out of the country, he spends his time promoting his charity. He owns a place in D.C. not far from where I live." Lindsey peered down at her fingers and fiddled with a gold ring on her right hand. "Cherise, my father is a brilliant engineer and the kindest, most gentle giving man I know. He could easily be taken advantage of."

Cherise pointed. "Did your father give that to you?"

"Beautiful, isn't it?" Lindsey held her hand out flat exposing a dazzling blood-red stone. "He gave it to me last Christmas. It's a Burmese ruby."

"I'm sure it means a lot to you. Tell me about the cruise."

"That was my idea. As I mentioned earlier, Dad lives close. Which makes it easy for us to keep in touch. He'd been home since

Christmas. Donations were down so I thought it might be good for him to get away and socialize with people outside his usual circle. Maybe even have a shipboard romance." Lindsey sighed. "Now this. Something bad has happened to him. I know it. And it's all my fault."

Cherise couldn't let her believe she was responsible. "We don't know that. And whatever *has* happened, it's certainly not your fault. I assume you have keys to his place?"

"When I didn't hear from him, that's the first place I went. Nothing I saw there indicated he had returned home. That's when I contacted the police."

"You mentioned the representative for Blue Water Cruise Line claimed he left the *Caribbean Star* in Miami along with the other passengers. And you claim he never got off the ship. Did they say anything about his luggage, whether it was still in his cabin or if he had taken it with him?"

"They said they checked his cabin and found his luggage gone."

"He took it with him?"

"That's what they implied."

"And you think they're lying?"

"Not necessarily about that. I'm sure his bags were gone. The question is: who got rid of them? Obviously, they want me to believe Dad disembarked the ship voluntarily, taking his bags with him. Granted, I haven't known him for a hundred years. But I know him well enough. And I'm saying that's simply not something he'd do. Not without calling me, or texting . . . something. Someone aboard the ship had to have gotten rid of his things long before there was any investigation."

Maybe. Maybe not.

Cherise convinced herself she had to trust Lindsey's perception as it related to her father's disappearance. Proof. Or no proof.

"You mentioned you received several texts from your father during his trip. Can I see them?"

"I received two or three from him every time the *Caribbean Star* made a stop in a port of call. Most are short, saying he's having a good time. That sort of thing. In one he sent from Key West, the first port of call on his trip, he did say he met a woman by the name of Amanda, and that they were spending a lot of time together. I'll let you read it. Seems he actually did strike up a shipboard romance."

"He didn't give a last name?"

"Unfortunately, no."

"How about her picture?"

"Sorry."

"And the text you didn't show the police?"

"It's this one here." Lindsey angled the screen toward Cherise.

"Do you mind?" Cherise held out her hand.

Lindsey passed her the phone. "I think you'll understand why I didn't show it to the police."

Cherise read the text:

I might have just done something stupid. I bought three ugly little figurines today. Primitive deities. Solid gold. All over four inches tall. Mayan, I've been told. Pre-Columbian. Corey swears they're authentic. If so, they belong in a museum. All I have to do is figure out a way to turn them over to the authorities without making trouble.

"Those gold figurines had to have cost a bundle," Cherise said. "And black market transactions aren't handled by check or credit card. Did your dad have the necessary funds available to make a purchase like this?"

"Apparently. He has money he inherited from his parents."

"The important part is he attached a photograph of the idols. From what I can tell, this was taken in his cabin. Which means he was back onboard the *Caribbean Star* when he sent this."

"Implying he hadn't run off with some woman."

"Not there, anyway. Do you have any idea who Corey is?"

"Scroll up to the text I received from him in Key West. He mentioned Amanda was traveling with her brother Corey."

Cherise found it. "No picture attachment, of course."

"As you can see, he sent a few pictures with his texts. But there's no way to tell if Corey or Amanda is in any of them."

"So we have no idea what either of them look like?"

"I'm afraid not."

Cherise returned Lindsey's phone and picked up her own. "I

think I know a way to get the information we need."

"So you're going to help me find out what happened to my dad?"

Cherise never doubted for a moment she would. She had several job offers in the queue. Any one of them would net her a very large payday. But none involved a dear friend's father having gone missing. She'd find out what happened to him. For better, or for worse.

With only one promise. The truth.

She leveled her gaze at Lindsey. "Linds, I wouldn't be here otherwise."

CHAPTER 11

On the way back to the *Adeona*, Jack thought about Cherise. He had no idea where her travels had taken her. Only that she was meeting her friend Lindsey. And that things could turn real serious for her real fast. He figured it would be a pleasant distraction for her to know he had flown to Key West to check out a boat he considered buying.

A surprise to her as much as it had been to hm.

He fished his phone from his pocket and tapped the text, wishing he could see the look on her face when she opened it.

Robert must have noticed him smiling because he asked, "What has you so amused?"

"I just sent Cherise a text letting her know I'm in Key West buying a boat."

"Isn't she involved with her friend?"

"Doesn't hurt to keep her in the loop. Besides, she might need a laugh."

"Buying a boat is funny?"

"Only that we flew five thousand miles to do it."

"You'd better put that phone away before you drop the thing over the side."

They were nearing the *Adeona*. Jack slid his cell into his pants pocket and said, "What would I do without you to look after me?"

"Get into trouble as usual, of course."

Jack scoffed. "Right."

He climbed aboard the *Adeona*, excited to be taking her out for a test run. With Robert's help, he winched the dinghy into place, astern. Once the Boston Whaler was secured, he hurried inside to the controls in the forward cabin. Robert and Salvatore followed.

Jack said, "Let's see what this goddess will do."

"You're the captain," Robert answered.

Salvatore took a seat on the sofa without comment, apparently content to sit back and let Jack take control of the yacht.

Jack started the engines and let them idle. The instrument panel came to life and he studied the gauges. All showed normal. Even the fuel tanks read a fraction under full. A fifteen-thousand-dollar bonus.

"Ready to raise anchor?" he asked Robert.

"I'll go out onto the bow and make sure the lines are clear." Robert stepped behind Jack and opened the starboard hatch, letting in a waft of hot, humid air heavy with the scent of salt and rotting vegetation.

Jack flipped the power switch to the anchor winch and watched the process through the windscreen. He saw Robert run his hand across his throat in a slashing motion and cut power. He could have handled the procedure by himself, but it was nice to have Robert on the bow to watch for foul-ups.

"Ready when you are," Robert said, stepping inside. "And now might be a good time to test the air conditioner."

Sweat had already beaded on Jack's forehead. He swiped it away with the back of his hand. "Good idea. You can do the honors."

Robert reached up and turned the system on. At once, cool air began flooding the compartment. Given the size of the cabin, it would take a while.

Jack listened to the unit run. Satisfied it operated properly, he eased the throttles forward and maneuvered through a flotilla of pleasure craft on a slow course for the Gulf of Mexico. When they were clear of the other boats, he pushed the throttles forward and brought *Adeona* up to ten knots. Then seventeen. Then the top speed of twenty-three knots. The speedometer inched forward to twenty five.

He ran the engines at that speed a few minutes then backed off to ten knots and kept it there. With the boat slicing smoothly through a calm sea, he turned the helm over to Robert and began a systematic check of all the onboard systems, including a thorough examination of the bilge and engines.

Not that he questioned the marine survey that had been done six months earlier, he just didn't want to chance having another boat explode under him.

Given his druthers, he'd rather live until he was old and gray.

CHAPTER 12

Cherise had her cellular in hand and her finger poised to make a call, when the phone chimed with a text. Seeing Jack's name appear on the screen brought a smile she hadn't expected. She read his note, surprised by its content.

"You're smiling," Lindsey said.

"I am."

That she had brightened so easily to receiving a text from him, surprised her. They had said goodbye on Oahu—had kissed long and sweet, and she had carried the memory of that final embrace with her into the waiting taxi . . . and later onto the plane. Then she had needed to put her thoughts on what lay ahead with Lindsey, and beyond. After all, their relationship was hardly one at all. More a mutual attraction they both acknowledged with no discussion of where it would lead.

"Well . . . ?" Lindsey continued to stare.

Cherise chuckled to conceal her nervous flutter. "Jack, a friend of mine, is in Key West buying a boat."

"I'm sure there is a story that goes with it."

There certainly is.

Cherise continued to grin, her thoughts on Jack. What would he have to say about the situation with Lindsey's missing father?

She had a pretty good guess.

"There's a story, all right. A good one," she said. "I'll share it with you later. Right now, Jack being in Key West might work to our advantage if he can have a look around down there and make some inquiries about your father. According to your dad's texts, he'd hooked up with Amanda by then. Which we agree is suspicious in itself. If she and her brother are part of an ongoing scam, perhaps something will pop."

"He'd do that?"

"I believe he will if I ask him."

Lindsey's lips curled up at the corners, having at last allowed herself a smile. "I take it he's someone special?"

Cherise almost laughed. "You could say that. I just spent three weeks with him island hopping our way up and down the Northwest Hawaiian Islands. That's where we were when you tried to reach me."

Lindsey arched a brow. "I'd say that qualifies. And judging from your expression, you're ready for that Grey Goose martini."

"Sounds like a great idea."

While Lindsey waved over their waiter, Cherise placed her call. She turned in her seat and stretched her long legs while she listened. The phone would buzz twice before it connected.

"Susan, it's me again." She kept her voice down. "I need you to access Blue Water Cruise Line's passenger list for the *Caribbean Star*. The ship returned to port two weeks ago. I'm particularly interested in a brother and sister traveling together. Probably in their thirties. Their first names are Corey and Amanda."

As usual, Susan had questions. Cherise listened, and added, "Sorry, I don't have their last names. But there can't be too many passengers by those names. It's even possible they have the same last name. Send their photos. Include one of Lindsey's father, Sam King. He was on the same cruise. Yes, I know. You're the best. Text the information to me as soon as you get it."

Lindsey was staring at her, so she asked, "Why the puzzled look?"

Lindsey leaned close. "Both the cruise line and the police refused to show me the passenger list for Dad's cruise. You make it look easy."

"Susan makes it look easy. Not me."

"The woman I spoke to on the phone?"

"She's a real treasure."

Their martinis arrived and Cherise pulled her legs in. A group of people walked by speaking German. Cherise couldn't help overhearing their conversation. Chatter about how much they enjoyed their tour of the Statue of Liberty. The waiter followed them to their table.

"To us," Lindsey said, raising her glass.

"To us."

Lindsey asked, "So Susan can hack Blue Water Cruise Line's computer?"

"Among other things."

"You sound confident."

Cherise checked her watch. "She's already in, I'm sure. Providing she doesn't have too difficult a time putting the first names with a last, we should have the information in a matter of minutes."

They worked on their salads until Cherise's phone chimed. She read the text and scanned the attachments. The first three stuck out.

"That was fast," Lindsey said.

Cherise smiled. "Actually I expected this information sooner. But it appears Susan did a little extra digging. She sent photos of Amanda and Corey. And one of your father. She also attached several promotional photos taken during the trip. She thought we might be able to make use of them."

"We could use some luck."

"Give it a chance. We're only getting started."

Cherise clicked on a photo taken at the Captain's dinner. She enlarged it. "That's your father, right?"

Lindsey studied the image. A smile formed. "He looks happy. Maybe that's Amanda sitting next to him?"

"Here's her picture. Looks like her to me."

"She's younger than I imagined."

"Do you find that odd?"

"Some," Lindsey said. "Dad's not bad looking in a rugged sort of way but he's no spring chicken, either."

Cherise took a closer look. Seated, the woman in question was close to Lindsey's father's height, thirtyish, possibly a few years older, voluptuous, styled dishwater blonde hair extending several inches below the shoulders, high cheek bones, a nice smile, and twin arches of thick graceful brows. Not hard to see why he found her attractive.

"Perhaps she likes older men."

"Yeah, maybe. So what do we do now?"

"Do you have to get back to work?"

"I asked for the afternoon off to give us plenty of time to talk."

"Did you bring your laptop with you? Mine's dead."

"In my car."

"Then let's finish our lunch. When we're done, we'll look over the information Susan sent us."

CHAPTER 13

Cherise took a seat at the table in her room. She could read the anticipation showing in her friend's expression.

"I'm also emailing the attachments. Won't take but a moment."

Lindsey pulled her laptop from her briefcase and quickly opened it on the tabletop in front of them. "Where should I start?"

"First read the text. Apparently there were a half-dozen Amanda's on board. But four of them were under ten and one was sixty-five. That left only the one possibility. Amanda Kelly. Fortunately, there was only one Corey. Corey Jameson."

"Brother and sister?"

"According to your dad's text."

Lindsey scanned the email. "Surely Amanda wouldn't have lied to Dad about her name . . . or Corey's."

"There's always that possibility, but I'm betting she didn't. Unless it was a lie from the beginning and they had fake IDs and passports."

"That's scary to think." Lindsey leaned close and scrolled the list. "Here they are. They had an aft suite on deck eight. Port side, number 8702, two queen beds and a large aft-facing balcony."

"Which cabin did your father stay in?"

"Here it is." She leaned close. "A suite all the way forward. Same deck. Number 8504."

"Practically neighbors."

Lindsey turned a confused expression on Cherise. "So what are you thinking? We know Corey's last name is Jameson and Amanda's last name is Kelly. We know the cabin they stayed in, and we know the cabin Dad stayed in. You obviously have an idea of where we need to go with this thing. I'd like to hear it."

Cherise placed her hand on Lindsey's arm. "Your dad had an on board romance with Amanda. Her brother Corey—if he is in fact her brother—was with your dad when he purchased the gold idols. I say we begin by talking to them. Find out what kind of people they are. How much time they spent with your father during the cruise. Maybe something was bothering him that you aren't aware of."

"Other than the idols?"

"Something that might have caused him to cut and run."

"I told you that doesn't sound like something Dad would do. And we've already determined he was on board after the stop in Belize, the ships last port of call. The text about the idols proves it. And he sure didn't disembark in Miami. That only leaves the middle of the Caribbean."

Cherise pulled her hand away. "I know what you're thinking. I'm thinking the same thing. But likely or not, it's possible your dad cut and ran all the same. Especially if he thought he was going to be arrested. Who, other than Corey and Amanda, can best describe your father's frame of mind? Particularly Amanda, if she and your father were sleeping together."

"Don't you think the police have already talked to them?"

"Seems like they would have, provided they put two and two together as far as their names. But you and I haven't. And I'd like to hear what they have to say."

"Me, too. Only how do you suppose we go about that without an address for Corey or Amanda? It'd be on the police report. But when I tried to get a copy, the police told me they couldn't release the information because Dad's missing persons case is officially an ongoing investigation."

"Only they're not investigating."

"Not until there's more for them to go on. At least that's what the detectives told me."

"It'd be nice to know what's in their report, but we don't need it. Susan, being the detail oriented person she is, thought ahead and attached the shipboard financials for all the passengers. Home address, credit cards used, a complete list of charges during the trip, total amount paid. According to the information, they live in Palm Beach. Or at least that's the address they gave. Should make it easy enough for us to locate them. Can you take some time off?"

"The meetings at the UN conclude tomorrow. I'll have to work all day finishing up, but I have a week's vacation coming. My boss knows about my dad's disappearance so there shouldn't be a problem with me taking it."

"A boyfriend you need to worry about?"

"No one I have a serious enough relationship with that it would interfere with anything I'm doing."

"Good. We need to move on this ASAP, so put in your vacation request."

Lindsey took Cherise's hand. "I think I already told you this, but even if I did, I'm going to say it anyway. It's like Afghanistan all over again. I don't know what I would have done if you weren't here to help me through this."

"I haven't helped anyone yet."

"But we're doing something. That's a step in the right direction."

CHAPTER 14

Jack took his time completing a thorough going-over of the yacht, bow to stern, before returning to the forward cabin.

"Well?" Robert asked.

Jack gave him a thumbs-up. "*Adeona* is in excellent condition."

Salvatore rose to his feet. "My cousin will be pleased to hear that. She is most anxious to conclude her business here."

Jack let the comment hang and turned to Robert. "Take us back in. And kick her up a few RPMs."

Robert winked and pushed the throttle levers forward an inch. The twin four-hundred-and-fifty horsepower diesel engines responded with a slight lurch of the hull and a lifting of the bow.

Jack adjusted his balance and refocused his attention on Salvatore. "I would like to give Ms. Faggini my answer in the morning, if that's possible. There is a lot to think over and I'd like to sleep on it before I make my decision."

"You do understand she hoped to conclude her business by this weekend. She has a flight to New York at noon tomorrow. The boat's captain and chef have already taken work elsewhere. If the *Adeona* isn't sold, she'll turn her over to a local yacht broker at that time."

Upping the pressure.

"She'll have my answer first thing. That's the best I can do."

"Very well. I will tell her she can expect an answer in the morning."

"Over breakfast. Say, at eight o'clock. My treat."

"I assure you that is not necessary."

"But I insist." Jack gave him a toothy grin.

My idea. My treat.

* * *

Three hours later, Jack rested his arms on a table inside Sloppy Joe's and gripped his glass of cold draft lager with the correct amount of head. He lifted the beer to his lips and savored a swallow that brightened his already great day.

Robert sat on the opposite side of the table, a pint of lager in front of him. He pointed at the photo gallery of Ernest Hemmingway hanging on the wall. "Appears nothing's changed since the last time we were in this place."

"Except Pillai and Kazuko aren't sitting here with us."

"Do you still hear from her from time to time?"

Jack shook his head. "Not so much this last year. She's engaged. Or even married by now. I wasn't invited to the wedding."

Robert chuckled. "Probably a good thing. Did you get hold of Doctor Goddard at the aquarium?"

"That's a bust. Monday, he flew to Australia for a conference on a broad spectrum of issues impacting the Great Barrier Reef."

"Missed him by a couple of days. The bright side is we're sitting in Sloppy Joe's drinking a cold beer."

Jack hoisted his glass. "Here's to *The Old Man and the Sea.*"

"A tried and true Hemingway fan," Robert said.

"Always have been. Always will be."

For maybe fifteen minutes, they had the place mostly to themselves before people began flooding in. Somewhere up the street, Jimmy Buffet sang a tune about cheeseburgers and paradise and a big glass of cold beer. Jack took another gulp of lager and quietly listened.

Robert made it to the end of the song before saying, "You're going to buy the *Adeona.*"

"Are you telling me or asking."

"I know you."

"So you think I should?"

"Nice boat. But it's your call."

A sunbaked couple walked past.

Robert looked around the room. "Place is filling up. You want to stay here or go someplace else and eat?"

"Mostly, I just want to sit here and enjoy a couple more of these." He held up his near empty glass.

"I can't argue that." Robert waved their waiter over. "Another round, please."

Jack downed his last swallow. "It'll be a long cruise getting her to Oahu."

"You could invite Cherise along. Or has she had enough of you?"

"Seriously?"

Robert shrugged. "It could happen."

Jack shook his head. "She's busy with her friend, but I could ask."

"Have you texted her a picture of the *Adeona* yet?"

Their beer arrived and Jack pulled his arms back to allow room for his freshly-drawn pint. "Not yet. Just the text I sent her earlier today."

Robert clinked his glass against Jack's. "I think it's high time you sent your lady a picture to go with that text, don't you?"

Jack pondered the question. "And say what?"

"That you've decided to buy a new boat."

"It's an old boat."

"Then tell her you're buying a new old boat."

Jack removed his phone, tapped out the message, attached a couple of photos of the *Adeona*, and sent the text.

"Done," he said.

Robert nodded. "Now you wait."

CHAPTER 15

Cherise stepped into the warm New York evening pleasantly content after enjoying a delightful dinner at Dino's Northern Italian Fine Dining located at the corner of Lexington and East 45th Street. She took Lindsey's hands in hers and held them gently in her fingers. "It was great catching up. And the food was fabulous. I only wish I was in town under different circumstances."

Lindsey's smile slipped. "I wish a lot of things were different."

Cherise felt a twinge of regret for her choice of words. "I'm sorry, Linds. I feel terrible about what's happened and should have . . ."

Lindsey sighed. "I suppose it's just me being melodramatic. But this situation with Dad has me wearing my emotions on my shirtsleeves."

"That's perfectly understandable." Cherise had been there herself and knew the sense of loss Lindsey struggled with. "I guess I should have said don't worry, together we'll find out what happened to your dad. . . . Because that's what we *will* do."

"You really believe that?" Lindsey's look intensified. "That we'll find out what happened to Dad?"

Cherise nodded, confident in her abilities. "That's what I do, Linds."

Lindsey peered into the night. "I guess I knew that. Otherwise I wouldn't have called."

Cherise heard a text come through on her phone. Sirens wailed in the distance. Cars honked at a taxi weaving through traffic on the street in front of them. New Yorkers going about their business in New York fashion. Everyone locked in their own true-life struggle.

"Up till now I've had little hope," Lindsey said. "I suppose it's time I have faith in something or someone."

"In me," Cherise said.

She never would have left town without first helping Lindsey find the truth, no matter how unattainable it seemed.

Continuing to ignore the text, she added, "I know you want answers, immediately if not sooner. All I can do is promise we'll go to whatever lengths necessary to get those answers. But it'll take time. Try not to give up hope."

"I know Dad's dead. That's the only answer that makes sense."

"We don't know that."

"Let's not kid ourselves, Cherise. Too much time has gone by. Dad's dead. Either by some horrible accident, or someone murdered him. If someone killed him, they need to pay for what they've done."

"And if he died by accident?"

"Then someone at Blue Water Cruise Line needs to answer for trying to cover up his death."

Cherise looked into her friend's eyes. It had taken time for Lindsey to arrive at the realization her father met with foul play. Or at the very minimum, to openly accept it. And now she asked for revenge.

In the back of Cherise's mind, she had believed the man had been killed. A belief that solidified when she learned about the golden idols. Information the police didn't have for their investigation.

She doubted it would have made a difference. It might have even cast a dark cloud of suspicion on her father.

A possibility that still needed to be addressed.

But it didn't change the distinct likelihood her father had been murdered.

Most likely for the gold.

Lindsey didn't blink or turn away and Cherise could see the determination in her stare. A new side to her. "You want revenge?"

"Isn't that what we've been talking about?"

CHAPTER 16

Jack collapsed into one of the two padded chairs inside their suite. Robert dropped into the other chair and leaned his head back. Above them, a ceiling fan whirled.

"We could have stayed here and drank," Robert said. "There's a perfectly good bar downstairs. Would have saved us the walk."

"A couple of blocks isn't that far. Not in Key West. And I didn't want to chance running into Ms. Faggini and her cousin. Not before I've had an opportunity to sleep on my decision to buy the *Adeona*. Besides, Ernest Hemingway drank in Sloppy Joe's."

"Meaning that's where you should drink?"

"Why not?" Jack sighed. "Honestly, I didn't want any pressure put on me to buy the boat. And listening to the nonsense going on in that place did the trick."

"I thought buying the boat is what you decided to do?"

"It is. But I might change my mind."

"You need another beer."

"I've had enough beer."

"Whiskey, then?"

Jack shook his head. "I'm going to bed."

"It's still early."

"Not that early. And I need my beauty sleep."

His phone trilled as he started to push out of his chair. Cherise's name flashed on the screen and he answered the call. "Did you get the picture of my new boat?"

"It's gorgeous," she said. "Sorry I didn't have a chance to text you back. I got caught up with Lindsey."

Her voice perked him up. "You called instead of sending a text, that's a whole lot better. I assume she's told you what her problem is."

"We were talking about that when I got your message. Her father went on a cruise and disappeared. Blue Water Cruise Line claims he got off the *Caribbean Star* in Miami with the rest of the passengers. The police believe he's on a romantic tryst with someone he met on board."

"Without telling his daughter? What would possess the man to do that?"

"That's only the half of it. Lindsey has a text she received from him after he went ashore in Belize and returned to the ship. He attached a photograph of three gold idols he bought at the recommendation of a man he met on the cruise. Probably stolen. Or at least sold illegally. The guy's name is Corey Jameson. He's traveling with his sister, Amanda Kelly. Apparently Lindsey's father struck up a romance with her shortly after the cruise ship left Miami."

"Sounds a little sudden. Still, you never know. But buying stolen artifacts? That makes zero sense to me."

"According to her father's message, he bought them with the intention of turning the relics over to the authorities, hopefully without making trouble for himself or anyone else."

"That's a one-way street to trouble. What about his luggage?"

"Gone. But a *Caribbean Star* employee could have seen to that."

"Or a passenger."

"If his death wasn't an accident. Which makes more sense, to me and to Lindsey. She believes her father died at sea and representatives from Blue Water Cruise Line are trying to cover it up for some reason. At this point, I have to agree."

"I suppose it's possible. Has the company had prior disappearances that you know of?"

"I called Susan and put her to work on that very question. And not just Blue Water Cruise Line. I asked her to look into all of them. She's still digging, but so far she's found three documented cases in the past year. The cruise lines involved received some really ugly press. And even though none of the cases were connected to Blue Water, that doesn't rule out one of their employees covering-up what happened to Lindsey's father."

"I can see why they would be motivated to keep an incident like that out of the news."

"Avoid responsibility and point authorities in a different direction," Cherise said. "Lindsey's father's case is officially filed under missing persons. Makes you wonder how many other incidents of this type have been written off that way."

"I'm sure Susan is looking into it."

"You know me too well."

"But not as well as I'd like. Key West was one of his ports of call, wasn't it?"

"His first stop."

"Send me their pictures. I'll flash their faces around down here and see where it leads while you dig deeper into this mess. Who knows, maybe something will surface. Hell, stranger things have happened."

"You never disappoint me, Jack."

"So you were hoping I'd offer to help."

"Saved me from asking."

"How's your friend doing? This has to be hard on her."

"She's had a tough time, but she's holding herself together. I'm texting you pictures of her father. His name is Sam King. I'm also sending pictures of Amanda and her brother Corey. And there's one of Lindsey's father having dinner at the captain's table with Amanda."

"I can't promise it'll do any good. But if it helps you and your friend make some sense out of what's happened, I'll do what I can. By chance, does her father have a beard?"

"A gray one, why?"

"A minor complication is all. The annual Hemingway Days celebration is getting underway down here and the town's filling up with men sporting gray beards."

He listened to silence.

"Figures," she said after a beat. "I'm sure you'll do the best you can. It's a shot in the dark, anyway."

"Sometimes even a wild shot hits the mark. With luck, I can shed some light on the situation. Anything else I can do to help?"

"Are you really buying that boat?"

"I haven't talked myself out of it yet."

"So you'll be there a few days completing the sale?"

"A couple, at least."

"Good. There's a chance I'll see you down there. If I do, I'll bring Lindsey with me. She'll love meeting you."

"Robert's here, too, so she can meet him as well. Any idea when you'll arrive?"

"If it works out, sometime this weekend. Bear in mind that's a great big *if*. I'll call or text to let you know."

He had to believe she'd make it down.

Positive thinking.

"See you when you get here." He disconnected the call and slumped in his seat.

"What was that all about?" Robert asked.

His question came as no surprise. It would have been more out of character for him if he hadn't asked. They had been friends way too long. And had shared far too many adventures.

Jack gave him the short version.

"What is it with you?" Robert said. "You're like a trouble magnet."

"You're the one who talked me into coming here to buy a boat."

"To buy a boat, yes. Not to play private eye for Cherise."

"Her friend needs help. We're here so it's only right we do what we can. I didn't plan this, but I'm not walking away from it."

Robert ran his fingers through his curly hair. "You said *we*. I suppose that means you want me to tag along with you?"

"Damn right."

CHAPTER 17

At ten minutes before eight the next morning, Jack stepped into the Beach Bar under a sunny sky and took a seat at an outside table. A waiter appeared with two menus, and he ordered a Bloody Mary. He wasn't accustomed to drinking this early, but would make an exception after the night before.

For medicinal purposes.

Robert sat down leaving two empty chairs across from them. He glanced up at the waiter and said, "I'll have one of those, as well."

"Will you be having breakfast?" the waiter asked.

"Not just yet," Jack answered. "We're waiting on a couple of people who will be joining us."

"No problem."

Robert looked at Jack. "A liquid breakfast, huh?"

Jack breathed in the salt air that helped dissipate some of the fuzz clouding his brain. "After last night, I thought a little hair of the dog was in order."

"Just so you keep it at one. You'll want a clear head when you talk business."

"Not a problem." Jack straightened in his seat. "Here they come."

They stood at Violetta Faggini's approach. She looked gorgeous. Jack imagined she always looked that way.

He slid back a chair for her. "Good morning."

A curt nod and she took her seat as though accustomed to the courtesy. "I have a busy day planned. Salvatore assured me you would give me your answer this morning. I suggest we get down to business."

The waiter returned with the drinks. Jack retook his seat and motioned at his Bloody Mary. "Would you care for one of these, or some coffee, or something to eat first?"

"I appreciate the offer, but I've already had my coffee and my breakfast. And I have a lot of business to take care of before I fly out this afternoon."

"I appreciate your position. And I apologize for making you wait until this morning to get my answer. The good news is, I believe the *Adeona* will serve my needs well. I assume you have the sales documents ready for me to sign?"

She nodded at Salvatore who then laid a manila envelope on the table. "You will find everything in order," she said.

Jack slid the papers from the envelope and thumbed through a registered copy of Antonio's death certificate, a notarized document giving Violetta Faggini the authority to sell the *Adeona*, and one stating Antonio's estate was free and clear with no liens on the boat. She had done her homework. He read over each document. All were acceptable. He slid the forms over to Robert for his opinion.

He scanned the documents and slid them back. "They look in order to me. She just needs to sign the bill of sale."

Jack tapped the mobile app for his bank, and smiled at Ms. Faggini. "If you give me an account number, I'll have my bank deposit the cash."

She read the numbers off her phone and he entered them. The transaction complete, he said, "I arranged to have the funds available for immediate transfer. The money should show in your account momentarily."

She studied the screen, tapped, and slid the device into her purse. "The deposit is complete."

"Excellent."

Salvatore handed him a pen, and he signed in the appropriate places. As did she. With the paperwork in order, Salvatore handed him a manila envelope containing an assortment of keys.

"I guess this concludes our business, Ms. Faggini. It has been a pleasure."

She stood, and he rose to his feet. Robert and her cousin followed. She offered her hand to Jack.

He took her fingers in his. "I do hope you have a nice flight. And all the best to you and Salvatore."

"My card is in with the papers," Salvatore said. "Violetta will not be available after we leave here. If you have questions, please direct the inquiry to me."

Jack shook the man's hand. "Thank you for all your help. It was nice meeting both of you."

Robert stepped forward. "Likewise."

"And thank you both. I'm glad I was able to be of service. Violetta and I will be on our way, then. Enjoy the *Adeona*."

As soon as Ms. Faggini and Salvatore were out of the area, Jack raised his glass to Robert. "I guess that's it for the moment."

"For the moment."

"I'm going to order something to eat. Taking care of all this business has made me hungry."

"Are you sure you can pay the check?"

"Smartass. Just for that, you're buying."

"Then what?"

"Then we show Sam King's photo around town and see if someone remembers him."

CHAPTER 18

Cherise stood at the window in her room. A flock of pigeons, perched on the roof of Grand Central Station, went about their business oblivious to the world's problems. Below, on 42nd Street and Park Avenue, traffic moved in cadence to the pulse of the City. A perfect July morning in Manhattan.

The view wasn't helping her impatience. Her conversation with Lindsey the day before ended blunt and to the point. Knowing the truth would never be enough for her friend. Deep down, she wanted revenge.

Cherise could live with that without reservation. Vengeance was as much a part of her life as it had become for Lindsey. A question remained.

Can Lindsey live with it?

She drained her coffee.

Idleness would never make Cherise's list of top-ten ways to spend a day. Neither would taking a sight-seeing tour of the City. She took a seat in front of her computer. She only had a few hours to plan out their next move.

During her conversation with Lindsey, they had agreed to begin by checking into Amanda and Corey's backgrounds. That brother and sister each owned a condominium in the same high-rise on South Ocean Boulevard, surprised her. Even more surprising, their condos were next door to each other.

Not what she would have expected.

Susan's email hadn't arrived yet, so she Googled Palm Beach, Florida. A place she'd never visited. She clicked on an article with a map and read that Palm Beach is the easternmost town in Florida, located on an eighteen-mile long barrier island with Lake Worth Lagoon on the west and the Atlantic Ocean on the east. Palm Beach had been ranked the twenty-seventh wealthiest place in the United States.

Her phone chimed. She scooped it off the table and saw Lindsey's name on the screen. She answered, "How is your day going?"

"A lot of work to finish up before I leave," Lindsey said. "I called to ask you the same thing."

"I'm at my computer doing a little research on Amanda and Corey."

"Did you get any sleep? You were dead on your feet when I left you last night."

"Slept in till nine. Then I made myself get up."

"Have you found anything interesting?"

"Maybe. Have you ever been to Palm Beach?"

"No. Is that important?"

"It's the twenty-seventh wealthiest place in the United States. A condo there surely wouldn't come cheap. Which tells me Amanda and Corey have some bucks. Inherited or incomes."

"So Amanda might not be the gold-digger we suspected her of being."

"And Corey could be on the up-and-up as well."

A second's pause, "But it doesn't make sense for that to be the case. They were hanging out with Dad. I'm sure Amanda was sleeping with him, dammit. It just doesn't add up."

"Still, you have to be ready to accept the possibility."

Another pause. "I guess we will find out what kind of people they are when we talk to them tomorrow. We're still flying down there in the morning, right?"

"Nothing's changed. In the meantime, Susan is running a background check on both of them. I expect an email from her any time."

"Great. We can discuss everything over dinner tonight. See you then. Gotta get back to work."

"Take care of yourself, Linds."

Cherise disconnected the call, still concerned her friend might not be able to handle the direction they were headed. Lindsey had convinced herself representatives from Blue Water Cruise Line lied to cover up her father's disappearance.

She believed him dead.

Most likely murdered.

Cherise knew full well what the chances were they'd find Sam King alive after two weeks missing.

They'd be kidding themselves to believe they would.

In the past, a job was a job. Nothing personal. No emotional attachment. Then came the situation with Admiral Casey's son. Now Lindsey's father.

The difficult kind.

* * *

Cherise climbed out of the taxi at the curb in front of the American Museum of Natural History. The gold idols provided more than enough motive for Corey or Amanda, or even one of the other passengers to want to kill Lindsey's father. Staring at the columned facade, she realized how little she knew about Mayan culture, let alone the deities in question.

To make a run at Corey and Amanda, she needed to learn as much as possible in the short time she had to prepare.

Her work had taken her into many people's private lives for a hundred different reasons. In all but a very few of those cases, strangers hadn't opened up until they felt it was in their best interest to do so. And even then the information needed to be pried out of them. Knowledge had been the pry bar. In each instance, she had to make them believe she possessed facts they needed to disprove.

Corey and Amanda would be no different.

She trotted up the stairs and took her turn going through a security bag check. Then, thanks to a fast-moving line, she paid her admission fee and followed the halls to the Mayan exhibit in less than ten minutes.

The pre-Columbian artifacts were displayed in a glassed-in enclosure in the middle of the room. She walked directly there and scanned the relics for deities similar to those in Sam King's text. Stone and clay figurines dominated the display, a breastplate, an obsidian knife, intricately decorated clay pots and jugs. Many with effigies of men and women. Royalty, she guessed. Some of dogs. One of a man with a jaguar head. Only a couple in gold.

"You interested in Pre-Columbian art?" a stranger asked in a pleasant voice a few feet away.

Cherise looked up from the display. The guy speaking to her was middle-aged and a couple of inches shorter than her. He had dark skin as though he spent a lot of time in the sun, and facial features clearly of Mexican Indian ancestry.

"I have to admit, I know little about the topic," she said.

He smiled. "Put simply, Pre-Columbian relates to the history and cultures of the Americas before the arrival of Columbus in 1492."

"I didn't know that," she lied and continued to scan the exhibit.

"My name is Pacal Balam." He stepped closer and handed her a business card. "Perhaps I can be of further assistance."

She figured she had nothing to lose talking to the man. "A friend of mine has three gold idols that are supposed to be Mayan. I came here hoping to find others in the exhibit. Maybe learn a little bit about them."

"If you can describe the pieces, it's possible I can help you."

"Better than that, I can show you a photo of them." She glanced at the man's card. "You're an expert in the field?"

"My ancestors were Mayans of royal blood. I'm a professor of Central American History. The museum's curator invited me here to authenticate several artifacts that recently came into their possession."

She accessed her phone and showed a cropped photo to Pacal.

"Interesting," he said. "It's unusual to find a collection of deities such as this. As you are probably aware, sixteenth-century Spaniards stole most of the gold in my country. Mayan . . . Aztec . . . Incan— melted everything down and poured it into ingots. Shipped the bars back to Spain."

"Are they rare?"

"Rare enough. Most pieces are found in museums and private collections. Many of the new relics that come on the market today were looted from archeological sites across Central and South America, much of it from the Yucatan. Treasures such as these belong in museums in their native country, to reflect the indigenous people's culture."

"Do you know which deity they represent?"

"May I hold your phone?"

She handed it to him, and he studied the image. "*Cum Hau* . . . *Cizin*, I believe. A god of death and the underworld—The Lords of Death. Many of the Mayan gods dwell in the underworld to rule over the dead. The Lords of Death are often depicted as skeleton people or—as in this case—ugly bloated beings adorned with ornaments taken from the dead."

"What would three solid gold idols like this be worth to a collector?"

His eyes flashed a flinty hardness. "The artifacts in that picture are pieces of Mayan culture. They belong to the Mayan people. My people. I would strongly urge your friend to see that the pieces are returned at once."

Something haunting in the tone of his words took her aback.

A veiled threat?

A warning of some kind . . . a malediction?

She didn't believe in ancient curses.

"We don't actually have the idols in our possession. We only know that the relics exist." She slid the man's card into her pocket. "If we acquire the pieces, I'll be sure and keep your suggestion in mind."

She left the museum and hailed a taxi. She knew more than she did going in. But not as much as she wanted.

She had one more place on her list to visit.

CHAPTER 19

Jack stood at the entrance to Mallory Square. Two weathered posts resembling the spars of a long-dead sailing vessel holding a colorful sign with spindles to resemble a ship's wheel. A cruise ship sat tied to the dock. A flock of eager travelers milled about the shops and square.

"I figure this is a good place to start," he said to Robert.

"I know you want to help. I do, too. But a lot of people go in and out of here every day. And we're talking a couple of weeks since he went missing."

Jack remained positive. This wasn't all that different than some of the other capers he'd been involved in.

"I understand what you're saying. But we can't let it stop us."

"Still, I'm a little confused about what we hope to accomplish showing Sam King's picture to people. We know he was in town and we know he'd struck up a shipboard romance with this Amanda woman. What does it prove to have a shopkeeper tell us they remember seeing them together?"

"Maybe nothing. Then again, maybe something that will turn out to be a piece to a larger picture."

"That's a lot of maybes."

"So it is." Jack motioned him to follow. "Come on."

The next few minutes passed uneventfully. Jack stopped in front of the Memorial Sculpture Garden and looked at his watch. They had gotten enough sad shakes of the head to discourage them. But that didn't mean the next person, or the next, wouldn't recall seeing Lindsey's father.

He scanned the monument dedicated to the age of wreck salvaging, and the bronze busts of the thirty-six men and women credited with having the greatest impact on Key West. He'd seen them before and knew which bust was of Hemingway. He asked himself what the writer would have thought had he been in this situation. *Man is not made for defeat. A man can be destroyed but not defeated.*

He'd memorized the quote.

"What's the plan?" Robert asked.

"We keep looking."

"How about the Shipwreck Museum and the Mel Fisher Museum? We haven't been to those places yet. I'm almost certain they would be on King's list of places to check out."

"Sounds logical to me. I know I would."

"You have been. To both of them."

"I meant if I was him." Jack started walking. "Come on."

At the Shipwreck Museum, they listened to the guide portraying wrecker tycoon Asa Tift tell the history of four-hundred years of wreck salvaging and how this unique industry provided for the livelihood of the entire island at a time when Key West had the largest population in Florida. An interesting story. One they'd heard before.

When the guide finished his talk, Jack made the introductions and showed him the photos, only to receive another shake of the head.

He wasn't ready to give up.

"Are you sure?" He showed the photos to the man a second time and scrolled back to the picture of Sam King. "It's been a couple of weeks, but it's important. This man's missing and we're afraid something bad has happened to him."

"Sorry," the guide said. "I really do wish I could help. But I honestly don't recall seeing him, or the friends he was with."

Jack took a calming breath. "I understand. Thanks for your time."

They stepped away and Robert said, "It's not looking good, is it?"

"We haven't tried the Mel Fisher Museum, yet."

It was mid-day when they stepped through the doorway of the museum. The weather turned into a scorcher with enough humidity from a bank of dark clouds out over the Gulf to make them happy to be inside.

"Good afternoon," Jack said to the man collecting admission. "My name is Jack Ferrell and this is my friend Robert Foster. We're not here to see the exhibits. But if you have a moment, I'd appreciate it if you would look at a couple of pictures and tell me if you recall seeing any of the people in the photographs. It's really important."

"I think most everybody who comes to town wanders through here at one time or another during their stay. My name's Ned. I'll be happy to take a look. Doesn't mean I'll remember their faces, though."

Jack showed him the photo of Lindsey's father. "This is a man named Sam King. He's missing. That's why we're looking for him."

"Missing, huh?"

"A couple of weeks ago. He was with two passengers from the cruise ship he was on. We fear something bad has happened to him."

Ned gave the photo a long look. "Nothing rings a bell. Course he looks like a lot of the Hemingway wannabes in town. And it has been a while. You have pictures of the people he was with, I suppose?"

Jack scrolled ahead. "We know he was with this woman. We're not sure about the guy."

Ned began to nod, almost imperceptibly at first. "I remember her. A real beauty. Stuck with me because of how she was dressed. Didn't hide much, I'll tell you that. She was hanging on to an older gentleman that could have been the man you're looking for. To be honest, I paid more attention to her than I did him."

"What about this guy?" Jack showed him Corey's picture.

"There was a big man with them. Tall. Looked like a body builder. Could be this guy. Like I said, I was looking at the woman."

"Anything special about them other than their looks?"

Ned shook his head. "I just remember they didn't stay long."

"I appreciate your time. You've been a big help." Jack laid a twenty on the counter. "A donation for the cause."

He stepped into the heat of the day. The weather hadn't cooled in the last fifteen minutes. He bought him and Robert a bottle of water from a vender and said, "This is good. We placed the three of them here together. Let's see what else we can dig up."

CHAPTER 20

The answers Cherise wanted weren't going to come from a hotel concierge or a professor of Central American History. They would come from a dealer in rare and unusual antiquities. Special items. A shop owner not concerned with how the relic was acquired, and no compunction about breaking up a collection to sell off each piece to someone rich enough to pay the money to acquire the artifact. With no troublesome morals to hinder cash flow.

Anything for a profit.

The driver of the taxi she'd ridden in on her way to the museum, suggested she pay a visit to Bristol Gallery in lower Manhattan. Purveyors of fine and unusual collectables.

Where she was headed now.

The driver of the taxi she climbed into seemed to know where he was going.

Several times during the ride, he attempted to engage her in conversation. And each time she avoided his questions, preferring to keep her business at Bristol Gallery private. The man was persistent if nothing else.

That annoyed her.

At one fifteen she left the taxi driver and the July heat behind and stepped into the air-conditioned comfort of Bristol Gallery located at Mercer and Bleecker. A subtle *bing, bong* announced her arrival.

The shop did not appear large at first. On closer examination, she realized how far back the room went. Porcelain figurines, colorful vases, primitive wood and stone carvings, tapestries and rugs, a suit of armor, and several small pieces of oiled wood furniture—probably colonial—were everywhere. Three large, glassed-in display cases loomed in back. Swords and antique guns hung on the walls.

A plump, spectacled, middle-aged man, well dressed with a large bald spot in the middle of a mat of graying brown hair, appeared from a dimly lit back room and walked toward her. A dab of mustard clung to the corner of his mouth.

"May I help you?" He talked in a quiet voice.

His tone implied this was a hushed place. She spoke just as softly. "Are you the owner?"

He gave a curt nod. "Harvey Bristol. Is there something in particular that you're looking for?"

"I understand you deal in items of archeological significance?"

He perked up. "That's my specialty."

She smiled and touched her fingertip to the corner of her mouth. "It looks like I interrupted your lunch."

He produced a handkerchief and dabbed at his lips. "I apologize for that. With my wife out ill, I rarely get time to actually sit down and eat."

"That's quite all right. I hope your wife feels better soon. Items of archeological significance are your specialty? How about solid gold idols—Pre-Columbian gods, devils, pieces like that? Mayan . . . or possibly Aztec or Incan."

His eyes locked on hers and held a moment before he made an appraisal—subtle but head to toe. Apparently satisfied with his assessment of her, he motioned with his head. "I have a couple that might interest you. This way, please."

She followed him to the display case at the rear of the shop and waited while he slipped from view in the back room. If he had to remove the items from a safe it could take him a few minutes. She spent the time perusing the gold and silver coins beneath the glass.

Five minutes later, he returned. "These are the only objects I have. They are completely documented and authenticated. Fourteenth-century Peru. Lovely craftsmanship."

She waited while he unwrapped the artifacts and placed them on a swatch of purple velvet. The first piece—maybe three inches tall—depicted a pregnant woman. The second looked male, also about three inches tall.

"What does something like this go for?"

"For you, forty-eight thousand each."

"And if the idol was an inch or two taller and more finely crafted than either of these two?"

His head tilted in a quizzical look. "A piece like what you describe could go for perhaps twice that. Of course I would need to see it. Are you saying you have the idol you're describing?"

"A friend does," she said. "Suppose my friend walked in here wanting to sell it on a cash basis, no fuss or questions asked on your part. What would you pay for something like that?"

His eyes shifted back and forth. Somewhere in the shop a clock ticked. "I assure you, madam, I do not receive or deal in stolen antiquities. If that is what this is about, I must ask you to leave the store."

Faked indignation.

Expected.

"I suppose my friend could always melt the idols down for the gold content."

The shop owner sucked in a breath, the flat of his hand pasted against his chest. "Idols?"

She had his attention. "Three of them, Mr. Bristol. All practically identical. And all over four inches tall. Solid gold."

He shook his head. "Surely your friend would never destroy an art treasure such as that?"

She shrugged. "My friend, of course, realizes they'd be taking a loss. But that might be the only way."

The little man leaned close. "You are obviously a careful person."

"When the situation calls for it."

"I would have to see the pieces, of course. But if they are what you claim them to be, a mutually agreeable arrangement could be made. Say, twenty-five percent over gold value. I'll give you my card. Have your friend call me."

She smiled at the shop owner's greedy little offer, slid his card in her pocket, and walked out of Bristol Gallery. Even if she had the idols, she'd never sell them to him. But she did have a better understanding of how much the relics were worth and how easily they could be disposed of.

Her phone chimed with an incoming email.

Susan.

There would be a lot to talk over with Lindsey at dinner.

CHAPTER 21

Jack stood next to Robert at the corner of Fleming and Duval Street. Directly behind them, Margaritaville blasted parrot music in full swing with the afternoon crowd. He looked back the way they had come and watched the busy street activity. Too early in the day to start drinking . . . except in Key West—especially with the Hemingway Days celebration right around the corner. An ice cold beer would do a lot to soothe his disappointment.

He'd held off long enough.

"Frustrating, isn't it." A statement not a question. "Unless you have a better idea, I suggest we walk back to Sloppy Joe's, get us a cold beer and something to eat, and talk this over."

Robert gave him a sideways look. "You do realize how lucky we were to stumble onto Ned, don't you?"

Jack huffed. "Sure I do. But I had my hopes up that we'd have something more substantial to tell Cherise."

"I think the optimum word there is *we*. And giving her something is better than zip. Makes me cringe to think of the disappointment Mel Fisher suffered."

"Be nice to have some of that gold about now."

"A little buyer's remorse?"

"Over buying the boat? Not even." Jack clapped Robert on the back. "Come on. We haven't had fun together like this in a while."

"Not your kind of fun."

"My kind of fun? All we're doing is showing the man's face to a few people. What can happen?"

"With you, plenty."

"Quit whining. Let's get that beer while we're still young."

"All the way back to Sloppy Joe's?"

"Hemingway drank there. I drink there."

"I keep forgetting. But you do know Sloppy Joe's was originally located on Greene Street where Captain Tony's Saloon now stands. Hemingway's close friend 'Sloppy Joe' Russell moved his bar a half-block to Duval Street in 1937 in order to get cheaper rent. So technically, Hemingway drank in both locations."

"You've been surfing your iPad again."

Robert shrugged.

They made it two blocks. Jack's chest and armpits were soaked. Getting to that cold beer kept him walking, until he saw three punks hassling a young lady in the alley behind the Hard Rock Café. One of the assholes stomped the girl's cell phone. Another groped her ass and laughed. The third held on to her arm, preventing her from running away.

"Dammit," he said. "And I was having such a good day."

Robert frowned. "Sir Galahad to the rescue."

"The woman clearly wants to be left alone."

"Looks like those assholes have a different idea."

"We can't stand here and not help her."

"Told you you'd get me into trouble."

Jack glanced back at him. "Stay here and watch, if you like."

"And let you have all the fun, no way."

Jack approached the men. College aged. Young and stupid. "I think you boys have had enough fun. Time to leave the young lady alone."

"Butt out, old man." The smallest of the three punks squared off at him. Always the small one with something to prove to his bigger buddies backing him up.

Jack didn't necessarily want to hurt these guys, but he didn't want to dance with them, either. "Walk away and call it good. Your friends, too."

"Fuck off."

Had the situation been more serious, Jack would have finished Big Mouth off already, along with the guy's two friends. Their hormones and the drinks they had downed got the best of them. He wanted to give the dudes every chance to walk away.

"Last chance. It's hot out here. You've obviously been drinking and I don't have time for any bullshit from you."

The other two punks joined Big Mouth and all three of them squared off with him and Robert. Shirtless to the right and Big Red to the left.

Dance time.

Big Mouth attempted a kick to the groin.

Jack expected the move, turned just enough, and took the blow on his thigh. At the same time he grabbed Big Mouth's ankle, pulled him in close, and hammered a hard right to the guy's nose.

His punch smashed cartilage and bone amid a gush of blood and put the loud-mouthed asshole down on his butt.

Shirtless telegraphed a roundhouse right that Jack ducked under.

The guy needed boxing lessons.

Jack answered with a right to the gut, followed by a left jab to the side of the jaw. The guy wobbled and Jack put him down with a hard right cross to the chin.

Jack hadn't forgotten about the third guy.

He pivoted, ready to take on the big red head.

But that wasn't necessary.

Robert stood over him, massaging his hand.

Three down.

"Hurt yourself?" Jack asked.

"Just my knuckles. What do we do with them?"

"I have an idea. Give me a hand."

Shirtless lay on his side, out cold. Big Mouth sat staring about through glassy eyes blank as slate and would likely remain that way for some time. Big Red didn't appear to be in any better shape than Shirtless.

"In there." Jack hefted Big Mouth over his shoulder.

He carried the guy's slack body to the dumpster at the rear of the Hard Rock Café and heaved him in. Robert did the same with

Big Red, and Jack went back for Shirtless.

With the three punks laying limp among the scraps of food and other garbage, Jack walked over to the young lady. Robert followed at his side. She hadn't run off. He was glad of that.

"They didn't hurt you, did they?"

"I like what you did."

Jack glanced at the dumpster. "Just taking out the trash."

She hugged herself tight across her breasts. "They deserved it."

"What's your name? That's our price for helping a damsel in distress."

"Lynn Hastings. I really can't thank you enough."

Robert scooped up the remains of Lynn's phone and handed the pieces to her. "Are you going to be all right now? Do we need to call someone for you?"

She shook her head. "I'll be okay once I have a chance to calm my nerves. I'm down here with a girlfriend. She's back at the room. We're staying at the Casa 325. It's not more than a half block from here."

"Then we'll leave you to your friend," Jack said. "Don't let this little incident spoil your vacation."

"I'll try not to." She smiled. "Thank you . . . both of you."

They watched her walk away. Several people had stopped. How long they'd been standing there and how much they had witnessed, Jack didn't know. But they all carried smartphones.

No doubt a ton of pictures would show up on social media.

Or already had.

He clapped Robert on the back and said, "Let's get that beer before something else happens."

CHAPTER 22

When the two policemen wearing uniform shirts, matching shorts, gun belts, cuffs, and two-way radios stepped into Sloppy Joe's, Jack and Robert were seated at a table. They sipped their beers as though nothing had happened.

Jack looked at Robert. "I think we have company."

"Probably here to talk to us."

"Suspect so."

The two officers scanned the room before walking over. The cop standing to Jack's right, towered over his partner who stood close to six feet tall. The taller cop said, "We need to talk to you two about the incident up the street."

Not any incident. *The* incident.

Jolly Green knew they were involved and knew there was no question in their minds which incident he referred to. There had been plenty of witnesses, and just as likely, plenty of pictures taken by bystanders' smartphones.

Jack asked, "Did you talk to the young lady those punks assaulted?"

"We did. The three guys you dumped in the trash bin, too. And now we're talking to you."

"Are any charges being pressed?"

Jack knew the drill. He dug out his Hawaii driver's license before being asked and handed it to the officer. Robert did the same. Jolly

Green glanced at the IDs and passed them to his partner who stepped back and radioed in.

"You worked over those three guys pretty good. The one whose nose you smashed is on the way to the hospital."

"We gave them every chance to leave the young lady alone. The short one thought he was tough. He started the altercation with us."

The shorter cop returned to the table, still holding on to the licenses. "You've had a few run-ins with law enforcement."

"Jack has," Robert said. "Not me."

"Thanks, buddy." Jack looked up at the officer's nameplate. "Officer Harper, I'm sure you also know, none of those incidents resulted in charges being filed."

"But you seem to get involved in questionable situations, which is of interest to me and my partner."

Jack glanced into the eyes of each officer. Both cops studied him with expectant expressions. Possibly sizing him up, pushing a few buttons to see what kind of response they would get.

A game he didn't want to play. "Why would that interest you?"

Jolly Green—Zackary from the nameplate pinned above the breast pocket of his uniform—said, "We don't want any problems. Once Hemingway Days is in full swing, we'll have plenty to handle without adding to them now."

Jack had no problem playing law-abiding citizen. "What you're saying is you want us to promise to be good boys and not get in any more fights. I can assure you, we'll do our best."

"See that you do." Harper handed back their licenses and motioned his partner out.

"That was fun," Robert said when the officers left the bar.

Jack stared at the open entryway. A group of twenty-somethings broke out in laughter on the sidewalk out front a second before stepping inside. "I'm surprised they didn't get around to us sooner."

Robert tapped the rim of his glass against Jacks. "Here's to being good boys."

Jack drained half his beer. "What do you say we take a couple of thick steaks and a six-pack of ice cold Red Stripe out to the *Adeona* and watch the sunset from her upper deck?"

"You do own the boat so we might as well make use of her. After today, I could use a quiet evening."

Jack felt the same.

But he still had a text to send before he could let go of the day. He just wished he had more to pass on to Cherise. Surely she would know he and Robert had done the best they could. And feel fortunate to have the information Ned had given them. It had been a stroke of luck to run into the man.

He knew it. Robert knew it.

If Sam King had bought into a con, he'd done so quietly.

CHAPTER 23

Cherise felt the need to walk. Jack's text gave her more to think about. One more piece to fit into a puzzle she was beginning to put together.

She met Lindsey at Toscana 49—classic Italian cuisine in a quiet atmosphere—seven blocks from the Grand Hyatt and one block from the Waldorf Astoria.

They settled into a back booth and each ordered a glass of red wine.

"I heard from Jack," she said. "He talked to a man who puts your dad with Amanda and her brother at the Mel Fisher Museum. It's not much but we at least confirmed they went ashore together."

"So they had become pretty good friends by then?"

"At the very least, Amanda and Corey wanted your dad to think they were."

"Those two didn't waste any time, did they?"

"They only had a few days. Did you get the time off you asked for?"

"All next week. My supervisor was totally understanding."

The waiter arrived with their wine. Cherise watched him set the glasses on the table.

He asked, "Are you ready to order dinner now?"

She shook her head. "We'll need a few minutes."

Lindsey studied her. "You have something else on your mind.

I can tell. Is everything okay?"

Cherise sipped, taking time to answer. "I did some digging today."

"All right. But this is Linds you're talking to. Something's eating at you. What is it?"

Cherise knew she couldn't move forward without being totally open about her concerns. And Lindsey was demanding it.

"There is something bothering me. I make it a point to know as much as I can about my cases. Normally I don't take clients along with me on a job. Too risky. I'm making an exception for you for old time's sake. But there might be a time when I need you to stand down and let me handle things, whatever that might entail."

Lindsey gripped the stem of her glass and peered into her wine. All at once her casual smile crumpled. "You're saying you don't want me along?"

"That's not what I'm saying. I'm saying I'm worried about you."

"That I'll get hurt?"

"Physically . . . there's certainly that possibility. But you could also be hurt mentally. I don't want that, either."

"I thought the matter was settled. That you understood how I felt."

Cherise peered into her friend's eyes. "You made it quite clear you want revenge. I get that. And I have no qualms about seeing that you get what you're after. But we can't without knowing for sure that Amanda and Corey are responsible. We need to go slow, work the angles. It could take time."

"How much time?"

"There's no way for me to know that going in."

"But they *are* responsible. We both agreed on that. How long can it take to pry the truth out of them?"

"*Pry the truth out of them* is an interesting choice of words."

"What are you saying?"

"I'm saying Corey and Amanda are a starting point. When you said pry, you were closer to the truth than you might realize. Because that is exactly what we could end up having to do. And bear in mind, some people don't pry as easily as others. Getting them to open up could be unpleasant. Are you prepared for that?"

"I thought with you helping me, it would be easy."

"That's why I had second thoughts about having you along. Now that I've laid everything out for you, do you still want to play? Or would you rather I handle this problem personally and provide you with a nice tidy box full of answers sealed with a pink ribbon?"

Lindsey looked like someone slapped her. "Now you're being nasty."

"That's not my intention, Linds. I'm just giving you the option to watch from the sidelines and still get what you're after."

"My mind hasn't changed. I grew up not knowing the love of a father. Then I found Dad. Now someone has taken him away from me. Damn right I want them to pay. And I want to be there when they do."

"Even if you have to settle in for the long haul?"

"No matter how long it takes."

"And you'll follow orders without question?"

"I'll do whatever I have to do to see this through."

Cherise nodded to herself. "That's what I needed to hear. Let's order and I'll fill you in on what I've found out."

"You got the information from Susan?"

"That's not all."

CHAPTER 24

Cherise closed her menu. A silent signal to the waiter they were ready to order. Lindsey did the same. "Disappointed?" Cherise asked.

Lindsey stared. "In what? You made no promises. Only that we'd try. We're doing that."

Their waiter appeared. "What may I get for you?"

"Linds?" Cherise said.

Clearly preoccupied, Lindsey said, "Go ahead."

Cherise turned to the waiter and took it upon herself to order for both of them. "We'll have the green salad and the spaghetti carbonara. And bring us two more glasses of wine, please."

The waiter left the table, and Cherise looked at Lindsey. "You *are* disappointed."

"I'm not, really." Lindsey drained her glass. "I just wish Dad would call and say he's all right."

"But you know that's not going to happen?"

"That's what makes me sad. . . . And angry."

"I understand how you feel. As you know, I've been there myself."

Lindsey didn't answer.

Cherise's concern for her friend resurfaced. She wished she was able to lend comfort. Find the right words. Share the pain. But she had buried her own feelings of loss and had no desire to dig them up and air them out.

Nothing would be gained.

For now, she needed to stop worrying. Lindsey had survived the military. She could survive this.

"Linds. Are you with me?"

Lindsey blinked. "I apologize. My feelings got the best of me for a second. It won't happen again."

"It's okay to have feelings, Linds. But we need to stay focused in order to make this work."

"You're right. And I am. What did Susan have to say about Amanda and Corey?"

"First, I want to tell you about my afternoon. I visited the American Museum of Natural History hoping to get some idea what these relics are all about. I spoke to a man by the name of Pacal Balam. A professor of Central American History. They're Mayan Deities. Gods of death and the underworld. According to him, solid gold idols such as these do not come on the market often. When they do, most of them have been looted from archeological sites across Central and South America, much of it from the Yucatan. He hinted that they're cursed."

Lindsey sipped her wine. "Do you believe that?"

"Not at all. But I'm sure some people out there do."

"Maybe those ugly little things *are* cursed. It could explain what happened to Dad."

"The only curse those idols possess is that they're valuable."

"How much money are we talking about?"

"A gallery owner estimated they were worth around a hundred thousand each. He wouldn't pay that much for them, of course. But he did offer me twenty-five percent over gold value. That's still a lot of money."

"Dad would know that. And I'm sure Corey and Amanda did, too. What did the background report tell us about them?"

"Susan included complete financials on both which saved time. Amanda is thirty-two years old. She's an independent chartered accountant. Single. Never married. Father's deceased. So are the grandparents. She specializes in saving failed companies by eliminating unnecessary expenditures. Quite a reputation, according to the internet. She has a high six-figure bank account and lots of credit. There were no suspicious transactions that I saw."

"What about Corey?"

"He's thirty-eight and a TV celebrity. He had his own reality series till a couple of years ago. A fishing show where he traveled the world catching monster fish. Canceled after a couple of seasons. That's probably where he got his tan. Now he's working in advertising—endorses fishing and sports equipment. As it turns out, Corey is Amanda's half-brother. And he has an arrest record for second-degree assault. A three-year-old case out of West Palm Beach. Pled no contest to a misdemeanor charge and received a year's probation."

Lindsey frowned. "That says something about him."

"Perhaps. But it depends on the circumstances surrounding the case."

"Still, it tells me he's not the nice guy you'd expect him to be."

Cherise shook her head, not wanting to jump to conclusions even though she found it difficult not to. "At the very least, I think it's safe to assume he exhibited a predisposition for violence."

"Like murder?"

"He might just be an asshole actor with a temper." Cherise paused in thought, then added, "Then again, he could be a sociopath with no qualms about committing murder. All we can really say about him is he appears to enjoy living the high life. His bank account fluctuates drastically from month to month. Lots of credit card expenditures at restaurants and clubs. But I didn't see any recent deposits that would correspond with the sale of the idols."

"Which means what?"

"It means that if they are responsible for whatever happened to your father, they managed to operate under the radar."

"You mean, hid the money? Amanda would certainly know how to do that."

"If that's what they're doing."

"There has to be something to indicate they are involved. What else do we know about them?"

Cherise admired her friend's persistence. "They have a sister named Jessica Finch. Husband deceased. Jessica is a travel agent at

Dream World Travel, a company owned by their mother Veronica Kelly."

"I saw an ad for that agency in a travel magazine. Dad booked his trip through them."

"That's extremely interesting. I never have put much stock in coincidences. They happen, I suppose. But this is way too fortuitous not to have some connection to your dad's disappearance."

"A setup from the beginning?"

"We'll find that out when we get to Palm Beach."

CHAPTER 25

The sun set in all its magnificence. Jack let go of the events of the day and sipped his beer on the upper deck of *Adeona*.

"Nice evening," Robert said.

"A great steak, a cold beer, and a perfect sunset." Jack sighed with contentment. "Doesn't get any better."

"So what's the plan?"

"At the moment, I don't have one. Cherise said she and her friend Lindsey might be meeting us here. If that happens, I suppose whatever we do will depend on what she has to say."

"So it's kickback time until then. I could get used to this."

"You own a house overlooking Kaneohe Bay. You're already used to it."

"But this is like a vacation."

"Then we'll make the best of it. How about going below and getting us another beer?"

"If it'll keep you happy."

"Just don't break anything while you're down there."

Robert chuckled. "O ye of little faith."

Jack listened to his friend thump and bump around below. A light came on and the noise stopped. He smiled to himself and propped his feet up on the railing and watched the last of the color fade in the western sky. He felt good having his own boat under him again.

"You need to see this," Robert called out. "You're not going to believe it."

Jack couldn't imagine what Robert referred to. He ducked through the top hatch and followed the steps into the salon. Robert stood, pointing to a wood panel on the forward bulkhead.

"What the hell? I haven't owned the boat twenty-four hours and you're already breaking stuff."

"I bumped into it in the dark, but it's not broken. Take a closer look."

Robert beamed with curiosity. An expression Jack had seen many times. He stooped to study the damaged panel. "What the hell?"

Robert stooped next to him. "See what I mean?"

"Looks like a secret compartment . . . some kind of hidey-hole." Jack slid the panel to the side, revealing a compartment roughly eighteen inches wide, twenty-four inches tall, and twelve inches deep. He reached inside and removed a watertight plastic container the size of a Clive Cussler novel and what looked like a bound journal or ship's logbook.

"Interesting," Robert said. "I'm guessing Ms. Faggini didn't know about her husband's hiding spot."

Jack set the box on the deck in front of him and leafed through the pages of the log. "This looks to me like a personal journal more than it does a ship's logbook. The entries are written in Italian. But most of the pages are blank."

"I know how good your Italian is," Robert said. "Better let me have a look."

Jack handed him the journal. "Let's take everything topside."

Under the stars and utilizing the light mounted above the flybridge helm, Robert perused the entries in the journal while Jack opened the watertight container.

"You're *not* going to believe this." He carefully lifted a novel from the box, drawing Robert's attention away from his reading.

"Looks old," Robert said.

"You have no idea." Jack turned the front cover toward Robert so he could see the title.

Robert rocked forward, nearly falling out of his chair. "No way."

Jack opened the cover and scanned the page. "It's a first edition and it's signed by Ernest Hemingway: 'To Miguel. My inspiration for Manolin.'"

"You're kidding?"

Jack closed the novella and ran his fingers over the cover. "I've seen copies of *The Old Man and the Sea* in nowhere near as fine a condition as this go for ten thousand dollars. I'm guessing this would go for a lot more."

Robert reached out. "Let me hold it."

Jack handed the novella to him as though the pages could fall apart in his hands.

Robert carefully opened the cover. "This inscription that Hemingway wrote credits Miguel, whoever he is, with being the inspiration for Manolin, the boy in the story. Hemingway claimed the old man, Santiago, was based on nobody in particular. Apparently that is not true for the boy."

"There's a letter addressed to Antonio Faggini inside the box, as well." He removed it from its envelope. "Maybe it sheds some light on what this is all about."

"It's probably in Italian," Robert said.

"Sure looks like it." Jack returned the letter to its envelope and handed it to Robert in exchange for the novella. "There's a photograph in here, too."

"Miguel?"

"That'd be my guess." Jack removed the photograph and returned the book to the box. "It's a boy of about twelve or thirteen. He's standing with Hemingway and another man. There's a marlin strung up between them."

Robert scanned the letter. "You'll want to hear this."

CHAPTER 26

Jack waited. Robert was taking his time. Perhaps he wasn't as versed in Italian as he claimed.

"All right already. I'm going gray waiting."

"Give me another second or two. From the name at the bottom of the letter, Miguel Garcia wrote it. But judging from the quality of the writing, he wasn't an educated man."

"But does he mention the book?"

"That, and quite a bit more. He starts by saying he knew Ernest Hemingway and he knew his sons. And he knew Gregorio Fuentes. Miguel says he's the young boy named Manolin in *The Old Man and the Sea*. That he carried their stout rods and reels down to *Pilar*, and caught the sardines and mackerel they fished with."

Jack pictured the boy fishing from the rocks along the beach— using a hand-line to catch the bait. Pictured him carrying the heavy rods and reels down to the boat. And he pictured the boy, Manolin, from the story.

He nodded. "Hence the inscription Hemingway wrote in the book."

"Exactly," Robert agreed. He traced the page with his finger as he read. "Miguel goes on to say that in 1951, when Hemingway started writing *The Old Man and the Sea*, he was eleven years old. And that he was six when Gregorio found him living on the beach and invited him into his home. He says that on his thirteenth birthday,

Hemingway gave him this first edition copy of *The Old Man and the Sea* and told him, 'There is no friend as loyal as a book.' "

Robert laid that page aside, taking care not to tear or crumple the paper.

Jack said, "No truer words were ever spoken. You being the exception, of course."

"But of course." Robert grinned. "There's more. Do you want to hear it?"

"Are you kidding? Keep reading."

Robert scanned the page. "Okay. Now we know how Antonio ended up with the book. Miguel writes that Antonio is his wife's brother's only son. Miguel explains his health is failing. He has no children of his own, and there is no family left. And though they have never met, he's passing this treasure to Antonio."

Jack peered down at the cover of the novella. "But how did the book wind up on the boat?"

"There's more," Robert said. "But I think the journal entries might answer that question. In the letter, Miguel says people have claimed that Ernest Hemingway based *The Old Man and the Sea* on his longtime friend and captain of his boat *Pilar*, Gregorio Fuentes. And even though Hemingway claimed the old man, Santiago, was based on no one in particular, Miguel claims he knows different. He says that for nearly thirty years, Gregorio Fuentes served as captain, cook, and friend to Hemingway. That Gregorio, alone, spent more time with Hemingway than any other man. And since Hemingway, upon his death in 1961, left *Pilar* and all his fishing tackle to Gregorio, there is no greater proof of the strong bond between them."

Jack leaned back in his chair, Red Stripe in hand. "So Miguel disputes Hemingway's claim."

"Appears so." Robert stared at the final page, clearly drawn in by what had been written there. "You'll love this. It says here that not long after Gregorio took possession of *Pilar*, the boat was requisitioned by Castro and eventually put on display outside the Hemingway Museum—Hemingway's former home in Havana. And during the days that followed, Rafael Fuentes, Gregorio's grandson, showed Miguel a leather-bound sheaf of papers Gregorio discovered on *Pilar* before the boat was put on display. Those papers, he claims, were Hemingway's handwritten manuscript notes for *The Old Man and the Sea*."

"What?" Jack almost choked on the swig of beer he'd just taken.

"That's what he claims," Robert pointed at the page. "Right here. And he finishes the letter saying, to hold the leather-bound folder in his hands and read Hemingway's handwritten words had such power, he found it difficult to return the pages to Rafael who swore him to secrecy out of fear Castro would seize Hemingway's story notes. A secret he has kept until now. He concludes with a quote from Hemingway: 'The best way to find out if you can trust somebody is to trust them.' "

Robert refolded the letter, inserted it in its envelope, and laid it in the box.

Jack watched, his mind whirling as his brain replayed everything Miguel had written. "Can you imagine getting your hands on those manuscript notes? They'd be worth a small fortune."

Robert picked up the journal and opened it. He slowly turned the pages. And after a moment, he said, "Apparently Antonio had the same idea." He read the entries aloud.

"September 6, 2017:
After three weeks at sea crossing the Atlantic, Violetta and I arrived in the safety of Havana Harbor ahead of the threat of Hurricane Irma. As we entered the harbor under the watchful eyes of the 16th-century stone fortresses—Castillo de San Salvador de la Punta and Castillo De Los Tres Reyes Del Morro—I felt their rusted cannon bear down on the *Adeona* as though the big guns would fire upon us at any moment. I have yet to tell Violetta my real reason for our visit to Cuba. She believes we are here for the shopping. As much as I want to tell her about Miguel, and share the letter I received from him, I feel bound by the vow of secrecy he entrusted to me.

"September 7, 2017:
We spent last night ashore in Havana. Violetta's mood

has improved. Today we visit the Hemingway Museum to see the famous writer's home, and to walk the grounds where Miguel played as a young boy. The handwritten notes mentioned in Miguel's letter are not at the museum but I hope to visit Cojimar, the coastal town ten kilometers east of Havana, where Gregorio Fuentes lived his entire life. It's also where Hemingway kept his yacht. And if I locate Rafael Fuentes, Gregorio Fuentes' grandson, and talk to him, maybe I can hold those story notes the way Miguel did and feel the power of Hemingway's handwritten words.

"September 8, 2017:
This morning, Violetta and I travel to Key West. If we leave Cuba now, we will arrive ahead of Hurricane Irma, which has destroyed Puerto Rico and is sure to hit Cuba. I know I am taking a chance leaving with the storm so close upon us, but I am anxious to find out if what I have learned from Gregorio Fuentes' grandson is true. Rafael was hesitant to give me specifics, even when I showed him the letter from Miguel. And though he did not doubt its authenticity and my vow to secrecy, he would only tell me the manuscript notes are in Key West where he took them to keep the papers out of Castro's hands. My quest has now turned into an obsession to locate them.

"September 9, 2017:
We arrived in Key West ahead of Irma. But the storm is due to hit the Keys some time during the night. My objective now is to ride out the storm in one of the shelters and hope the town is not destroyed. I must find those documents."

Robert closed the journal and sighed. "Those are the last entries Antonio made before he died."
And now we have the rest of the story.
Jack leaned back in his chair and stared at the town lights. "So Hemingway's story notes are hidden here, someplace."
"According to Rafael Fuentes they are. Only Antonio didn't

know that for sure and neither do we."

"Still, Antonio came here in search of them."

"You have that glint in your eyes. If you're thinking of turning this into one of your Jack Ferrell treasure hunts, sorry. Looks like a dead end to me."

"Not a dead end," Jack said. "A place to start."

CHAPTER 27

Jet Blue touched down in West Palm Beach at 10:23 AM. A half hour later—and a quick stop at baggage claim—Cherise stood next to Lindsey in the moist air at the curb waiting for the hotel shuttle that would take them to The Breakers Luxury Palm Beach Resort. The weather felt more like the Hawaiian Islands and less like New York City. A cloudless blue sky overhead. A storm brewing on the eastern horizon.

Lindsey exhaled a deep, audible breath. "Why do I feel strange now that we're here?"

"New York wasn't reality. This is."

"This kind of work doesn't scare you?"

"I'm used to it, I guess."

"So not even a little?"

"Okay. Just enough to keep me from getting overanxious and careless. Not to mention, dead." Cherise pointed at an on-coming passenger van. "Our ride is here. You'll relax once we get checked into the hotel."

Lindsey took hold of her luggage. "I hope so."

The Breakers turned out to be every bit the luxury resort Susan said it was. Cherise made a mental note to send her a nice bottle of Santa Teresa rum along with a thank-you note.

She also needed to calm Lindsey's nerves. "This place is unbelievably fantastic."

Lindsey glanced around as though taking in the hotel's magnificence in a single sweep of her head. "Makes me feel like I'm on vacation."

"If it were only so."

"Doesn't mean we can't enjoy the stay while we're here."

Cherise agreed. "No it doesn't. And who knows, one of these days we might have an opportunity to return under different circumstances."

"I'd love that."

Cherise saw genuineness in her friend's smile. And in her eyes, the nervous uncertainty of a quest with no guarantees. Merely a series of blind corners with no way to see what's coming, only what's been.

"It's early," she said. "Let's see if we can check in?"

The dark-haired man at the registration desk greeted them. David, according to his brass nameplate, wore a wide smile.

"We have a reservation." Cherise gave David her identification and watched him tap the information into his computer.

Again, with his too-friendly smile. "We have you in adjoining ocean view rooms. Numbers 426 and 427. A nice location away from the elevators. Unfortunately, it will be a while before they're ready. If you excuse me a moment, I'll check with housekeeping and see if they can give me an idea when your rooms will be available."

"Thank you." Cherise turned to Lindsey. "We can always have lunch while we're waiting."

"Just so it's not too long. I'd really like to freshen up after the flight."

Cherise winked. "I have a feeling we've been moved to the top of the list."

Her phone chimed. She read the text, smiled, and sent a reply.

"You're smiling, so let me guess. Jack?"

"Checking up on us."

"He's worried?"

"Just curious if we made it here."

David reappeared from a back office. "The guests in those rooms have only just now checked out. I asked that the rooms be cleaned right away. But I'm afraid it'll be another hour before they're ready.

Perhaps you would like to have lunch in the Beach Club Restaurant while you're waiting? I can call you and have your luggage sent up when the rooms are all set."

"Thank you. Now if you point us toward the restaurant, we'll take you up on your lunch suggestion."

The heavy, moist air had a salty smell. Overhead, the sun had grown hotter as the time neared mid-day. They had their choice of a table inside the airy, beach-chic dining room, or on the patio to take in the view of the pools and the oceanfront. In spite of the heat, they opted to sit on the patio deck at one of the many tables shaded by umbrellas. Their waiter handed them each a menu and left them alone to decide.

Lindsey picked up her menu, gave it a glance, lowered it, and looked around. "You're spending a lot of money helping me out. I know we're friends, but . . . What I'm trying to say is people pay you for what you do, right?"

"A percentage, usually. It varies from job to job, depending on the degree of danger involved and the estimated value of the recovery. But that doesn't apply in this case."

"You're saying that because you think you owe me?"

"Maybe that's part of it."

"You can't keep feeling guilty about what happened to me. We agreed . . ."

Cherise remembered their conversations. The promises. Good intentions, but she doubted she'd ever be free of the guilt for what happened that day.

She gave herself a moment, then said, "Since you insist, I'll put it to you straight. I'll front the expenses, which could be considerable. What we're doing can easily come crashing in on us or even get somebody hurt. But if we're fortunate to recover the three idols your father bought, we split the value right down the middle. Half for you and half for me. Agreed?"

"I think that's more than fair. What about expenses?"

"I'll cover them out of my share. This is not about making money. It's all about helping you find out what happened to your father."

"And if we don't recover the idols?"

"We'll cross that bridge when we come to it."
Lindsey's gaze met Cherise's and held. "What can I say?"
"Just say you understand how I feel."
Keep it together, Linds.

CHAPTER 28

Late the next morning, Jack motored him and Robert ashore in the dinghy. A slow start on the day after a great medium-rare steak, a few beers, and a late-night brainstorming session.

Robert hopped out with the bow line and secured it to the dock. "Still think we can find Hemingway's manuscript notes?"

"It's worth a try."

"We taking the Cooper this time?"

"Leave it. The exercise will do us good."

"Do *you* good. I'm just fine."

"So you say. Ready?"

"As I'll ever be."

Jack paused and scanned the town. "Sounds like Cheeseburger in Paradise is hopping."

Robert looked in that direction. "I think that place is always busy, especially on a Saturday. And keep in mind, the town is filling up for the festival next week."

"A blowout for sure."

"And this time we'll be here to take part in it."

"You know what I keep wondering? Why'd Rafael tell Antonio the papers were here but didn't tell him where?"

"Maybe because they aren't in Key West."

"As in, they never were?"

"That's what I'm saying. Rafael probably has the leather folder tucked away under his mattress in Cuba."

"And sent poor Antonio in search of something that isn't here."

"Yup."

"That's some wild goose chase. But if he just wanted to blow Antonio off, he could have said any number of things. Why specifically Key West?"

"Jack, my friend, that's the ten-thousand-dollar question. And also why we'll spend some time poking around, and have fun while we do it."

Jack nodded. "Let's start with the Hemingway Museum. You never know. We got lucky with Ned."

They walked the six blocks to Whitehead and Olivia Street. By the time they got there, Jack was eager to spend some time in the shade under the trees. He scanned the buildings and the grounds. A six-toed cat lounged on the front steps licking its paws. Five minutes later, he and Robert paid their fourteen dollars each and joined a group of people on a tour of the two-story house.

It was easy for Jack to envision Hemingway living there. Of particular interest was the author's writing studio in the loft of the carriage house. Decorated in pure Hemingway style, the room reflected a man who lived life large and then wrote, in his short, declarative writing style, some of the most extraordinary experiences a person could have.

Not unlike my own.

He could almost hear Hemingway's big fingers banging away on the Underwood typewriter sitting idle atop his desk.

When the tour concluded at the top of the stairs leading down to the basement Hemingway used as a wine cellar, Robert agreed with Jack that they were grasping at straws. Had Hemingway's manuscript notes been placed among the items on display in the museum, a treasure like that would not have gone unnoticed. The entire world would have known about them by now.

They stood in the shade and Robert asked, "Okay, Jack. You're leading this expedition, where to next?"

"So now we're calling this an expedition, and I'm in charge. I thought we were just checking a few places to see if something clicked."

"I like the idea of you being in charge. That way if we come up empty, it's your fault."

"What happened to the enthusiasm you had back on the boat?"

"That was before you made me walk six blocks in the sun."

"What you're saying is we should have taken the car?"

"You made the call. And I'm sweating. Any ideas?"

Jack checked the time on his phone. "Sloppy Joe's for a beer."

"And then what?"

He shrugged. "I'll let you know as it comes to me."

Five blocks later, they stepped into Sloppy Joe's and edged their way past a half dozen Hemingway lookalikes crowding the only empty table.

"People are starting the celebration early," Robert said. "If you wanted a quiet place to have a beer and brainstorm, this isn't it."

Jack slid back a chair and took a seat. "Good thing this place has plenty of help or a person could run the risk of dying from thirst."

"There's a few empty stools at the bar if you want to move."

"This is better for people-watching."

Robert motioned with his head. "Like this happy bunch next to us."

Jack scanned the room and the people occupying tables and those hugging the curved bar. "I'm sure the crowd will only get worse."

A young black girl dressed in a green Sloppy Joe's t-shirt, dark shorts, and a ball cap, stopped on her way past their table and took their order.

"That was quick," Jack said. "Looks like I won't die from thirst after all."

"She's not back yet."

"No, but here she comes."

They sipped their lager and watched the crowd. The group of Hemingway lookalikes had grown more boisterous. Two of the beefy men were engaged in a debate over fishing and boats and which one of them had caught the bigger marlin. After a minute or two, they got up from their table and stepped to the wall of framed photographs where they continued their argument.

Jack recalled most of the photos from his and Robert's prior visits. Enlarged black and whites of Hemingway posing with enormous billfish, with his drinking buddies, or alone with a drink raised to his lips, always peering into a camera. A rogue's gallery of Hemingway's life and of 1930's Key West.

The men's voices got louder, the tone of their dispute growing more heated. Three more from the group joined in the discussion.

Jack tried to tune them out, but couldn't.

He leaned close to Robert. "I think I need another beer."

Robert drained his bottle and set it aside. "I'm not sure it will help."

Jack kept his arms planted on the tabletop. "I've been thinking. If Antonio came to Key West to find Hemingway's manuscript notes, he must have had an idea of where to look. Otherwise, he'd have been in the same boat we are."

"Right, with no frigging idea where to begin looking."

Jack leaned back, distracted by the argument. "Maybe we're missing something in that letter?"

Robert nodded, his frown betrayed his own annoyance at the escalating tension. "Or Antonio's journal."

"Exactly . . . a clue or something that we'll pick up on when we look at it with a fresh set of eyes."

"It's worth a try." Robert scooted his chair back. "Shall we?"

They stood and made an effort to excuse their way past the crowd of rowdy writer lookalikes. The man closest to them stumbled to the side, in an effort to make room. In the process, he bumped into the man next to him. That brought a litany of swearing and shoving.

Jack tried to edge by and was pushed against the wall by the rest of the group who had joined the quarrel. The photograph he slammed against fell to the floor, in spite of his attempt to catch it. Glass broke, but the frame remained intact. He tried to rescue the photo from the herd of shoes and got kneed for his effort.

He made another grab for the photograph and got hold of it.

The drunken brawl escalated. He pushed aside the men closest to him, ducked a roundhouse right from one of the guy's, and saw Robert shove the man to the floor.

Jack reached for Robert's arm to pull him out of the place and was stopped by one of the police officers from the day before. Jolly Green—Zackary.

"Wait over there," Zackary said.

Jack backed away and watched the officer and his partner separate the bearded combatants. Robert joined him, ruffled but unscathed, and together they waited for the officers to get around to talking with them.

"You okay?" Robert asked.

"Bastards broke the glass on this picture of Hemingway." Jack handed the photo to Robert. "Stupid assholes."

Robert studied it. "This is an enlargement of the photograph we found inside the box along with the letter and the book."

"Let me see that." Jack took the picture back from Robert. "I've seen this photo on the wall in here a dozen times and never made the connection before now."

"Me, too. But that was before we stumbled onto Antonio's hiding place on the *Adeona*."

"More like stumbled into it. What's confusing is that photo was taken in Cuba when Miguel was twelve or thirteen. A year or so after Hemingway wrote *The Old Man and the Sea*."

"Then how'd the enlargement get here?"

"And with the date 1963 written on it?"

"Both good questions," Robert said.

"Very good indeed." Jack poked at a tear in the paper backing. "And I may have found the answers to both. There's a folded piece of paper wedged in here. If I can get it out—"

"Be quick about it. Your two cop friends are on their way over here and they don't look happy."

Jack freed the paper and slipped it into his pocket.

Zackary fixed his gaze on him. "I thought we were done with you two?"

"I know we promised no more fights. But we weren't fighting." He nodded at the group of men. "They were."

"How do you explain that?" Zackary pointed at the broken picture. "Appears you were involved more than you want to admit."

"We were trying to walk out of the place when one of those bearded yahoos pushed me into the wall, causing me to knock this to the floor, breaking the glass. The photograph and frame appear to be okay. Just needs to have the glass replaced."

Officer Harper, who'd let Zackary do the talking, took the picture from Jack and eyeballed it.

"You talked to the witnesses, right?" Jack looked back and forth at the officers. "I'm sure they vouched for us."

"Your waitress did. And so did the bartender who called 911."

"Does that mean we're free to leave?"

"As long as you don't want to press charges against anyone. Which I would strongly discourage you from doing."

"We don't," Robert answered for Jack. "And I'll make sure my friend here stays out of trouble."

"Do that." Zackary motioned toward the door. "Now be on your way."

Robert gripped Jack's arm and pointed him toward the doorway. "You heard the officer. Time to go."

Jack needed no further encouragement.

When they stepped into the mid-day heat, Robert stopped and looked at Jack. "That's twice now."

Jack knew what he meant. "You're saying we're pushing our luck?"

"That's what I'm saying."

"Then we had better not wear out our welcome with the local cops any more than we already have. Let's go back to the boat and take a look at what I found."

CHAPTER 29

Cherise got the call from the front desk at ten after one; five minutes later they followed the bellman to their rooms. Lindsey in room 426. Cherise in 427. The rooms were identically configured, mirror images with a connecting door.

The bellman set their luggage inside and unlocked the glass slider leading to the Juliet balcony off of each one. Cherise wanted to get showered and changed. She didn't need to wait for him to go through his routine.

She handed the man a twenty. "Thank you. That will be all."

He accepted the money from her outstretched hand and said, "Enjoy your stay. If you need anything, please ask."

"We'll be fine, thank you." She pushed the door closed behind him and engaged the lock.

"These rooms are really nice," Lindsey said from the interconnecting door.

Cherise laid her briefcase-sized tactical bag on the bed, stepped to her glass slider, and pulled it open to let in the meager ocean breeze wafting in off the water. The sheer curtains billowed slightly with a puff of warm wind that dissipated in the cool of the air conditioning.

She turned to Lindsey. "Even better if we were on vacation."

"Which we're not." Lindsey leaned against the doorjamb and crossed her arms. "What would you like to do first?"

"For starters, I want to shower and change. Then we'll check out Winslow House Condominiums."

"Do you intend to talk to Amanda and Corey?"

"Possibly. But not before I get the lay of the place."

"You have a plan, of course."

"I do."

Lindsey rocked away from the doorjamb. "I'll be ready in ten."

Cherise showered quickly and changed into a sheer turquoise silk blouse, medium blue slacks, and a lightweight, white silk jacket. The right look, she thought, for a woman in the market for a multi-million dollar condo.

There was a knock at the interconnecting door and she opened it. Lindsey stepped into the room dressed in white shorts, a sleeveless yellow blouse, and a sun visor most people would expect to see on a tennis player.

Lindsey's version of Florida beachwear.

The colors deepened her mocha skin.

Cherise checked the time on her phone. "We have an appointment with a salesperson at 2:30. Get your purse and we'll go."

"To the Winslow House?" Lindsey seemed confused.

Cherise slung her Kate Spade bag over her shoulder and picked up her Burberry sunglasses and a big white sunhat. "Can you think of a better way to have a look around the place without arousing suspicion?"

"It's perfect."

On the way downstairs, Cherise phoned the realtor to let the woman know they were on their way.

The taxi driver drove south along the beach and dropped them off in front of an eight-story condominium building located on the corner of Worth Avenue and South Ocean Boulevard. Cherise paid the fare in cash and exited the cab. A platinum blonde, nearly as tall and trim as her, and maybe a couple years shy of her age, approached carrying a Gucci briefcase.

"I'm Carla Simmons," she said. "We spoke on the phone."

"Nice to meet you." Cherise motioned toward Lindsey. "I'm Cherise Venetta and this is my friend Lindsey Taylor."

"A pleasure," Lindsey said, stepping forward to greet her.

After a quick round of hand shaking, Carla said, "I have several properties that I feel will interest you."

"That's good to hear," Cherise said. "I did specify that I was interested in a unit on the seventh or eighth floor with an ocean view."

"You did. But as you might imagine, prime ocean-view condos on the upper floors don't come available often. Fortunately, 608, a two bedroom, two bath unit on the sixth floor, came on the market a week ago. I also have a couple of places on the second floor that might interest you."

Cherise turned to Lindsey. Time to bring her into the conversation. "What do you think, Linds, unit 608?"

Lindsey pursed her lips in a prearranged pouty face of a spoiled life partner and said, "I did have my heart set on one of the upper floors."

Their little act put an eager smile on Carla's face. The desired effect Cherise was after. If Carla believed she had a prime opportunity to make a sale, the more helpful she would be.

"You know I'll get you what you want," Cherise said, setting the hook. She arched a brow at Carla.

The woman bit. "Let's do a walk-through of unit 608. I think the two of you will be impressed. It's an exceptionally nice unit with updated marble counter tops and fixtures, tile and hardwood floors, multi-zone air conditioning, and stainless steel kitchen appliances."

"Sounds like they put a lot of money into the place. May I ask why the owners are selling?"

"They're trimming their portfolio. But I have to tell you, they aren't desperate to make a sale."

"Perhaps a generous offer will change their minds." Cherise looked up at the seventh floor where Amanda and Corey lived. Their only reason for being there. "How about building security?"

"You'll be pleased to know Winslow House has a twenty-four-hour doorman and an in-house manager. If you're ready, I'll take you up."

Cherise glanced at Lindsey and got an eager nod in return. If she had a problem playing along, she didn't show it.

"We'd love to. Thank you."

"Winslow House is one of the most impressively located residences in Palm Beach." Carla talked while they walked. "You'll have direct access to an abundance of shops, elegant boutiques and restaurants. The building has a heated pool, a private tunnel for beach access, a fitness center and club room, a rooftop sundeck, and garage parking for residents, up to two cars."

"Impressive," Cherise said. "Linds loves to shop."

"Don't we all." Carla handed the doorman her business card and motioned them inside.

He eyed the card, studied the three of them, and flashed a row of even, white teeth. "Ms. Simmons, you've been here before. I assume you're familiar with Winslow House?"

"Quite," Carla said.

Cherise mentally noted the exchange between the agent and the big, black fellow manning the door. He seemed pleasant enough. Especially to a pretty face. Information that could prove useful.

They followed the realtor up and Cherise had Lindsey take the lead. She gave an Academy Award performance, with well-placed *oohs* and *ahhs* to achieve the anticipated response from Carla.

"I just love it," Lindsey said from the balcony.

Cherise took her cue. "I agree the place is quite nice. And I'd love to buy it for you, honey. But I do have concerns." She turned to Carla. "Do you know anything about the neighbors? We do enjoy our privacy."

"The couple in 607 are rarely here. From what I've been told, he owns a bunch of oil wells in Texas and uses the condo for a vacation home. There's an older couple in 609, both retired."

"How about above us. 708 and 709. Do you know anything about them?"

"I don't. Sorry. But if you are truly concerned, the manager might be able to answer your questions better than me." Carla made a sweeping gesture with her hand. "So what do you think?"

"Linds?" Cherise asked.

Her smile looked convincing. "I want it."

Cherise turned to Carla. "Looks like we'll be making an offer. But I'd like to talk to the manager, first. I still have concerns."

CHAPTER 30

Cherise stood a half step back from Bob Whirling's door and waited while Carla pressed the buzzer.

"I've met Mr. Whirling a few times," she said. "He's always been very helpful."

"That's good to hear." Cherise suppressed a smile.

I can only hope.

True or not, she had nothing to lose by talking to the manager, except a few more minutes of playing her and Lindsey's charade in anticipation of extracting worthwhile information from him.

Amanda and Corey. Brother and sister. He should know plenty.

It all depended on his willingness to be candid about his tenants.

"Is Mr. Whirling married?" she asked.

"Divorced," Carla answered a second before the door opened.

He looked to be about forty-five. Fit. And on the handsome side. That she and Lindsey were pretty, would help. So would the outfits. Providing his ex-wife hadn't castrated him in their divorce. His extra-wide smile and roving eyes indicated she hadn't.

Cherise wanted to laugh. Five minutes alone with this fuckwad and he'd tell her everything she wanted to know about Amanda and Corey. Even stuff she didn't care about knowing. But she'd play nice until it was time not to.

"I apologize for dropping by like this," Carla said. "This is Cherise and her friend Lindsey. They're interested in unit 608 and have some questions they'd like to ask you. If that's all right."

"Of course." His smile seemed to broaden to the point his face would split in half. He stepped to the side and opened the door wide. "Please come in. Can I get you ladies something to drink?"

Cherise felt like a lamb being led into the wolf's den.

If they only knew.

"Nothing for us, thank you." She answered for her and Lindsey, keeping up pretenses.

"Water for me," Carla said. "If it's not too much trouble."

"No trouble at all." He made a sweeping gesture toward his small sofa. "Make yourselves comfortable. I'll only be a moment."

Cherise led Lindsey to the settee and Carla settled into one of two matching padded armchairs.

"You have questions?" Bob directed the question to Cherise who was still standing when he returned with Carla's water. He had one for himself. "Ask away."

"As Carla explained," Cherise said, as he settled into the other chair and she took a seat next to Lindsey. "My partner and I are extremely interested in unit 608. Our concern is what kind of neighbors we'll have. We've had problems in the past and don't want them repeated."

"I assure you, all our residents are well behaved. And I can definitely guarantee that your neighbors in 607 and 609 will not cause you any problems."

He clearly wasn't going to offer the information she wanted.

"And the people living above and below us?" she prodded. "Sound carries through floors. I certainly wouldn't want to be disturbed by loud music or television or a lot of stomping around. We enjoy our quiet."

"Corey, the gentleman above, is single. A television star. But I've never received any complaints. As far as I know, he doesn't spend a lot of time there. His sister lives next door."

Nothing she didn't already know. "What can you tell me about his sister?"

He shrugged. "She's an accountant. Single, pretty, and always extremely nice to me. From what she's told me, she specializes in saving failed companies. Quite a reputation, according to her."

"Does she have a lot of male visitors?"

He gave her an odd look. "And why would that concern you? I told you she's a nice person."

And you told me way more than you should have.

Cherise feared she may have probed too deeply into a personal side of Amanda he didn't want to divulge. He had made a special point of saying she was pretty. Maybe he secretly admired her. A romance conjured up in his mind, growing, waiting for that special moment when he felt he could finally reveal his affection for her.

"I believe you." She thought quickly, and added, "It's just that I had a young lady for a neighbor once. Lovely in every way. She always had something pleasant to say to me. But she also had a different man over every week. Sometimes two or three. Therein lay the problem. She was—to put it delicately—extremely overenthusiastic in her sexual encounters with her male visitors."

His tan reddened. "Amanda's not like that. When she's at home, she uses the gym and the pool. Otherwise, she stays pretty much to herself. I think her work keeps her busy."

"How about her brother. Does he have much of a social life?"

"You're referring, of course, to women visitors?"

Cherise smiled, letting the question hang.

"Occasionally." Bob shifted nervously in his chair. "But like I said, he travels a lot. Are you sure you wouldn't like something to drink? It's no problem for me to mix us up a rum punch if you'd care to stick around."

"Actually, I'd like to meet Amanda and Corey if that's possible."

She noticed his shoulders slump, and resisted a smile.

"Amanda, maybe," he said. "But Corey is on location at a lake in Alabama filming a commercial. He's not due back for a couple of days. If you like, I'd be happy to give her a call and tell her you're dropping by."

Cherise stood. Lindsey followed her lead. "That would be wonderful."

CHAPTER 31

Cherise didn't know what to expect. But she definitely didn't like having Carla Simmons tagging along. Even so, there would be no getting rid of her. Not with the scent of a huge commission hanging in the air.

To get to Amanda's unit, they had to walk past Corey Jameson's place. Cherise couldn't help wonder what lay beyond his door. If their hunch about what he and his sister were up to, would play out? If she kicked the door in right now, would she find those crude gold figurines hidden there? Chances were he had already fenced them to a collector. Or someone like Harvey Bristol.

Amanda could tell her. But not without some serious convincing. The best way would be to pick the lock and search his place.

She held on to that thought and pressed the buzzer to unit 709.

The woman who answered the door stood tall enough to look her straight in the eyes. Six feet, at least. Her dishwater blonde hair looked darker in person. And with little or no makeup, she wasn't as striking as she appeared in the photos Susan had sent.

But quite pretty all the same.

Slightly taken aback by the woman's height, she said, "My name is Cherise Venetta and this is my friend Lindsey. Are you Amanda?"

"The couple the manager told me about?"

Cherise swept her hand toward Carla. "This is Ms. Simmons, our realtor. She showed us a place for sale on the floor below you and we wanted to meet our upstairs neighbor."

Carla wasted no time handing her a card.

A nice touch.

Amanda glanced at it and said, "How very nice of you. Please come in."

Cherise's first impression of Amanda as she invited them into her living room was not that of a femme fatale. Beyond the woman's obvious beauty, she did not appear to possess the mysterious, seductive charms that would lure unsuspecting men into compromising and deadly situations. Though her hands and fingers were shapely, the nails were manicured short. Those of a working girl. She wore no visible jewelry, very little makeup beyond a pale lipstick, and dressed in clothing that did nothing to flatter her voluptuous figure. Her decor was tasteful but not over the top. Comfortable more than elegant.

Certainly not what Cherise expected.

"Please have a seat." Amanda motioned toward a cushioned sofa and two facing padded armchairs. A furniture arrangement similar to the one they'd just left. "I was surprised to get a call from the manager informing me you were on your way up and wanted to meet me."

"He seems like a nice man." Cherise noticed Amanda referred to Bob Whirling as 'the manager' instead of by name. "As I said earlier, Linds and I are considering making an offer on the unit below you and your brother. We enjoy a quiet lifestyle and wanted to meet our potential neighbors before making a final decision."

"I suppose that's wise." Amanda motioned again. "Please sit."

"Yes, of course."

Cherise led Lindsey to the sofa. Carla and Amanda settled into the armchairs. Cherise noticed Amanda still hadn't acknowledged Lindsey or Carla. A lack in social skills?

She wondered.

"I'm glad you dropped in. Too bad Corey isn't home. You and your friend could have met us both."

"We were told he was away."

Amanda furrowed her brow as though they had missed something. "Mr. Whirling didn't tell you my brother is Corey

Jameson, the actor?"

Finally, his name.

"Actually, he did mention it. What kind of acting does your brother do?"

"He had his own fishing series until a couple of years ago. Now he advertises fishing and sports equipment. That's why he's not home now."

Cherise detected a hint of loneliness in Amanda's voice. A social void created by her brother's absence, possibly. "You sound as though you don't have a lot of visitors?"

Amanda's lips curled into a shy smile. "Not many."

"According to Mr. Whirling, you travel a lot."

"On jobs mostly. Sometimes for a month or more. I'm sure he told you I'm an independent chartered accountant."

"I find your work quite interesting," Carla said as though she didn't like being excluded from the conversation. "Mr. Whirling thinks highly of you."

"That's nice of him." Amanda's smile returned, more confident this time.

Cherise couldn't shake the feeling she wasn't talking to the woman who had lured Lindsey's father to his death. Yet, she was undeniably the person sitting next to him at the Captain's table. And she had been identified as being with him at the museum in Key West.

She heard her phone vibrate twice inside her purse. A text.

Ignoring the message for now, she said, "Mr. Whirling also mentioned your brother is away a lot."

"Much of his advertising work is done on location. That's why he's not home now."

Cherise felt she had gotten about as much as she was going to get, and decided it was time to ask the all-important question she'd been avoiding. Contrary to what she wanted Amanda to believe, she wasn't there to make friends.

"That sounds interesting," she said. "Does he ever find time to vacation abroad, take cruises, that sort of thing?"

She noticed a flicker behind Amanda's blue eyes, a fraction of a second delay in responding. "What concern is that of yours?"

"Just curious," Cherise said. "The way Mr. Whirling made it sound, your brother's rarely home. I'm sure his work keeps him busy, but I can't imagine him traveling that much filming commercials."

"Mr. Whirling had no right to infer anything. And you have no right to speculate on anything he said."

"You're right, Ms. Kelly. Pardon my pretentiousness."

"Seriously, Ms. Venetta?" Amanda stood and peered down at her. "I found your question quite rude. Now, I'd like you to leave before this goes any further. If we're going to be neighbors, I really don't want us to start off on the wrong foot."

"I assure you, neither do I."

Cherise got up and Lindsey followed. Carla had a stricken look on her face. Clearly, she feared the imminent sale had spiraled downward in serious jeopardy.

Amanda let them out and eased the door closed.

"She seems nice," Carla said, when they were in the hallway.

Damage control.

"I appreciate your position," Cherise said. "I'd like to meet Corey before I give you my decision."

CHAPTER 32

Jack wanted to stop walking and read what had been written on the folded, yellowed piece of paper concealed in his pocket. Most people who travel to Key West go home with t-shirts, shell ashtrays, or even a metal token stamped to look like a seventeenth-century Spanish coin from the *Atocha*.

He would be going home with a boat, and hopefully the discovery of a lifetime.

To Robert, he said, "I think we'll be spending our nights aboard *Adeona*. We can stop at the market and pick up enough supplies to keep us going while we sort out this riddle."

Robert stopped him with a hand on his arm. "First, I want to see what's on that piece of paper. This is one hell of a coincidence."

"You got that right."

Jack gave in to his own curious urge. He dug the yellowed paper from his pocket, unfolded the note, and held the message so they could both read it.

Papa bought *Pilar* when he lived in Key West. It was from *Pilar*'s deck that he began his pursuit of the big fish that, with the help of my grandfather, became the subject of his last great novel. So it is only right that this photo belongs in the bar he spent so much time in. As does so much more.

"You know I don't believe in coincidences." Jack refolded the note and slipped it into his pocket. "But I have to say, there's no other explanation."

"I have to agree," Robert said. "There's no way that bar fight could've been staged. Or that you'd end up knocking that picture off the wall and find the note. Let's get our things from the hotel and the supplies we need and sort this out over a cold one."

Jack nodded. "Good idea."

* * *

Below decks, the *Adeona* was hot and stale and damp. It had taken the entire prior evening to cool the interior and dry out the dampness, and Jack wished he had thought to leave the air conditioner on with the thermostat set at a reasonable seventy-eight to keep out the day's heat and humidity.

He started the generator and reset the thermostat to sixty-five. It would be an hour before the temp inside was comfortable.

While the air conditioner struggled to cool the forward salon, they stowed their food. Then each of them carried their gear down to the staterooms they'd stayed in the night before. Jack put his things away, checked on the first-edition copy of *The Old Man and the Sea*, and met back up with Robert in the galley.

"Ready for that beer?" Jack asked.

"Beyond ready." Robert opened a couple of Red Stripes and handed one to Jack.

"He was a wise man who invented beer," Jack said. He tapped his bottle against Robert's and toasted, "To us and a successful treasure hunt."

They took a gulp and carried their bottles aft to folding chairs sitting in the shade under the upper sundeck. The temp outside was still warm but a reasonable on-shore breeze cooled the air enough to make sitting there bearable.

The cold brew helped.

"You're the brain," Jack said. "What do you think?"

Robert took a moment before answering. "Hemingway moved here in 1928. He and his wife Paulina lived in an apartment on

Simonton Street before moving into the two-story house on Whitehead three years later where they lived until 1938, when the Hemingway's moved to Cuba. His close friend, Charles Thomson, is the person who introduced him to sport fishing. The waters off the Florida Keys and the nearby Caribbean being his favorite places to fish."

Jack tapped his foot. He almost regretted asking Robert for his thoughts on the matter, knowing his propensity for detail—understanding the cause as well as the effect. At times, it could be exasperating waiting for him to get to the point.

He said, "I assume you're going somewhere with this history lesson?"

Robert sighed. "It's important we explore every detail."

Jack understood the logic in his friend's response. But it didn't make it any less irritating.

"Sorry," he said. "Finish your thought."

Robert swigged his beer and continued, "Hemingway and some of his best friends were known in Key West as the *Mob*. They spent a lot of time together fishing for marlin and tuna from the deck of *Pilar*. This is also when Hemingway got the nickname, *Papa*. In addition to fishing, Hemingway and the rest of the Mob spent considerable time drinking in the Silver Slipper, a saloon owned by his good friend Joe Russell. It was Hemingway's urging that prompted Russell to change the name of the bar to Sloppy Joe's."

The tide change swung the stern toward shore, sparing them the glare from the sun that had dipped low in the sky. Jack planted his elbows on his knees and stared at the bottle he'd emptied while listening to Robert.

Robert continued, "In 1962, a year after Hemingway's death, his fourth wife Mary traveled to Key West and took possession of a pile of boxes he had left in a back storeroom at Sloppy Joe's bar. It almost makes sense Rafael Fuentes would hide them there."

Makes sense.

Jack stood. "I'm getting us another beer."

Robert handed his bottle to Jack and said, "We've been chasing longshots. What's one more?"

CHAPTER 33

Cherise and Lindsey took a cab back to the resort. On the way, Cherise read the text she'd received. A message from Susan, it turned out.

> Emailed you additional information on Corey and Amanda.
> I think you'll find the info interesting.

She read the email. But for the time being, kept the news to herself. Lindsey gave her a casual glance, but didn't press.

They were both ready for a cold drink.

After a quick trip to their rooms to freshen up, they wandered down to the Beach Club patio. The sound of breaking waves had a soothing effect on their day. Though warm, the temperature had dropped a few degrees now that the sun had dipped low in the sky.

Lindsey collapsed in her chair. "What do we do now?"

Cherise brought up the email she'd received. "Susan sent additional information on Corey and Amanda. Quite interesting, really."

Lindsey sat up straighter. "The message you were reading in the cab?"

"Appears Corey and Amanda have been busy. Susan confirmed they have taken nearly two dozen Caribbean cruises over the past two years. Different cruise lines, always traveling together, and no cruise longer than seven days."

"Did they correspond to any missing person's cases?"

"Only the three we know about. But we know not all cases are reported."

"So . . . ?"

"So we keep digging," Cherise said. "But I have to admit, Amanda confused me. It's too bad we didn't have a chance to feel out Corey."

"He's supposed to be back in a couple of days. We can wait."

Cherise shrugged. "If that's what it comes down to."

"You have another plan?"

"I do. Tomorrow morning I'm searching his condo."

Lindsey sat upright, clearly stunned by what she heard. "You mean you're breaking into his place?"

Cherise smiled. "Unless you have a key."

"I assume you know what you're doing?"

"It's what I do. Remember?" Cherise looked Lindsey in the eyes. "If the idols are there, we know who killed your father."

"And if they aren't?"

"Assuming he's involved, he's already sold them."

Lindsey slumped, the surprise gone from her expression. "Where would that leave us?"

"I can't say until I've had a look inside his condo."

Silence fell on the table. Lindsey faced the ocean as though seeking the solace of the breaking waves. Something in her mood had changed.

Cherise waited.

Lindsey sat staring at the ocean for a full two minutes. When it seemed she had become lost in thought, she said, "All of a sudden this feels very real. The way those months in Afghanistan felt."

"Any conclusions?"

"When we started, all I could think about was revenge at any cost. It seemed right to make someone pay for the loss of a father I had so little time with. But it's not that black and white, is it?"

"You mean a line drawn in the sand with the good on one side and the bad on the other? No, it isn't. Not everyone turns out to be who you think they are."

"Like Amanda?"

"Exactly like Amanda. Only we know she was on the cruise with your father."

"You said she confused you. This entire mess is confusing."

"We'll sort it out one way or another."

"I wish I had your confidence."

Cherise offered a smile of support. "You did great today. Now, I'm going to order an iced tea. Care to join me?"

"I think that's a wonderful idea."

Their order arrived, and Cherise sipped from a tall fluted glass with a lemon slice on the rim and a colorful miniature paper umbrella. To anyone watching, the beverage could easily be mistaken for a fancy rum drink.

The sun continued to set, spreading color across the sky. Clouds over the Atlantic reflected a pale wash of reds and oranges. And though the sun had set behind them, she remembered the sunsets she and Jack shared until a few days ago. He never wanted to miss the spray of color that came at day's end.

And she quickly understood the magic.

"Excuse me," a male voice said.

Cherise turned to see a tall, blond, deeply tanned, handsome young man wearing a tennis outfit and carrying a rocks glass, walk up to their table. He swayed just enough for her to know that wasn't his first drink of the afternoon. Some type of whiskey over a few cubes of ice, she guessed.

He pointed with his glass, sloshing a bit of the amber liquid over the rim. "Aren't you the actress who plays the spy in that new movie?"

Cherise knew he directed his question at her. "I'm afraid you have me mixed up with someone else."

He reached for a chair and attempted to slide it back. She locked it in place with her foot. "This is a private party and we'd like to be left alone."

"No reason to get nasty," he said, anger creeping into his voice. "I was only being sociable."

"I understand that. We'd just like you to be sociable someplace else."

"Your pretty friend hasn't asked me to leave." He directed his gaze at Lindsey. "Maybe she'd enjoy some male company."

"She doesn't have to," Cherise said. "I'm telling you."

He stared a moment. Then huffed. "You bitch actresses think you're so hot. Well I have news for you. Your movie sucks."

Cherise smiled. "Thank you. You can leave now."

"Bitch," he mumbled as he turned and walked away.

"You sure handled him," Lindsey said.

"Not much to handle."

"But he could have been trouble."

Cherise noticed the young man glaring at them from his table twenty feet away.

Asshole.

She said, "I'll be right back."

"Where are you going?"

"The ladies room. Stay here and save our table."

She got up and strode past Asshole without as much as a sideways glance at him. After a few steps, she heard a chair scrape back and figured he had an idea of catching her alone. Exactly what she thought he'd do.

A part of her hoped she'd figured wrong.

She continued along the empty corridor as though unaware of his presence. The scuff of the soles of his shoes scraping on the tile floor told her he had quickened his pace. Intoxicated, but not that intoxicated.

Game on.

She let him come.

Her next move was up to him.

"Hey," he said, his hand on her arm.

She spun and grabbed him by the throat.

His eyes widened; he tried to pull her hand away.

She didn't give him a chance.

"Fuck off," she said, slamming him against the wall.

He shook his head violently from side to side. "I . . . I—"

"You had your chance, asshole." She kneed him between the legs and let him slide to the floor.

He rolled onto his side and moaned with both hands gripping

his groin.

Satisfied the obnoxious idiot would give them no further trouble, she returned to her iced tea. Taking her seat, she saw a look of concern on Lindsey's face.

"What?" she asked.

Lindsey stared, concern turning to surprise. "I saw that young man get up and follow you."

Cherise noticed he hadn't returned to his table. She smiled. "No worries. He has his hands full."

CHAPTER 34

At eight the next morning, wearing black compressive running tights, a short-sleeved gray T, fanny pack, and running shoes, Cherise joined Lindsey at the patio restaurant for breakfast. Mr. Tennis sat three tables away, nursing a Bloody Mary. He shot a couple of nervous glances in their direction, got up without his drink, and strode off toward the Surf Break bar.

"Isn't that the guy from yesterday?" Lindsey asked.

"His color's a little ghostly this morning." Cherise watched him walk away. "Must have been something I said."

Lindsey chuckled. "I'm guessing he won't be making any rude passes at women anytime soon."

"With that Ken-doll look and all those perfect white teeth, he's probably not used to women rejecting his charm so readily." Cherise focused her full attention on Lindsey. "That's enough about him. Let's talk about today."

"You're still going through with your idea?"

"Just as soon as we finish breakfast."

"Then there's nothing to discuss."

"You made it quite clear you're not happy having to stay behind. But that's the way it has to be. And we talked about that."

"We did," Lindsey said. "And I agreed. It's just that last night I got to thinking."

"And?"

"You're insisting there's no other way?"

"There's always another way," Cherise said. "Only I'm not willing to wait for Corey to get home to have a look around his apartment. Time is of the essence. If we're chasing a dead end, we need to refocus our investigation."

"Amanda lives next door. She'll hear you."

"Not if I'm quiet."

"How long will you be gone?"

"No more than an hour. Two, tops. Use the time to relax as if you're on vacation. Kick back by the pool. Treat yourself to a massage. Just try not to worry."

Lindsey faced the ocean, her eyes concealed behind the dark lenses of her glasses. "Just be careful."

"You know I will."

After a quick fruit and coffee breakfast, Cherise left Lindsey sitting at their table and walked to the portico. Lindsey had the wait ahead of her to deal with. Probably the hardest part.

Cherise had to wait for her taxi to arrive. The easy part. She checked her watch. Dispatch had said ten minutes. She thought about the big, black man at the doorway into Winslow House and looked inside her fanny pack to make sure Carla Simmons' business card was there, just in case.

The only wildcard was Amanda.

"Excuse me," a male voice said.

Cherise recognized it immediately.

Mr. Tennis: AKA, Asshole.

She detected something different about his tone. Not the pushy young man from the night before. A note of apprehension. Hesitation. She turned and waited to hear what he had to say.

He stood five feet away, appearing hesitant to step a foot closer. "I'm sorry to interrupt your morning, but I'm checking out of the hotel and I want to apologize for my behavior last evening. I acted totally inappropriate."

"I won't hold it against you," Cherise said.

"Thank you. And please extend my apology to your friend."

"I'll be sure and do that," she said. She heard a vehicle stop behind her with the engine running.

He pointed. "I believe your taxi is here. Do have a good day."

"Thank you. I will."

She climbed into the back seat and the driver sped away.

Lesson learned.

She exited the cab at the same location she and Lindsey had the day before. She knew what she'd say to the doorman. Surely he'd remember her.

Provided someone new hadn't taken his spot.

To her relief, she saw the familiar black face smiling at her from the doorway. "My friend and I were here yesterday with Ms. Simmons, our real-estate agent. You probably remember me."

"I do," he said. "And where is your friend?"

She smiled. "Lindsey had business to take care of this morning or she would have come with me."

"That's too bad. Have you decided to purchase a unit?"

"Actually, I dropped by because I wanted one more look around before I make my final decision. Ms. Simmons would've been here, but she had a prior appointment. I hope it's all right with you that I came alone."

He flashed his toothy grin and said, "Of course. Take your time."

"Thank you. I'll be sure and tell my friend you asked about her."

She went directly to the seventh floor and paused twenty feet from Corey's door to look and listen. Hearing only muffled TV sounds coming from one of the other units and seeing no one, she decided to walk straight to the door, pick the lock, and get inside before someone stepped into the hallway.

A minute, maybe two.

She took three steps and stopped when she saw the doorknob turn.

CHAPTER 35

Cherise only had a couple of seconds to decide her next move. She considered turning and stepping away in the opposite direction. But Corey didn't know her. She could walk right past him if he'd returned early from his trip. He'd be none the wiser.

His sister would be a different issue.

She and Amanda hadn't exactly parted on the best of terms.

And it wasn't all that unlikely Amanda had slipped next door to check on her brother's place. Surely they had exchanged keys for just that reason.

Cherise decided to play out the situation and walked calmly, focusing her eyes on an imaginary point several doors farther down. A half-dozen steps away, the door swung inward. And a half-second later, a Latino woman holding a basket of cleaning supplies stepped into the hallway.

The woman's gaze met Cherise's and registered surprise. Clearly, she hadn't expected to practically run into someone passing by.

"*Buenos dias*," the woman said, easing the door closed behind her.

The encounter, purely innocent. The woman, friendly. Cherise smiled and replied in a hushed tone, "*Buenos dias*."

Wanting to avoid further conversation so close to Amanda's door, she continued walking. To her relief, the cleaning lady strode off in the opposite direction.

Cherise continued on past Amanda's door to not draw attention, chanced a glance over her shoulder, and noticed the woman was gone. What had seemed a stroke of bad luck, might actually work in her favor. She planned to search Corey's condo quickly and silently. But there was always a possibility she wouldn't be the quiet little mouse she intended to be. Should that happen, Amanda would likely know about the cleaning lady being next door.

One noise the same as the other.

But she needed to work fast.

She hurried back to Corey's door, picked the lock, and slipped inside.

A burglar alarm seemed like a real possibility. No loud ringing. A silent signal relayed to a monitoring company miles away. A contingency she had planned for. The cleaning lady might have the code. Or more likely, Amanda would have disarmed the system in preparation for housekeeping service.

She located the control panel and found the alarm had been turned off.

Though she had been saved the risk of bypassing the system, Amanda could return any moment to reset it.

A real possibility she didn't want to think about.

She stepped into the living room and slipped on a pair of thin leather gloves. The floorplan looked to be a duplicate of the unit she and Lindsey had walked through the day before. An unanticipated advantage that would help simplify the search.

She scanned the furnishings, and mentally noted how different they were from his sister's.

Egotistic. Narcissistic.

Definitely full of himself.

Pathetic.

She had no interest in Corey's plethora of fishing memorabilia, the two-thousand framed photographs of him posing with monster fish, or his abundance of high-end electronics.

But his décor said a lot about him.

She had handled a couple of recovery jobs for a millionaire named Peter Jackson, fifty-two years old, visibly fit, obsessed with holding onto his youth, much like Corey. A year later the inevitable caught up with him. In spite of his exercise regimen, vitamins, the plastic surgery, and the hair dye, his heart exploded in a massive coronary. Family genetics he couldn't beat.

Moving fast, she searched the display cases. Brass fishing trophies, a mounted black piranha the size of a dinner plate, a squat half-man/half-beast carved in stone, but no gold idols. She looked behind pictures for a wall safe, searched drawers in the sofa tables, the kitchen, the guest bedroom, closet, and bath.

Nothing to link him to Lindsey's father's death.

She moved on to the master bedroom and found a two cubic foot floor safe in the closet. Large enough to hold the idols. For the heck of it, she stooped and tried the door handle.

No surprise.

Without a combination and no time to crack the locking mechanism, she moved on to a desk sitting in the corner of the room. People hide combinations. She held onto that thought as she searched the drawers. She sat on her heels, exasperated. That's when she noticed the envelope tucked into the corner of the desk blotter.

More so, the name Dream World Travel embossed on it.

She slid her fingertips under the flap and removed a single ticket aboard the *Caribbean Sensation* in Corey Jameson's name.

A four-night cruise departing July 18th, returning July 22nd.

Another pigeon for the plucking.

How many victims have there been?

She might never know.

A bigger question remained. Would Corey and Amanda continue killing until someone stopped their deadly game?

She snapped a photo with her phone, slid the ticket back into the envelope, and returned it to the corner of the blotter. Corey, she understood. Amanda remained a mystery.

She didn't fit the mold.

Cherise glanced at her watch, feeling she had pushed her luck.

She hurried to the front door. Her hand inches from the knob, when she heard the door to the adjoining unit, close. Amanda's condo. Amanda the accountant would be conscientious about resetting the alarm in her brother's place.

Cherise bolted for the balcony.

CHAPTER 36

Jack stared over his cup of morning coffee at the note he'd removed from the torn backing on the photograph. Could the answer really be that easy?

Possibly.

That notion left him thinking of ways to sneak into the back room at Sloppy Joe's. Each time, the scenario ended with Officers Zackary and Harper leading him and Robert out in handcuffs.

Which is what would likely happen.

Considering.

He sighed, giving in to resolve. Perhaps the best way would be to simply ask permission.

And hope for a sympathetic ear.

He waited for Robert to finish his phone call. When he laid his cell down, Jack asked, "How's Kazuko?"

Robert sighed. "Wondering when I'll be home."

"Other than that?"

"She had a fantastic week in Monterey."

"Does that mean vacation is over?"

"She's home. If that's what you're asking?"

"I meant for you."

"I'd kind of like to stick around and find out if the manuscript exists."

"So you haven't given up hope?"

"That the pages exist? Hell, no. But when she asked what we intend to do with them, I got to thinking. This isn't exactly finders-keepers. There's the Fuentes family, Hemingway descendants, even the owner of Sloppy Joe's to think about. Any one or all of them could lay claim to the manuscript."

"I thought it was more or less understood what we'd do with it. And the novella. In the past, we always made every effort to return whatever treasure we found to the rightful owner. Nothing's changed."

"Never saw it any other way," Robert said. "And I suppose that's why the question never came up until she asked me."

"She worries. And that's okay. Now, let's figure out how we're going to get into that back room."

"We're not planning on keeping what we find, so why not just ask the bartender or manager for permission?"

"I've been tossing around that same idea. But they might want to try to get their hands on the pages first. Can't trust anyone these days."

"Wasn't Hemingway the one who said you don't know who you can trust until you trust them?"

"Close. But more accurately: 'The best way to find out if you can trust somebody is to trust them.' "

Robert shrugged. "So we trust them."

Jack nodded. "That's what I'm thinking. Get into the dinghy before we change our minds."

They left the thirteen-foot Boston Whaler tied to the wharf and walked the now familiar two short blocks to Sloppy Joe's. Jack tried to imagine finding the pages. Would he feel the power of Hemingway's handwritten words the way Miguel had?

Robert paused outside the entrance and said, "This is your show, so you do the talking."

Jack grinned. "Old buddy, I never figured it any other way."

He walked directly to the large horseshoe-shaped bar in the center of the room. Two bartenders—one on each side. The bartender working his side was female, tall, thirtyish, pretty, with dishwater blonde hair tied back in a ponytail. He sidled up to the counter and took a seat. Robert joined him.

"What can I get you?" Her green eyes flicked back and forth between them.

Jack took notice of her nametag. "An ice cold Red Stripe."

"The same," Robert said.

She stepped away, and Robert chuckled. "A woman with green eyes and thick manicured eyebrows. I'm not sure if that's good or not."

"How is me being a sucker for green eyes a problem?"

"Just saying, that's all."

She returned with their beers. "Can I get you something else?"

Jack smiled. She did have nice eyes. "You can, Vicky. A small favor if you would. I'd like to speak to the manager, if that's possible."

"The manager's not here at the moment. Perhaps I can help?"

"I believe you can. My friend and I would like to see inside your storage room in back."

She looked him up and down, then Robert. "I suppose you have a good reason?"

He and Robert had decided he'd provide as much information as he felt was necessary to get them into that back room. Nothing more. "We believe a leather folder containing a rare, and quite possibly, valuable Hemingway manuscript has been stored in there."

Vicky glanced in the direction of the other customers seated at the counter a few stools away. "Excuse me a minute."

"Take your time," Jack said as she stepped away.

He went back to his beer.

"Good morning," a female voice said from behind him.

He turned, and was surprised to see Lynn Hastings and another young lady smiling at him. Their cropped t-shirts and short shorts looked as though they had been sprayed on.

"And a good morning to you. No more guy problems, I hope?"

"Not since you handled those creeps the other day." Lynn gestured toward her companion. "This is my friend, Sandi. When I saw you sitting here and pointed you out to her, she just had to meet my knight in shiny armor."

"Rusty armor, more like it." He smiled at Lynn's friend. "Nice to meet you."

"The pleasure is mine. I can't thank you enough for helping

Lynn. I wish there were more guys like you."

He chuckled and jabbed a thumb at Robert, who sat watching. "Let's not forget my friend Robert. He helped."

"Of course." Sandi smiled. "You're both wonderful. And I want you to know, you saved our vacation."

"Glad we were able to help," Robert said.

"So are we." Lynn took Sandi's hand. "Thanks again. Now, we'll let you get back to your beers."

Jack faced the counter. "Nice, polite young ladies."

"And cute."

"That, too."

Vicky rejoined them and said, "You do know all of Hemingway's belongings were removed from the storeroom by his wife decades ago?"

Jack nodded. "In 1962, by his fourth wife, Mary Welsh. A pile of boxes he'd left in the back storeroom. We believe the folder containing the manuscript was put in there sometime after that."

"And you have good reason to think it's still there?"

"The only way to know for sure is to look."

"I guess it won't hurt. Though I can assure you it's a waste of time. I've worked here five years and have been all over that storeroom and haven't seen anything that doesn't belong."

"Then you don't mind if we poke around in there and have a look for ourselves?"

"I suppose not. For a minute or two, anyway." She motioned with her head. "Back here."

Jack followed her into the storeroom and scanned the interior. Cases of beer, aluminum kegs and tappers, assorted bottles of liquor, open cardboard boxes of coasters and napkins, exactly what he expected to see.

Robert stepped inside behind him and said, "I'm guessing the folder will be sealed inside a box of some sort. Wood or metal. Not cardboard. Probably labeled as belonging to Rafael Fuentes."

"Sounds reasonable."

Jack looked at Vicky. "Is this the only storeroom?"

She glanced around. "Only one I know of."

He turned to Robert. "Take that side and I'll take this one. Those pages have to be here somewhere."

Robert began pawing through his side of the room and Jack went to work on his. There were only so many places in the storeroom to look. He didn't feel it would take long to locate the document if it was there. A big *if*. Especially given how much time had passed.

Jack held onto hope as long as there was one more place to look. But after a couple of minutes, and with Robert coming up empty as well, he conceded the manuscript notes were not there. Not now, anyway.

Were they ever?

He had to wonder.

It had been a longshot and he assured himself that they had not wasted their time.

Their beers were sitting on the bar where they left them. They retook their seats in silence. Jack pondered the futility of their quest. Too much of a time lapse and too little information for them to work with. But enough to keep him interested.

Vicky resumed her place behind the counter. "Sorry. But then you'd have had just as much luck catching a marlin the size of that one up there."

Jack followed her gaze to the massive fish mounted high on the wall behind her. And the brass plaque that read: *In Memory of Papa*. "Was that one of Hemingway's prize catches?"

"Can't say. It was hanging there when I started work here." She picked up Jack's empty bottle. "Can I get you another Red Stripe?"

He considered a second round and looked at Robert. "What do you think?"

"That, my friend, is a double-ended question. Are you talking about not locating the documents or ordering another beer? If it's the beer, why not? And you can tell me where we go from here."

"We're still making it up as we go along."

CHAPTER 37

Cherise worked the latch on the glass door, tugged the slider open, and pulled it closed behind her a fraction of a second after the front door to the condo cracked open.

She bolted for the safety railing at the end of the deck.

Timing meant everything.

She covered the distance in four long strides, planted a foot on the railing, and leaped across the gap between balconies. She landed running. Two more strides and she reached the glass slider leading into Amanda's condo.

And gambled the door had been left unlocked.

She grasped the handle and pulled.

The door slid open with ease.

Three more seconds and she would be in the clear.

She slipped inside and pulled the slider closed. Thirty feet stood between her and the front door. A clear pathway, if she remembered correctly. The last thing she could afford was crashing into a piece of furniture in her haste.

Now her successful getaway hinged on Amanda taking an extra minute or two to complete a walk-through of her brother's condo to reassure herself that all was as it should be after the visit from the cleaning lady.

She hurried to the front door, worked the knob, and stepped into the outside hallway a second before Amanda emerged from her brother's place.

She spun her head to the side and peered into Amanda's startled expression.

"There you are," Cherise said, thinking fast. "I got to worrying about your comment that you didn't want to start off on the wrong foot. It bothers me that we might have, so I dropped by to apologize. Hopefully, we can start over."

Amanda appeared to calm. "I've already put the incident behind me."

"That makes me feel better." Cherise motioned her hand toward Corey's condo. "Is your brother back?"

"Not until tomorrow. I just popped in to check on his place."

And found everything in order, I trust.

Cherise figured it would be best to keep the conversation going to further avoid suspicion, but she also didn't want to hang around a moment longer than absolutely necessary. They weren't friends.

And she had no desire to be.

Regardless . . .

She smiled. "No doubt you have things to do, so I'll not bother you further."

"No bother. I'm glad you dropped by."

"Thank you," Cherise said. "I'm sure I'll be seeing you again. Have a good rest of your day."

She backtracked out of the building and walked to the corner of Worth Avenue and South Ocean Boulevard. Taking shelter in the shade of a trio of palm trees to escape the sun's heat, she called for a taxi.

Then she placed a call to Susan.

* * *

Cherise found Lindsey sitting at a table by the pool. She nervously flipped the pages of a magazine open in front of her. Not exactly looking like she was on vacation.

"I figured I'd find you here," Cherise said. "But I expected you to be in a swimsuit soaking up the sun."

Lindsey's gaze came up and she tossed the magazine aside. "You knew I wouldn't relax until you got back here. What did you find?"

Cherise took a seat. "I didn't locate the artifacts you father purchased. That would have been too much to ask for. But I did find a ticket in his name for a four-night cruise departing July 18th, returning July 22nd. And the trip had been booked through Dream World Travel."

"That's this Thursday. You think he's after another pigeon?"

"That would be my guess."

"But, so soon."

"Sad, isn't it. We've learned just enough to know Corey Jameson lives large. It's my feeling he doesn't have the income necessary to support the lifestyle he's grown accustomed to when he had his TV show, and subsidizes it with scams like the one he and Amanda pulled on your dad."

"That means the killing will continue until somebody stops them."

"That's the long and the short of it."

"What do you have in mind?"

"I have to expose their scam so that a competent police detective will see them for the killers they are. And I need to do it in a way that the charges stick."

"How do you propose we do that?"

"Not *we*. Amanda knows us. We'd be done before we started."

"Then who?"

"We need to stick to what we suspect. Amanda's the key. She sets up a romantic relationship with a likely mark. Then Corey moves in to finish the con and see to it the poor guy is not around to testify against them."

"Meaning we need a man smart enough and crafty enough to beat them at their own game."

Cherise knew several good, hard men who would be eager to help her. Tough, experienced soldiers. Men who could assault a fortified villa and rescue a hostage.

This was not one of those situations.

She said, "I know just the person."

CHAPTER 38

Jack took a gulp of his Red Stripe and stared at the bottle. "I guess there's no reason for us to waste any more time looking for those papers. If you ask me, Rafael Fuentes fabricated the entire story just to screw with Antonio."

"A nasty trick if he did," Robert said. "But Antonio believed him."

"Doesn't make it so. Still, if there is an element of truth to the story, there's a chance those notes will surface sometime down the line. It just won't be us bringing them to light."

"You're just feeling hit," Robert said. "What you need is to think about something else for a while."

"What I need is to get this boat registered and back to Oahu."

"And forget about finding Hemingway's manuscript?"

"That's what I'm saying."

"And you can do that?"

Jack shrugged, lifted his bottle to his lips, and said, "Sure I can."

Robert chuckled. "Right."

"O ye of little faith." Jack heard his phone chime. He slid his cell from his pocket, saw Cherise's name, and tapped on. "Perfect timing. How are things going with you and Lindsey?"

"Sounds like you're in good humor," Cherise said. "Linds and I are getting along just fine. But I've hit a snag regarding her father."

He hadn't forgotten about Sam King. "What do you mean by

'snag'?"

"I hear music. You sure I'm not interrupting anything?"

"That's nothing. Robert and I are entertaining ourselves with an early beer at Sloppy Joe's. Go ahead and talk."

She summarized the events of the past couple of days and he listened, sober faced. Parts were repetitious of what she'd already told him. But when she began talking about breaking into Corey Jameson's condo, he paid close attention. Several times he wanted to interrupt and ask questions, but resisted the urge. That was how she operated. She thrived on danger.

He'd not second-guess her.

Yet.

When she finished bringing him up to date, he asked, "And you think I'm the ideal person to be the pigeon in your little scheme?"

"Can you think of someone better?"

He wanted to chuckle. "What fun would there be in that? But do you honestly believe I'm the best choice to pull this off?"

"Trust me, Jack. You have the background and the experience to handle yourself if something goes wrong. Plus, women are attracted to you."

"Meaning I'm a ladies man?"

"I think we both know the answer to that."

"And you think that'll be enough?"

"Believe me, I can't imagine anyone else I know being able to pull off what I'm proposing."

"Shouldn't I give some thought to my answer before I give it?"

"You can. But understand, you were my first and only choice."

Am I really the right person to make this work?

Or will I let Cherise and her friend down?

There was a lot to consider.

He thought about all the reasons not to get involved. But if Cherise was correct, the killing would continue, and he couldn't accept the guilt of knowing he could have helped prevent even one more person from dying, and didn't.

There's only one choice.

"All right, you can count on me. But we need to meet and discuss how you plan to pull off this charade of yours."

"How about meeting us up here in Palm Beach?"

"When?"

"Tomorrow? Sooner, if you can. The cruise ship sails Thursday."

"Three days to prepare." He thought about what they would be up against. "You think that's enough time?"

"It'll have to be."

"We'll make it work. I'll check flights and let you know."

"Thanks for helping. With you on board, I feel we at least have a chance. I'll rent us a car, and Lindsey and I will pick you up at the airport. I assume Robert's coming with you. Be great if he did. He and Lindsey can keep each other company."

"Can't say for sure he will until he and I talk."

"I understand completely. Talk to you soon."

* * *

Back aboard the *Adeona*, Jack and Robert sat on the deck aft of the cockpit. A bright blue canvas awning stretched tightly between stainless steel runners provided shade from the unrelenting afternoon sun. A cool breath of Gulf breeze fluttered the canvas overhead before moving past. They nursed cold bottles of lager and kept their voices down as they talked.

Robert said, "I thought they were meeting us down here?"

"Obviously, that's changed." Jack picked at the label on his bottle. "You think I'm foolish for wanting to help Lindsey? For getting involved in Cherise's scheme?"

Out on the bay a speedboat kicked up a spray of foam. When the engine roar faded, Robert said, "Need I remind you that you genuinely like women? You believe they're equals. You don't think of them as sex objects placed on earth to satisfy your every desire. But you enjoy the inevitable romantic game."

"That's what I'm doing by going along with her plan?"

"Partly. Plus, you like action."

Jack studied the speedboat that had reversed course on another run. "Sir Galahad, according to Kazuko."

"She has a knack of putting things in a way that fits."

"Tarnished armor and broken lance, perhaps."

"So we accept who you are."

Jack raised his bottle in salute. "And we bust this operation wide open."

"We?"

"Cherise suggested I bring you along. Besides, it'll be nice having you there to balance out my habit of kicking in kitchen doors and smashing dishes."

"Then all that's left for us to do here is to button up this tub and catch a plane north."

Jack set down his bottle. "I'll go online and get us a flight."

"You do that," Robert said, and slid down in his seat. "I'll sit here and watch you."

"I'm sure you'll do a good job of it, too."

Jack dug his phone from his pocket and began searching airlines. After several minutes and a lot of tapping on the screen, he paused and checked the time.

"You found us a flight?" Robert asked.

"And we have to hurry if we're going to make it," Jack said. "I've booked us on a Southern Airways Express flight that leaves in a little over two hours. Plane lands in West Palm Beach at five fifteen. We might hit a little traffic from people heading home after a day in the city, but it should be relatively light since it's a Sunday. That'll give us plenty of time to have cocktails before dinner."

Robert pushed himself upright in his chair. "Didn't Cherise ask us to meet her tomorrow?"

"Or sooner, if possible."

Jack hadn't forgotten. He'd already concluded he and Robert had exhausted their search for Hemingway's manuscript notes. An intriguing prospect in the beginning, but no cigar. And no reason for them to wander around Key West in a blind search when he and Robert were needed elsewhere.

The business they had left to do here could wait.

He added. "There's no reason to sit around staring at each other's ugly mugs. We'll let her buy us dinner."

"Won't it be the other way around?"

"Either way we'll be dining with a couple of beautiful women. Why don't you start packing and I'll give Cherise a heads-up call

that we'll see them tonight."
    "You're just a sucker for a pretty face."
    Jack had to laugh. "What can I say?"

CHAPTER 39

At five-thirty, Jack and Robert stood at the curb outside baggage claim. Jack's mind drifted back to the days he had spent island hopping with Cherise. And how much he missed her.

Cherise, he realized during their time together, allowed only a few men close to her. She'd given him the impression she believed it best to keep her emotions to herself. Devoting her existence to helping others while she ignored her own needs.

Then she had allowed him to get close.

At least briefly.

Now she was placing trust in him.

"So you've never met Cherise's friend Lindsey?" Robert's question pulled Jack from his thoughts.

"I only learned about her a few days ago. They became friends in Afghanistan. At the time, there weren't a lot of women at the base so they naturally gravitated to each other. I understand it was common for female soldiers to bond with other female soldiers."

"That's not hard to believe. A man's world for the most part. All the pressure that goes along with that added to the prospect of being killed in battle."

Jack nodded. "We're not just talking about sexual pressure. There's a lot of male soldiers who would jeopardize their life to protect his female counterpart."

"Which is what you'd do."

Jack studied the traffic. His friend was right.

He said, "Only in this case, it was Lindsey who ended up being wounded in the leg by a sniper's bullet that'd been intended for Cherise. Bottom line is you can see why Cherise feels she owes her."

Robert's expression sobered. "Totally. What's odd is Kazuko and I had this very discussion not that long ago. Women have played a vital role in every military conflict from the Revolutionary War to the current war on terror. Initially, they served as cooks and nurses. But their roles in combat have evolved, along with the military, to what they are today. I'm afraid women casualties is something the country will have to get used to."

Jack spotted Cherise in her rental three cars back in the line of vehicles driving toward them. He picked up his valise. "Looks like our ride is here."

Robert closed his eyes. "I'm envisioning an exotic raven-haired beauty."

A change of subject. Jack had to chuckle. "You've been away from Kazuko way too long."

Robert furrowed his brow. "Doesn't hurt to dream."

"Definitely. Just don't let her catch you doing it."

"You're who she worries about."

"For good reason, I'm sure." Jack stepped to the edge of the curb. "And I'm sure you provide her with plenty of incentive."

"You take care of that well enough by yourself."

"Screw you."

Robert laughed. "Remember, you promised cocktails."

"At the very least."

Cherise pulled parallel to them in a blue Dodge Charger and stopped. A beautiful young lady he figured had to be Lindsey sat in the front passenger seat. Robert would be pleased. The door window on her side rolled down and he leaned in. Cherise looked as gorgeous as she did the last time he saw her.

"Going our way?" he asked, peering across at her.

"Mind riding in back?" Cherise grinned.

He remembered the last time he rode in the back seat of a Charger she drove. An orange rental. And not that long ago.

He asked, "Do I have a choice?"

"Not if you want a ride."

She slid from behind the wheel and hurried around the front of the car. Lindsey got out on her side.

A stunning pair.

Cherise gave him a hug and a kiss. "It's good to see you. This is Lindsey. She's been anxious to meet you both."

"And we looked forward to meeting her." To Lindsey, he said, "I guess you figured out I'm Jack. This is my friend Robert."

Robert stepped up. "The pleasure is all mine."

She said, "Nice to meet you both."

"You'll have plenty of time to get acquainted," Cherise said. "Grab your things and let's go. We have a lot to talk about."

CHAPTER 40

Jack un-wedged himself from the rear seat and waited while Cherise turned her car over to the valet. She re-joined him and they walked into the lobby together. Robert and Lindsey followed a half-step behind them.

"Nice resort," Jack said.

"Extremely nice, actually." Cherise led them to the elevator. "I took the liberty of booking you and Robert into an ocean-view room on the fourth floor down the hall from ours. I have your key cards with me."

"Can't I bunk with you?"

She gave him a dismissive stare. "I'm sure you and Robert will be quite comfortable."

"You'll get no complaints from me," Robert said.

Jack noticed him smiling at Lindsey.

And her smiling back.

Cherise dug two key cards from her purse and handed them to him. The elevator doors opened and they stepped on. She pressed number four. "I got you the room that was available. Two queens and a mini bar. I took the liberty of having a bottle of Knob Creek sent up."

He handed Robert his key card. "Seems you've thought of everything. How about we get freshened up and meet in the bar in thirty minutes?"

"Make it the Beach Club patio deck. And thanks again for coming. I know it is a lot to ask."

He winked. "You knew you could count on me."

"Knowing you the way I do, I figured I could. Besides, you did offer to help if I needed it."

He grinned. "And I don't break my promises."

The doors opened and the four of them stepped off. She pointed. "412 is right over there. Ours is down the hall; 426 and 427."

"So they are." Jack looked in that direction wondering which door was hers. "We'll meet you on the patio deck in thirty."

* * *

Twenty-five minutes later, Jack and Robert stepped onto the elevator. Jack pressed the button to take them down, and said, "Lindsey is a pretty girl."

"So is Cherise."

"Meaning we're both lucky. Just don't let it muck up our reason for being here."

"Not going to happen."

Jack wanted to believe that.

They stepped off, followed the signs to the Beach Club, and found Cherise and Lindsey sitting at a table with an unobstructed ocean view. Both looking like models on holiday.

"Hope we didn't keep you waiting long." Jack slid the chair next to Cherise back and sat.

"Not long at all," she said. "I'm relieved you're both here."

Lindsey swiped at the corner of her eye and gave them a shaky smile. "And I want you to know I'm so very thankful you're helping us. Not many men would get involved in something this dangerous."

Robert took the seat next to her. "That's who we are, Lindsey. We would have flown here from Oahu to help."

Jack signaled a waiter over and looked at Cherise. "Let's order drinks and then you can tell us all about this plan of yours."

The waiter, a tall redhead with a pleasing smile, stopped at their table and the women each ordered a glass of Sauvignon Blanc. Jack decided to stick with beer since that's what he'd been drinking and ordered a Red Stripe. Robert did the same.

"I take it I can talk freely?" Jack directed the question to Cherise.

"You're referring to me of course," Lindsey answered for her. "I know Dad's dead. He was on that ship in Belize and no one can convince me he left the ship with some woman in Miami."

He studied the resolve in her eyes. "Over eighty thousand people are missing in the US at any given moment. Sixty percent are adults. Many of them stay lost. You honestly believe this Corey Jameson guy is responsible for whatever happened to your father?"

Her expression hardened. "And his sister Amanda is in it with him."

"At least it looks that way," Cherise added. "I figure this scam has been going on for some time. Corey is Amanda's half-brother. She's clean as far as I know, but he has an arrest record for second-degree assault. Three years ago, in West Palm Beach. Pled no contest to a misdemeanor charge and received a year's probation. At the very least, I think it's safe to assume he exhibited a predisposition for violence."

"Including killing people?"

"Lindsey asked me the same question. Corey could just be an asshole actor with a temper. Then again, it's also possible he's a sociopath with no qualms about committing murder."

"And you believe the latter to be the case."

"I do. But all we can really say is he appears to enjoy living the high life. His bank account fluctuates drastically from month to month. Lots of credit card expenditures at exclusive restaurants and clubs. I didn't see any recent deposits that would correspond with the sale of the idols even though Susan confirmed he and his sister have taken nearly two dozen cruises to the Yucatan over the past two years. Different cruise lines—the two of them always traveling together with no cruise lasting longer than seven days."

"What—?" The flat of her raised palm stopped him.

"Before you ask, the three missing passenger cases I told you about all correspond to cruises Corey and his sister were on. But that doesn't mean there weren't more victims. It's likely that not all cases of this nature are reported."

"What else can you tell me about him?"

He's thirty-eight and is, or was, a fishing celebrity. Had a TV show where he traveled the world catching monster fish. The network canceled the show after a couple of seasons. That was two years ago. Now he supposedly makes his living advertising fishing and sports equipment."

Jack understood the implication. "And you find that questionable?"

"Besides living the high life and a lot of credit card expenditures at restaurants and clubs, there's his Palm Beach condo to consider. As well as his sister's place next door to him."

"Pricy, I imagine."

"Very."

"I assume you got into his bank accounts. If he's working, even promoting sports equipment on TV, he should be bringing in a decent income."

"Maybe enough isn't enough. I'm no accountant, but even I can see he lives way above his means."

"And you figure he smuggles to supplement his lifestyle."

"Traveling the world fishing would be the perfect catalyst to get him started. Only that ended and he had to find another way."

Jack digested the information. Some of which she had already told him. "Seems like graduating to murder is a pretty big step."

"Money is a powerful motivator."

"How do you think his sister became involved?"

"When we talked to her, I couldn't help thinking she wasn't the woman who had lured Lindsey's father to his death. Yet you and Robert placed them together in Key West. And she's undeniably the person sitting at the Captain's table with him. Plus, her name and her brother's name are on the ship's passenger manifest."

Their waiter appeared and set their drinks in front of them. When Redhead walked away, Cherise tapped the screen of her phone and turned it toward Jack, "This is another photo Susan sent of Amanda. One you haven't seen."

Robert leaned in for a look as well.

Jack gave him room.

In the picture, Amanda stood next to another woman. Shorter and not nearly as attractive.

"She's pretty," he said. "And taller than I imagined."

Cherise arched a brow at him. "I noticed that, too. Amanda is a self-employed, independent chartered accountant. She's thirty-two and single. Never married. Her mother, Veronica Kelly, owns Dream World Travel. Her father's deceased. So are the grandparents. In addition to her half-brother Corey, she has a sister, Jessica Finch, who works at the travel agency. Husband deceased."

"And her financials?"

"She has a high six-figure bank account and a half dozen major credit cards, all in good standing. There were no suspicious deposits that I saw."

Lindsey leaned in. "What she hasn't told you is Dad booked his cruise through Dream World Travel. That can't be a coincidence."

And probably wasn't.

He looked from Lindsey to Cherise. She knew he didn't believe in coincidences any more than she did. "Have you checked out the place?"

Cherise shook her head. "Only Dream World's financials. The business is located on Washington Avenue in Miami Beach. Apparently they cater to people booking cruises. Unlike many of the travel agencies across the country that are struggling to stay afloat while competing with the discount travel sites on the internet, the company is doing well. But not so good as to raise any red flags."

"Still, it might pay to dig a little deeper."

"I truly believe someone at the agency is connected to what's going on. The question is who. There's also a matter of proof."

"Which will take care of itself. Once we take down Corey, the rest of the group will unravel and fall apart."

"I agree." She angled her phone toward Jack. "You only had a headshot of him. Susan pulled this one from his website. I'm almost sure he's the cornerstone to their operation."

"A big son-of-a-bitch. Ned wasn't lying when he said Corey looked like a body builder."

"With playboy good looks," Cherise added. "When I went through his condo, I saw a lot of photos of him in exotic locations posing with fish he'd caught. Built like a linebacker for a pro football team."

He took the phone from her hand and studied the face. "And more than capable of dropping a body overboard."

CHAPTER 41

Jack had Corey Jameson pictured in his mind when he noticed Robert's penetrating stare. He had seen it countless times over the decade they had been friends. That look of the perplexed bystander aching to speak up.

"Out with it," he said to Robert. "I'm surprised you haven't given us your two-cents worth already."

Robert leaned in. "You're setting yourself up as bait. Clearly, these two have been at this game for a while. How do you plan to get them to bite? It's doubtful you can just walk up to Amanda and introduce yourself."

"It might come to that." Jack looked at Cherise. "But I suppose you have a better plan?"

She smiled. "You're good, Jack. But not that good."

"Well now," he said. "There might be one or two young ladies who would disagree with you."

"The less discerning ones, I'm sure." She rolled her eyes, obviously for the benefit of the others seated at the table, and said, "Let's not confuse the issue. The Dream World Travel connection is far too coincidental to ignore. I'm guessing the entire family is in on the scam. The agency provides the perfect cover for them to compile a list of potential targets. Probably wealthy men looking for on board romance. Older men who would be easily charmed by an alluring beauty like Amanda."

"Preferably men without families," Robert added. "There would be less chance of children or a sibling pushing for an investigation."

Lindsey said, "Only with my dad they screwed up."

"They did, and I'm sorry for your loss." Robert's expression softened. "My understanding is you were still getting to know each other."

Robert pushed. "And you want revenge?"

"Dad either died from some horrible accident or someone murdered him. If Corey killed him with Amanda's help, they need to pay."

Jack understood revenge. And he knew Cherise did, too. To her he asked, "How many men do you figure they've murdered?"

Cherise took a moment to answer. "If necessary, Susan could compile a list of cruises Corey and Amanda have taken in the last couple of years. Even if only half of those trips paid off, a good guess would be a dozen."

Jack believed her. "The bottom line is they have to be stopped."

"And without evidence, the authorities are powerless to do anything."

"You were saying something about a plan?"

"As you know the *Caribbean Sensation*, *Caribbean Star*'s sister ship, departs from Miami on Thursday. Corey and Amanda will be on it, and so will we."

"I know. I'm the bait. But how is this going to work?"

"I had Susan pose as your secretary and book your ticket through Dream World Travel. Your cover story being you are a wealthy marine biologist who's widowed and hopes to connect with a woman on the cruise."

"In those words?"

"Not exactly. But to that effect."

"And you believe they'll buy that I'm a wealthy marine biologist. That's almost an oxymoron."

"Jack, you are wealthy, and you are a marine biologist. You can tell them you inherited the money from rich parents. Susan also planted information on social media to support your cover story."

"If they go as far as checking my background."

"My guess is your name will go on the list. Hopefully at the top.

They'll have your passport photo, and it will be up to them to make first contact. You have their pictures so if they don't, it will be up to you to be your usual charming self. It's only a four-day cruise so things should happen pretty fast."

"What about having sex with her?"

"Suffice to say, you'll have to rely on your personal discretion if and when the matter comes up."

"I guarantee it'll come up. That's the trap."

"Surely you haven't forgotten I'm well aware of how the game works."

He could see she wasn't happy. He didn't care much for the prospect, himself. But this was her game.

"I suppose you and Lindsey will make yourselves scarce since Amanda knows both of you?" He grinned at Robert. "That leaves you to be my backup."

"I'll be on the sundeck playing bodyguard for Lindsey if you need me."

"That will be my job," Cherise said. She swept her gaze over Lindsey and focused on Robert. "You stick close to Jack."

Jack felt all right with her decision. But just all right. Robert had covered his back more than once. And jumped in when needed. Still, he knew full well what Cherise was capable of in a sticky situation, and couldn't deny he would feel better knowing she was close by.

A whole lot better.

He said to her, "Robert's a great friend. He's always stood by me when the shit hit the fan. I'll never forget that. But I'm sure he would agree, we both will sleep better knowing you're there to jump in if your plan goes sour. And we all know how quickly that can happen."

She met his gaze and held it. "You know I'd never put either one of you in a position to get hurt. Not without being there to make sure that doesn't happen. You just might not be able to see me."

Robert chuckled. "So the sundeck comment was a joke."

She shook her head. "Really . . . ?"

Robert smiled and winked at Lindsey.

But not without Jack seeing him.

"Enough said for now." Jack sucked down his last swallows

of beer and swiped his forearm across his mouth. "That officially makes me the mackerel dangling on the hook. You ready to have dinner?"

He saw fifty questions in Cherise's eyes. Then she smiled, lifted her glass, and said, "While we have time to enjoy it."

CHAPTER 42

They ordered another round of drinks prior to leaving for dinner. Jack switched to Knob Creek on ice in the spirit of keeping in tune with the bottle in his room. Robert joined him. Cherise and Lindsey stayed with wine.

Cherise asked, "How is your new boat?"

"My new old boat will work out nicely," he said, happy to have the conversation on something else. "And you're welcome aboard anytime you're ready for another tour of the islands."

"Cherise told me you're into sharks," Lindsey said.

"Apex predators, actually. Sharks are only one group of many on the list. You might find it interesting to know that the other day divers filmed a twenty-foot female Great White named Deep Blue off the south coast of Oahu."

"You give them names?"

"Not always. This particular shark is one that was tagged twenty years ago. She's believed to be over fifty years old. The best part, she's pregnant."

"I can't imagine how you do it. A shark that size . . . any shark scares the hell out of me."

"They're fine as long as you keep your distance and don't serve yourself up to be dinner."

"Is that what you do, keep your distance?"

"Not always. But I've been lucky."

Cherise took a sip of wine. Her gaze found his. "Let's hope your luck holds a little longer."

"I'm afraid it will take more than luck to pull this off."

They finished their drinks and made the short walk down the resort's palm-lined drive to the steakhouse for dinner. The maître d' led them through the packed dining room with its beamed ceiling and oversized chandeliers to a table on the terrace where they had a view of the golf course and the Palm Beach skyline.

Jack admired the vista. "An excellent choice."

"Lindsey made the reservation," Cherise pointed out.

"Then my compliments to her."

"Thank you," Lindsey said. "Let's hope the food is as good as the ambiance."

They ordered a bottle of Sauvignon Blanc and, amid pleasant conversation, feasted on a shrimp cocktail, Caesar salad, and pan roasted Chilean sea bass. The food turned out to be excellent.

When the last of the dishes had been taken away, Jack asked, "Anyone for a brandy?"

Cherise picked up her cell and glanced at the screen. "I've got business to take care of on the phone. I think I'll call it a night."

Jack noticed a hint of color remaining in the sky. "It's still early. Not even one drink?"

She shook her head. "Sorry. It's been a long day."

He paid the bill and they walked into the hotel lobby. Cherise stopped them there and said to Jack, "Thank you for a wonderful dinner. You three have that nightcap and I'll see you in the morning."

He motioned at the elevator. "I'll ride up with you."

"Sorry. Some other time."

"Really?" He felt the sting of disappointment. And couldn't help thinking something had changed between them. "So this is it. You've donned your armor and you're not going to let me back in?"

She pecked him on the cheek. "You're persistent if nothing else." The elevator doors opened and she stepped on.

He watched them close.

"You ready?" Robert's voice brought him back.

He swallowed his frustration. "I guess."

"To the bar, then?" Robert said.

Lindsey turned to Jack. "You'll join us?"

"You two go ahead." Without Cherise there with him, a brandy lost its appeal. "I think I'll go for a stroll around the grounds."

"Don't wait up," Robert said, as he and Lindsey headed for the bar.

It was dark when Jack walked out onto the sand where the outgoing tide left it damp and hard. He understood the risks Cherise asked him to take and wanted to hold onto his erotic fantasies of her and carry them into the night. If he didn't, the faces of the dead tucked away in his memory would surface to replace her. He slid his hands into the pockets of his Dockers, and let the cadence of breaking waves and the hiss of the retreating surf work their magic.

Until they didn't.

Robert was sitting up in bed reading when Jack got back to the room. He'd been gone an hour. It was still early.

He noticed a glass on the nightstand next to his friend. The remnant of an ice cube floated in the last quarter inch of a watered-down drink.

"You and Lindsey seem to be hitting it off nicely." He poured an inch of Knob Creek into a glass with ice and took a seat.

Robert lowered his book. "She's a nice lady. It's a shame what happened to her father."

Jack took a sip, waiting for Robert to say more.

He didn't.

"Did you call Kazuko?"

"If you're asking me if I told her about Lindsey, I did. Everything. And I filled her in on what we're doing to make sure no one else falls victim to these two. You can guess she wasn't thrilled to hear you're off on another dangerous escapade."

"I'm sure she wasn't happy hearing you're in it with me."

"You know how she is."

"And we love her for it."

"Thanks for reminding me."

CHAPTER 43

Jack woke to sunlight streaming into his room and the sound of his phone vibrating on the bedside table. Robert stirred in his bed. The phone vibrated again and Jack picked it up. He read Cherise's name on the screen and answered the call.

"What'd I miss?"

"A beautiful sunrise," she said with a healthy amount of cheer. "How did you sleep last night?"

She'd obviously slept well. Maybe having him there helped. He eyed the bottle of Knob Creek, down by a third. "A bit too soundly, I'm afraid. Robert and I stayed up and had a few."

"Did you solve the ills of the world?"

"We worked on it. But alas, no. Did you make your calls?"

"We can talk about it over breakfast."

"Just you and I?"

"Linds will be joining us. Bring Robert."

"Do we have time to shower?"

"Of course. We'll be waiting for you on the patio deck."

Forty-five minutes later, Jack and Robert joined them at the same table they occupied the night before. The women stood to greet them. Lindsey smiled at Robert. Cherise kissed Jack on the cheek.

She said, "So the Knob Creek was a hit."

"I don't know whether to thank you or curse you."

"Have a Bloody Mary. You'll feel better." She turned to Robert. "How are you feeling?"

"Fine." He leaned toward Lindsey. "I trust you slept well?"

"Very," she said. "That nightcap did it."

"Wonderful. We'll do it again tonight."

"Only no fancy meal first. Let's keep it simple."

"Speaking of eating," Jack said. "Let's order and get down to business. I believe Cherise has something to tell us."

They all ordered light. And he asked for a Bloody Mary.

"I spoke to Susan on the phone last night," Cherise began when she had his full attention. "Everything is a go. She received confirmation on our tickets and texted the boarding passes to me. Corey and Amanda are booked into cabin 7678, a portside aft suite on deck seven. Jack, for appearance purposes, you're in 8520, a large balcony stateroom portside on deck eight. Robert, you're in 8527, an inside stateroom a few cabins aft of Jack's. Lindsey and I will share a 0cean-view cabin on deck four, number 4054, mid-ship on the starboard side. Which, with any luck, will minimize the likelihood of either of us running into Amanda or Corey in a passageway."

Jack thought about the money being spent on their not-so-little sting operation, and couldn't help wonder who paid the tab. He decided it best not to ask.

He said, "I'm a bit confused on how you plan to coordinate this."

"Susan overnighted me a wire you'll be wearing. Remember the humming bird we used on that job on Oahu? The miniature technology is similar and extremely difficult to detect. The one I've selected for you is mounted in the face of a waterproof Doxa dive watch to maintain your cover. Should work nicely with you being a marine biologist. The rest of us will have a receiver that looks like a cell phone and allows us to hear you and anyone close to you, loud and clear. A video camera is mounted in the face as well so we can see everything it's pointed at. Unfortunately you won't be able to hear us since we can't chance you wearing an earpiece."

"So even if I take all my clothes off, I'll still be wired?"

She looked at him as though she read his mind. "Just remember to put your watch on the nightstand."

He grinned. "With the camera turned away?"

"If you're shy." Her lips curled a fraction.

Seeing her crack a smile made him feel a whole lot better.

The situation will get serious soon enough.

He asked, "How about GPS?"

"We'll be able to track your movement within reason."

"Meaning?"

"We'll know that when we start tracking you."

"So from here on out, it's a matter of playing it by ear?"

She nodded. "The *Caribbean Sensation* is in port in Miami now. I figure we'll drive down tomorrow morning, check into a hotel, and be ready to board the ship on Thursday . . . hopefully before Corey and Amanda arrive."

"If I'd only known, I'd have brought my tux."

Her smile returned, broader. "You have to own one first. But I can fix that."

CHAPTER 44

The following morning at ten, Jack stood in the portico with Cherise while the valet hurried off to bring her rental car around. Robert and Lindsey stood ten feet away engaged in conversation.

It felt good to have time alone with Cherise.

If only a minute.

She turned to him and said, "I really appreciate you helping out."

"You keep telling me that." He felt he needed to say more. "Honestly, nothing would have kept me away."

"You're sure about that?"

"Having spent three weeks alone with you on a small boat, I'm sure."

The hint of a smile curled her lips. "You have a point. Only it's not like I asked you to do something as simple as going for a stroll in the park."

"What we're doing is the easy part," he said. "The difficult part for me has been knowing you're lying in bed a few doors away and not being able to go to you."

"Don't think I haven't had those same thoughts."

"We're both consenting adults. Why have you kept me away?"

She took a moment. "I think it's better if we don't confuse the issue. You can't risk being emotionally involved with me any more than I can with you."

"Maybe I'm ready."

"What if I'm not?" She peered deep into his eyes. "You mean a lot to me. Maybe to the point of being the closest I've been to being in love with a man. Out there on the water I thought I'd love for us to go on like that forever. But then this situation with Lindsey came up and I realized that wasn't possible. There would be no room in either one of our lives for the kind of love we're talking about."

"Maybe," he said. "And then again, maybe not."

"Face it. We operate on different tracks."

"Yet here I am."

She continued to peer into his eyes. For a slow five count, she said nothing. Then her expression softened. "Yes, you are."

He held her gaze, not wanting her to look away.

Ever.

"The other night you called me persistent," he said. "You at least got that part right."

The valet arrived with her car.

This time, Jack sat in the front seat.

* * *

Jack welcomed the seventy-five mile drive to Miami. Liked watching Cherise maneuver the Charger past slower-moving traffic. She was an excellent driver.

And beautiful.

On the outskirts of town, they passed a billboard advertising airboat tours of the Everglades. Robert pointed out the sign. "A few days ago, I read a news feed on the internet that said a man lost an arm on one of those."

Jack twisted in his seat. "In the propeller?"

"Wasn't close to the propeller," Robert explained. "The guy reached over the side and had it bit off by a ten-foot alligator."

Jack faced the front. "I've heard of sharks doing the same thing."

When she turned into the portico at the Intercontinental Hotel Susan had booked them into, he almost wished the drive down the Florida turnpike had taken longer than an hour and a half. He made no further complaint about having to bunk in a room with Robert.

Or about not being invited to Cherise's room.

That discussion had been tabled for now.

Cherise, he figured, appreciated that.

She left the car with the valet and they stepped inside. A bellman walked ahead of them pushing a cart loaded with their luggage. The opulence of the hotel's interior was not lost on them.

"Nice digs," Jack said.

"You ever been here before?" Cherise asked.

"To Miami? Never had a reason to."

"Till now."

He didn't need to be reminded.

"We're early," she said, and started toward the front desk. "I'll let the agent know we're here and ask for an early check in. We can have lunch while we're waiting for our rooms."

"Burger and a beer by the pool works for me," Robert said.

Cherise looked at Lindsey who glanced back and forth at her and Jack. "I vote to keep it simple."

"Works for me," Jack agreed.

"Good enough. I'll get us checked in." Cherise left them standing there.

Jack watched her step away, but only for a second. He caught up to her and slowed at her side. "I'll keep you company."

This time she had no objection.

When they got to the Blue Water Café, they found the place busy with the noon crowd. "What do you think," Jack asked.

"There's only one couple in line ahead of us," Robert said.

Jack got nods from the others.

"Okay, we wait."

Twenty minutes later they were seated at a table overlooking the rooftop pool. Jack stared out the window at the cruise ships sitting in port. The *Caribbean Sensation* stood out among them. Thursday's cruise. Ready for the next flock of happy travelers to board.

Among the passengers, two possible killers.

And the four of them to prevent yet another murder.

Cherise was strong-willed, tough, intelligent, and gutsy.

She had survived far rougher situations than they were facing now.

Her life revolved around danger.

It's what she did for a living.

And her luck held.

But even great hitters don't bat a thousand.

He suddenly realized his life would never be the same if anything happened to her.

CHAPTER 45

Jack got out of bed early to stand at the window of his eighteenth-floor room and watch the horizon lighten until the sun peeked between the cluster of hotels to the east. The morning dawned clear and bright. Another perfect day in Miami Beach.

Robert yawned and sat up a few minutes later. "You're awake."

"I wanted to see the sunrise. You never know, it might be your last."

"You're full of cheer this morning."

"Actually, I feel good. And as soon as I have a cup of coffee, I'll feel even better."

"You can text Cherise and see if they're awake. They might like to join us for an early breakfast."

"She's up. You can bet on it. We have a lot to do today."

* * *

Jack studied the cruise ships from the front passenger seat while Cherise drove them across the bridge to Miami Beach. Robert and Lindsey sat in back.

Robert made a whistling sound. "Big suckers when you get up close."

Jack thought the same thing. "Bigger than any of the research vessels I've been on."

"Wait until you're on board with four thousand other people," Cherise said. "The ship might not seem so big then."

She followed the A1A across Biscayne Bay and into South Beach, turned left at 12th Street, drove two blocks west to Washington Avenue, and parked next to the World Erotic Museum. Dream World Travel Agency—they discovered when they walked around the corner—sat sandwiched between the museum and a Starbucks. A forest-green canvas awning ran the length of the building, shading the sidewalk in front.

Jack extended his arm and stopped them short of the travel agency. He saw no reason to rush. To Cherise, he said, "No one here knows us, but I think it'd be wise to play it cautious."

"I agree," Cherise said. "Let's do a walk-by and check out the place before we go in. You and I will go first. Robert, you and Lindsey wait a minute before taking your turn. We'll meet up inside the coffee house on the other side."

Jack walked beside Cherise, Washington Avenue on his left. Her height added a degree of difficulty when he looked past her to scan the business.

He did his best to not appear obvious.

The place had a glass entrance door with ten feet of window on each side of it. A pair of desks and several straight-back chairs were visible inside. Travel posters and racks of colorful brochures lined the walls. A lone woman sat behind one of the desks. An open laptop in front of her. She had a cell phone pressed to her ear.

As they walked past, a second woman stepped out of a back room and joined her. Tall. Younger. He recognized her from her photo.

Cherise hurried past the window and ducked inside Starbucks five feet ahead of Jack.

He caught up to her at the rear of the coffeehouse and faced the door. So much for luck. "Wasn't that Amanda?"

Cherise kept her voice down. "And that was probably her mother. I hope she doesn't recognize Lindsey."

"We'll know in a second." He kept his eyes on the door.

Not even a minute later, Lindsey hurried inside with Robert following a few feet behind her. She rushed up to Cherise, grabbed hold of her arm, and whispered, "Did you see Amanda?"

Cherise laid her hand on top of Lindsey's. "She didn't see you, did she?"

"She was busy talking to the other woman, so I don't think so." Lindsey shot a nervous glance at the door. "But that was close."

Jack saw the worry in the women's expressions.

"The two of you obviously can't go in there," he said. "And Robert should avoid being seen as well. But I see no reason why I can't. I'll simply introduce myself and say I dropped in to thank them for arranging the cruise."

Cherise nodded. "Having Amanda there may well work in our favor. You meeting her could be the ice breaker we need."

"One thing is for sure," he said. "It should prove interesting."

He couldn't wait to put the charm on Amanda.

CHAPTER 46

Jack stepped into the cool interior of Dream World Travel feeling confident.

The woman he recognized as Amanda and the older woman were standing by the desk he'd seen them at earlier. The laptop open. They turned and looked in his direction when he stepped through the doorway. Both of them smiled. He flashed one back.

"Good morning," Amanda said.

"And a pleasant morning to you."

She continued to peer at him out of the corners of her eyes as she leaned close to the older woman and whispered something he couldn't make out. Without waiting for a response, she turned and walked toward the back room.

"May I help you?" the older woman asked.

"My name is Jack Ferrell." He approached her desk. But his eyes were focused on Amanda as she walked away. Her hair appeared blonder than it had in the photos he'd seen of her. And more stylish.

Even prettier in person.

Before leaving the room, she gave him a long pleasant appraisal and smiled.

He held her gaze.

Great lips.

"My name is Veronica Kelley, I'm the owner." The woman's voice drew his attention back to her.

He had no choice but to follow through with the charade. Amanda had left the room. But contact had been made. And that was enough for now.

Her smile said it all.

"I apologize for becoming distracted," he said. "It's wonderful to meet you. My secretary—actually she works for a colleague of mine—used your agency to book me on a four-day cruise aboard the *Caribbean Sensation*. The ship sails tomorrow and I just wanted to pop in and personally thank you for all your assistance."

"That's very nice of you. We get a lot of phone customers, but rarely have the opportunity to meet them in person. Sorry my daughter had to leave, I could have introduced you."

"I'm sure she's busy. Perhaps I'll get the chance another time."

"Is this your first cruise?"

"Actually it is."

"From your tan, I'd have guessed you spend a lot of time on the water."

"You're very observant. I'm a marine biologist. Much of my work is done on the ocean."

Her manicured brow arched. "And you've never taken a cruise? I find that somewhat surprising."

"Truth is, owning a boat as well as spending time aboard large research vessels, put taking a cruise way down on my list of to do's. But I did think about it a number of times . . . when my wife was alive. After she passed away, I lost interest. My colleague's secretary is the one who suggested I splurge on a Caribbean vacation to cheer me up. I figured I'd start with a four-day cruise. If it turns out to be something I want to do again, I'll work up from there."

"Your colleague's secretary is a wise woman. I'm sure you'll enjoy the experience, immensely."

He glanced around to appear uneasy and lowered his voice. "I probably shouldn't say this to you, but I hope to meet a lady aboard ship. Someone I can share the cruise with. That sort of thing happens, right?"

"Sometimes." She retook the seat at her desk and began tapping on the keyboard of her laptop. "Jack Ferrell, right?"

"Correct." He waited and saw her smile.

"You have one of the larger forward outside cabins with a balcony. You should be quite comfortable."

"Thank you. I really have no idea what I'm getting into."

"I can help." She got up, pulled several pamphlets from the rack and handed them to him. "Look these over. One of them covers everything you need to know about the boarding process, security, and what you can and can't take on board with you. The other one describes the ship and its amenities. There's also several tour options available to you when you arrive at Cozumel."

Amanda hadn't returned. He'd hoped she would.

He tapped the brochures against the palm of his hand. The game had been played. "I can't thank you enough."

"My pleasure." She escorted him to the door and held it open while he stepped outside. "Have a nice trip, Mr. Ferrell."

He gave her a casual wave and watched her return to her desk. When he was out of sight of her, he stepped back into the Starbucks.

"You were in there a while," Cherise said.

"You were worried about me?"

"A little. You can be a dork at times."

He liked that she had joked with him. "You can relax. Mission accomplished."

"And . . . ?"

"They are a cool pair, those two," he said. "I've been through enough scrapes to not be fooled by looks, but Amanda—her eyes . . . they draw you right in. She's pretty. Even prettier than she is in her photos. There's no denying, I would never figure her for a murderer."

"Neither does a male black widow spider," Cherise pointed out. "Right up to the instant he gets eaten by his lover. You said Amanda left a minute after you walked through the door. Were you able to introduce yourself to her or not?"

"Formally, no. But there was enough eye contact going on between us to guarantee she'll remember me when we meet on the boat. I planted some seeds with her mother, too. She went as far as checking which stateroom I'm staying in. I'll be surprised if Amanda doesn't show up at my door asking me to have a drink with her."

Cherise raised a brow at him. "Care to take bets?"

He ignored the dig.

"Whether she shows up with a bottle of wine or not, running into her at the travel agency opened the door for me to approach her."

He pictured Amanda. All six feet of her. If everything went according to plan, they'd be spending a lot of time together over the next four days. Time when he needed to be at the top of his game.

It could mean his life.

CHAPTER 47

Cherise saw the door open a crack and Jack's face appear . . . one cautious eye and a cheek. Then she saw more of his muscular body when he pulled the door open wide enough to reveal all of him.

She took a deep breath and held up the bottle of champagne she purchased at the gift shop. "Peace offering?"

He stood back, saying nothing. But his smile did. She took that as an invitation to enter and stepped inside.

He pushed the door closed behind her. "This is a pleasant surprise."

She noticed beads of water on his muscled shoulders, his biceps, in the mat of black hair on his chest. The towel wrapped around his waist. "Did I interrupt your shower?"

"I was ready to get out, anyway. But I certainly didn't expect to see you standing at the door. Let alone with a bottle of Dom Perignon."

"I can leave if you want me to."

"I've got a better idea." He took the champagne from her hand, carried it over to the ice bucket, and jammed it in. He held up two squat tumblers and added, "They're not stemmed flutes, but they'll work."

She felt a surge of heat go through her watching him walk barechested across the room, wearing only a towel. The same rush she felt the first time she saw him step toward her, naked.

She walked over to him and draped her arms around his neck. "Wouldn't it be better to set that on the bedside table?"

"What about Robert?" His voice soft and dreamy.

He stood so close to her she could feel the heat from his body. She slid her hands from his shoulders and raked her fingers through the hair on his chest. "I asked Lindsey to keep him company for a couple of hours."

"Only two hours?" He pressed her hand against him.

She could feel the rapid thump of his heart beneath her palm. "I suggest we make the best of it."

His hands dropped to her hips and pulled her to him as he leaned in and kissed her.

She closed her eyes, fully embracing him. And when they separated, she drew in a deep breath to ease the sudden tightness in her chest. Always the same. He had a talent for taking her breath away.

"What about the champagne?"

"Do we really need it?" He kissed her again.

His embrace sent a surge of lust through her body. Her fingers unhooked his towel and let it drop to the floor. At the same time, he went to work on her clothing. Seduction playing as important a part as removing each item.

She eased him away enough to allow her bra to slip from her arms. And buried her face in his shoulder as his lips found her neck. Sex with him had been intense and overpowering . . . and pleasurable. The overpowering as much her sexuality as his. He had never tried to dominate her. For him sex was as much about following as leading. He was the most seductive man she had been romantically involved with.

Yet when he arrived at the hotel to help, she had resisted his advances. Made him upset that she didn't share his desire.

She'd sensed it. Heard it in his voice.

And the fit of anger he'd let slip had been her fault.

She wouldn't allow that to happen again.

They fell on the bed and this time he took her rougher and deeper and harder. And she found herself responding with even greater passion than she had before. They kept at it for a long time.

Until he finally collapsed on top of her.

Spent.

With his arms at her sides and his hands supporting her shoulders, he lay laboring to catch his breath. Until finally he rolled onto his back, freeing her of his weight.

But not their feelings for each other.

She, too, had been consumed by their lovemaking.

When at last her heart rate and breathing slowed enough for her to talk, she turned to him and said, "I don't know what possessed me to say something like that. It upset you and I'm sorry."

He rolled onto his side and looked at her with eyes that sent another ripple of heat through her. "What was it you said?"

"That we should guard our feelings."

"I might have sounded angry. And I probably was a little. But I understood what you were saying. Even though I don't agree."

"You know what we both want. I couldn't let you board the ship and face those two without an understanding between us."

He laid his arm across her breast and kissed her shoulder. "I think you made that understanding quite clear."

She resisted a tingling of desire. "You're missing the point."

He began drawing circles on her flat stomach with his fingertip. Traced a line from her breasts to her bellybutton. "If you're worried about me having sex with Amanda, don't. What is it Bond says? 'For king and country.' "

"It's not that simple."

"You did what you had to do on Oahu. I'll do what I have to do. But only if that's what it takes to make your plan work."

She sighed. "It will probably be easier for you than it was for me."

"Because I'm a guy?"

"Because you're you."

"I haven't forgotten Amanda's a cold blooded murderer. She's no different than Yang Li. Honestly, I don't know how you did it."

"Like you said. I did what I had to do. I thought of it as being part of the job. Like you'll have to do."

"A job, huh. I only hope I can get it up."

"Believe me, Jack. That's one problem you don't have."

CHAPTER 48

Jack awoke with a start at one in the morning.

His heart raced.

Something was terribly wrong.

A nightmare?

The disturbing shreds of the dream that lingered made no sense. Nothing more than bits and pieces of long-dead memories juggled by his subconscious and put into an order that flowed logically while he dreamed them.

But not now.

He scanned the room and found Cherise gone and Robert asleep in his bed. The unopened bottle of Dom Perignon still in the ice bucket.

Nothing to cause him alarm.

Only pleasant memories of two wonderful hours entwined in Cherise's arms.

So why had his subconscious ventured into the nether regions of his mind?

A vision?

A revelation to caution me against repeating past mistakes.

He slid on his boxers. And for the better part of an hour, he lay on his back in the darkness with his arm across his forehead and fantasized about Cherise until finally he dozed off.

When his phone alarm jarred him awake at six, Robert was

already in the shower. Five minutes later, he walked out with a towel around him.

He stood at the foot of his bed running a brush through his wet hair. "Enjoy yourself last night?"

Jack tossed back the sheet and slid his legs off the side of the bed. "How'd you know?"

"The champagne. You didn't buy that for me."

"I didn't buy it for Cherise, either. She brought it with her."

"You might want to get in the shower. We're meeting her and Lindsey for breakfast."

At seven-thirty, he and Robert rode the elevator down to the Blue Water Café. They had time to sit by the pool and talk over their plan at least one more time before preparing to leave for the ship.

Jack thought how nice it had been on the *Sun Dancer* to wake up with Cherise in bed next to him, dark hair splayed on the pillow. He looked forward to seeing how she would act now that they had come to an understanding.

Cherise and Lindsey were already seated with cups of coffee in front of them. He saw no reason for pretenses. They were all aware of what transpired the night before. Robert sat across from Lindsey and Jack settled into the chair across from Cherise. She looked wonderful.

"Good morning," he said. And it was.

"Sleep well?" Cherise asked.

For about an hour, only he wasn't about to tell her that. "Like a baby."

"You were snoring when I left."

He grinned. "And ten minutes before that?"

He didn't believe it was possible to make her blush.

But she did.

She leaned in and pecked him on the lips. "You definitely weren't snoring."

* * *

At twelve thirty, Jack and Robert meet Cherise and Lindsey in the lobby to catch their shuttle ride to the cruise terminal. Two other

195

couples hoping to be among the first to board were waiting there as well.

Jack had to stifle a laugh when he saw Cherise and Lindsey.

"You're a sight," he said. Both women wore wigs a shade too light for their skin tone. "If you two ever think about going blonde, forget it. The color doesn't do a thing for either of you."

"You're saying we look like New York hookers?"

"I wasn't going to say that, but yes."

Cherise slipped on a pair of sunglasses with lenses large enough to cover a third of her face. "If they get us on board without Amanda recognizing us, they'll be worth the ridicule."

"You have a point," he said. "At least you're boarding ahead of me."

She peered at him over the frame of her dark glasses. "And I thought you were a nice guy."

He grinned.

The shuttle arrived on time. When they got out of the van at the cruise terminal, the place was already a hive of activity. Cherise and Lindsey got in line, Robert directly behind them, and in the rear, Jack. They turned their checked baggage over to a porter and joined the flood of people going through security.

Jack held back, letting his friends and a couple dozen other passengers proceed through ahead of him. Unlike Cherise and Lindsey, he wasn't concerned about being seen by Amanda. Exactly the opposite. There were a lot of anxious people in line, but neither she nor Corey were anywhere in sight.

He plodded through security and entered the room where passengers waited their turn to check in. Cherise, Lindsey, and Robert weren't among them.

Once he had his turn with an agent, the process went quickly. His picture was taken and downloaded into the ship's computer. The woman gave him his credit-card style room key and he proceeded to boarding.

The walk to the *Caribbean Sensation* turned out to be surprisingly long, and included going up several stories to reach the boarding deck amidships. When he at last reached the ship, he scanned his room card to let the cruise line know he was aboard, and received directions to his cabin.

The stateroom was bright and, he supposed, by cruise ship standards, spacious. Two twin beds pushed together to form a king, a desk and seat, and a full bath with shower. And three tiny closets. He checked the balcony and found it reasonably equipped with two patio chairs and a small table for cocktails.

Home sweet home.

His bags were still on their way to his room so he locked up and walked aft to 8527 to check on Robert. He probably felt entombed having been stuck in an inside cabin.

He knocked and Robert let him in.

"Comfortable?"

Robert scoffed. "If you like sleeping in a box."

"Your bags aren't here yet, either?"

"They have a lot to bring aboard. Want to grab a beer?"

"Sure. We'll get a couple and take them to my cabin. It has a decent balcony and we won't be seen together."

CHAPTER 49

Jack didn't see Amanda until after six. The ship had already begun its southerly course. He stood forty feet away from where she sat half-turned on a tall cushioned chair at the bar. She wore a red sleeveless blouse that had a pleasing sheen when she moved under the muted glow of the lounge lights—silk, maybe—and a black skirt that rode three inches up on her trim thighs. A bald, middle-aged man with far too much belly sat on the edge of the next stool, leaned over, talking to her.

She didn't appear interested.

He saw her turn her head and scan the guests seated at the tables. Her gaze swept past him and returned. She held on him a moment before smiling and giving an almost imperceptible nod of recognition.

He checked the time and angled the face of his watch toward her.

His friends were somewhere listening and watching. He tried not to think about where they had positioned themselves or what they were doing.

But now they all knew he'd made contact.

The bald man continued to talk without her paying the least amount of attention to him.

Jack saw her glance in his direction a couple more times.

And each time she smiled.

He figured she'd had enough of Fat Man and would brush him off at any moment.

She did exactly that, and he watched her in action.

Fat Man finally stopped talking long enough to sip his drink. She took advantage of the moment to whisper something in his ear. Jack couldn't hear what she said, but he saw her mouth move, and whatever she said had to be something so utterly disturbing it drained the color from the poor guy's face.

Fat Man recoiled from her as though he had peered into the burning eyes of the devil. She stared at him with cold efficiency and smiled an evil little smirk that must have made him a believer.

He reached for his drink, fumbled the glass spilling some, stood, and hurried out of the lounge.

A smile from her signaled Jack over.

He took Fat Man's seat, rested his elbow on the bar, and angled the face of his watch at her. "You were pretty rough on him."

She peered into his eyes and sipped her martini. She returned the glass to the counter and brought her gaze back to meet his.

Seductive. Practiced.

She smiled. "Should I invite him back?"

He signaled the bartender and refocused his attention on her. "I believe our paths crossed yesterday at Dream World Travel. My name's Jack."

"I'm Amanda. What a lovely coincidence we're on this cruise together."

Till now, he'd only seen her from a distance. Up close, he noticed she had smooth skin with minimal makeup, the type of full lips that made a man want to kiss them, thick brows—darker than her hair—manicured into heavy arches over hazel eyes.

The bartender stopped across the counter from him and asked, "Would you like a drink, sir?"

"Vodka martini." Jack glanced down at Amanda's near empty glass. The olive gone from the toothpick. "Make that two."

She finished hers off and returned the glass to her cocktail napkin. When she brought her gaze up to meet his, he noticed an explosion of tiny green flecks in the hazel of her eyes. He wondered how he had missed the added color when he first looked into them.

He'd have to pay closer attention.

"How'd you know I was drinking vodka?" Her voice took on a suspicious, seductive tone.

Charlize Theron without the accent.

Or Lauren Bacall.

He liked listening to her talk.

Those tiny green flecks drew him in. "I'm guessing Grey Goose, right?"

"You didn't request Grey Goose."

"Trust me. The bartender knows what you're drinking."

"So is this what you do? Take cruises and pick up unsuspecting women."

"God no." He laughed. "Not even close. Truth be known, this is my first cruise. Besides, I haven't been romantically involved since my wife died of cancer a few years ago."

"I'm sorry for your loss. Is that what brought you over here to me?"

"When I saw you in the travel agency, you were the most beautiful woman I had ever seen. And when I noticed you sitting here, I just had to talk to you."

"I'm flattered." She sipped her martini.

He nodded at her glass. "Grey Goose, right?"

"You're a good judge of bartenders."

She had a natural erotic charm. He enjoyed the game. "Can I ask how tall you are?"

Knowing he would not be able to resist looking, she extended her long luxurious leg with practiced casualness, raising the hem of her skirt another few inches exposing the dark band at the top of her stockings. The clasp of a garter belt posed a subtle challenge to the prospective lover.

"Six-three," she said. "In heels. Taller than most men I meet."

He swept his gaze over trim thigh and muscled calf to a single black ladies' pump with a deadly spike.

"I must say you carry your height beautifully."

"Again, I'm flattered. That's not a compliment I hear often."

"Each man to his own tastes."

"And yours is tall women?"

"This is new territory for me. Mostly I concentrate on my work."

"Which is?"

"I'm a marine biologist." He took a risk. "And sometimes treasure hunter."

The subtle upward curl of her lips suggested his gamble paid off. Or he had lost it all.

"I find that quite interesting," she said. "And it explains your tan."

"Which part is that . . . being a marine biologist, or amateur treasure hunter?" He felt the way he had at a craps table in Reno when his twenty-dollar bet on eleven swelled to three hundred and he let it ride, only to hit it again.

That seductive conspiratorial grin of hers returned.

"Both," she answered in her wonderful voice.

He took a sip of his drink and peered at her over the rim of his glass. "I can't believe a woman as pretty as you is traveling alone."

"Actually, I'm on the cruise with my brother." She glanced at a small rectangular wristwatch with a thin, black band. "And I'm sorry to say, I have to go. We're meeting for dinner."

"No boyfriend?"

She finished her drink, stood, and turned her sparkling eyes on him. "Have a nice evening, Jack."

CHAPTER 50

Jack watched Amanda leave the lounge. Having stared at those long legs, it was difficult for him to think of her as a cold blooded killer.

Femme fatale . . .

A real man-eater.

He didn't have to remind himself she had lured more than one poor soul to his death. Men who had gazed into those dazzling eyes and kissed her plump lips, had unclasped the garter belts and rode the silkiness of those thighs, and thought how lucky they were.

He raised his left hand to bring the watch close to his mouth, and cupped his chin between his thumb and forefinger as if in thought. And for his friends' benefit said, "A stellar performance, I'd say. Anyone interested in a drink?"

They were surely listening, and had seen her walk away. He wondered who would show up to stick the gold star of achievement on his forehead.

Robert made his appearance a minute later. Jack watched him all the way to the bar. He sat down leaving an empty chair between them. The bartender greeted him and he ordered an IPA.

Jack signaled for another martini. He'd stop at two.

He asked, "What do you think?"

Robert shrugged. "Seemed to me you went at her like a bull moose in rut. It'll be a miracle if you didn't chase her off."

"I just followed her lead."

"Guess I had to be there."

"Trust me. She's a real piece of work."

"Well, you got her interested. I'll give you that much. The question is, will she take the bait?"

Jack nodded. "I suppose that depends on whether or not they have some other poor sap lined up."

"That's always a possibility."

"More than a possibility, I'm afraid. My guess is they have several potential marks picked out long before they board the ship."

"But you got to her first. And after listening to her, I think that moves you to the top of the list."

Their drinks arrived and they sipped in silence that lasted all of thirty seconds before three nice looking ladies sidled up to the bar. Thirtyish. They ordered shots of tequila.

Jack asked Robert, "Have you seen Cherise or Lindsey?"

"After you left your stateroom, I called Cherise while we still had cell service. She and Lindsey were in their cabin and planned to monitor you from there until we knew how your little foray around the ship turned out. At least they have a window to let some light in."

"You're still complaining?"

"You ever hide inside a cardboard refrigerator box when you were a kid? Feels a whole lot like that."

"Then it's a good thing you won't be spending a lot of time in there."

"A very good thing. I swear it's like being confined to steerage."

Jack watched the women toss back their tequila. A kick-start on the evening, he guessed. They seemed to be enjoying themselves.

Not sisters. Close friends.

They ordered another round and a couple for them. He heard one of the ladies say, "Maybe these two good-looking guys want to take us dancing."

The brunette next to Robert smiled and asked, "How about it, handsome? Would you and your friend like to join us at the club?"

The shots arrived. Robert had his earpiece out but that didn't mean Cherise and Lindsey weren't still monitoring everything being said. They were getting an ear full as well as an eye full.

Jack let his friend answer.

Robert looked at her and said, "Sorry, ladies. Thanks for the drink but I'm afraid we'll have to pass on the club."

"You sure?" She looked at Jack. Her friends watched over her shoulders.

He shrugged. "I'm afraid we already have dates."

"Your loss."

The women looked at each other and the tallest of the three said, "To the club, ladies."

They downed their tequila and walked away amid happy chatter.

To Robert, he said, "That was entertaining."

They tossed back their tequila and Robert said, "I saw Amanda show you her legs. You could have tilted your watch so I could have a peek."

"Didn't those ladies take some of the steam out of you?"

"Keep those ladies out of it. When a beautiful woman shows off a leg that magnificent, it's something you share with a buddy."

"Friends do that for each other?"

"They do." Robert drank more of his beer.

Jack casually picked up his glass and pulled the olive off the pick with his teeth. "The best part was the garter belt."

Robert choked.

"Get serious," Jack said. "This woman is all sugar frosting and sprinkles outside. Inside she's pure evil and we have to keep that in mind."

"Jack, my friend, sex is a perfectly human desire. It's something men think about every ten minutes. With you, every five. And thinking about having sex with a beautiful woman is a great defense against having to think about putting her in prison or worse."

"It's the 'worse' part that bothers me."

"And it should."

CHAPTER 51

Jack saw Amanda again at dinner.

He took a seat at a table for two and stared across the empty chair at her and her brother sitting three tables away. She had changed into a long, white, backless evening gown with straps that fastened behind her neck. Corey Jameson was a big son of a bitch even sitting down. A wad of muscle bulged his pale yellow knit sports shirt, giving it the appearance of being one size too small. Which it very well could have been. But he had a Ken-doll face, sun-bleached brown hair, and a baked on tan that would turn a woman's head.

Looking at them together, Jack realized the con could go either way. The mark could easily be a woman, with Amanda and Corey's rolls reversed.

Something he and Cherise hadn't talked about.

He'd find out soon enough.

Her gaze kept shifting in his direction. She and her brother appeared to be having an innocent dinner conversation. But she clearly showed an interest elsewhere.

Each time she smiled, he returned the gesture with one of his own. Keeping in mind they were not the nice people they appeared to be.

Halfway through his beer, Jack saw Corey turn and wave him over. Evidently, he was no longer at the top of the list.

He was the list.

He gave them a casual nod as to not appear overly anxious and carried his beer to their table.

"Good evening," he said to both of them.

"Please join us." Corey motioned at an empty chair. "My sister told me the two of you met earlier in the lounge."

Jack found it difficult to not focus his full attention on Amanda. The dress did for her ample breasts what her blouse hadn't. A subtle shadow of areola and nipple showed through the fabric to hint at the bounty beneath. He sensed a complete awareness in her of being watched.

She let her smile slip long enough to say, "Do sit down, Jack. My brother wants to hear all about your work."

He slid back the chair and settled onto the cushion. To Corey he asked, "You're interested in marine biology?"

"I'm interested in really big fish. Grouper, tuna, marlin, sharks, barracuda—I've caught them all. Until recently, I had my own reality program where I traveled the world catching monster fish. Another network has expressed interest in picking up the show but they're still in negotiations. In the meantime, I make appearances at outdoor fishing and camping shows, as well as doing TV advertisements for sports equipment."

"How interesting." Jack had the feeling of being appraised. "If I'm ever in need of a new rod and reel I'll know who to ask. But why do I have a sneaky suspicion that's not all you're interested in?"

That brought a long look and a sly smile. "Because I'm a treasure hunter, of sorts, myself. I thought we might talk about that."

Amanda not only took the bait, Corey had grabbed hold and was running with it.

Jack grinned. "Now you've peaked my interest."

"You ever do any treasure hunting in the Yucatan?"

"For Mayan artifacts, no? It's my understanding the Mexican government frowns on that sort of thing."

"If you get caught."

"And you don't get caught?"

Corey let the question hang and scanned the room. "Let's order dinner. I'm starved."

Jack sipped his beer. He had no idea if Corey was playing him as much as he played Corey. Kind of like hooking a thousand-pound marlin. Who ends up playing whom? The hunter or the hunted?

He let the subject drop and waited for Corey to make his move.

Halfway through the meal, Corey said, "What part of treasure hunting do you enjoy most? The challenge of sorting through all the clues and finding it? Or the treasure, itself?"

Jack carved a bite of lamb chop and forked the meat into his mouth. He chewed longer than needed and washed the tender morsel down with a sip of beer. "Interesting question. I suppose the answer depends on the treasure. If we're talking gold, that's a subject all its own. There's nothing like the weight of it in your hands."

"That's always been my opinion." Corey went back to his steak.

Jack didn't push. He sliced another bite of lamb and forked the meat, along with a sprig of roasted asparagus, into his mouth.

Amanda broke the silence. "Tell me about some of the treasure you've found? I'm sure you have some amazing stories."

He finished chewing and swallowed. "I wouldn't know where to start."

"Meaning you've been quite successful."

To tell her about every adventure he had been on and the details of the treasure he found, wasn't what they were interested in.

They were talking about gold.

He said, "They weren't always gold coins and trinkets. Certainly nothing like what's been salvaged around here."

"Did they make you rich?"

"Not once the government took their share off the top. But I still managed to turn a tidy profit."

"You don't think Uncle Sam deserves his share?"

He noticed Corey watching him.

And keeping quiet.

They had been sizing him up all through dinner . . . her from the moment he sat down next to her at the bar. Nothing had changed. This was part of the game.

And he knew the answer she fished for.

"Maybe if the IRS was reasonable about it. Which they aren't."

"You don't have to report everything you find."

"Who said I did? I pretty much believe a person should be able to keep what they find and any money they make off it."

He thought he saw her smile ever so slightly as she went back to her lobster.

Another roll of the dice and another win.

He finished off his last bite of lamb and downed his beer. "This treasure talk has made me thirsty. I think it's time for a real drink."

"Have you ever seen the Mel Fisher Maritime Museum," Corey asked.

"I haven't had the pleasure," he lied.

"The ship docks in Key West in the morning. Why don't you accompany me to the museum? There's something I want to show you."

CHAPTER 52

Jack remained at the table a couple of minutes longer before excusing himself. Amanda and her brother had enough to chew on for the time being.

And he'd be seeing Corey in the morning.

Under different circumstances, he would have wanted that drink. Knob Creek on ice, a double. He grabbed a couple of St. Pauli Girls from the lounge, raised his watch to his mouth, mumbled his destination, and carried the beers back to his cabin.

Robert stood at the door waiting. Cherise and Lindsey disguised in their blonde wigs, hovered behind him. They had left the sunglasses behind.

"I should have brought a couple more beers," he said, using his card key on the door.

"Lindsey and I won't be staying long," Cherise assured him. "You and Robert enjoy them. We're going to the Cadillac Diner for pizza. I'm sure we won't be running into Amanda there."

He let them inside and latched the door behind him. Cherise walked directly to the door leading to the balcony and pulled it open. A cool ocean breeze curled back a lock of her blonde wig. She turned to the group and let the salt air into the cabin.

He saw resignation in her expression.

"You were listening," he said. "Quite a performance, I have to say."

"Hers or yours?"

A tone of jealousy?

"Both of ours."

She took a deep breath. "Amanda's going to be all over you, Jack. You better be ready."

Was she telling him that for his benefit . . . or hers?

"You're saying she'll want to up the stakes right out of the gate?" He looked away long enough to hand Robert his Pauli Girl, and opened his own.

She crossed her arms. "That's how those two operate."

A very vivid image of silky thigh and garter belt came to mind. "So it's the logical next step."

She huffed. "And Amanda won't hesitate for even a second. I guarantee you, she believes that once she gets her hooks into you, there's no way you'll pass on whatever scam they have planned."

Into the spider's web . . .

Bright and cunning and beautiful. A woman so perfectly put together no man can refuse her.

He regretted needing to have this conversation.

Robert and Lindsey seemed content to watch. All they lacked was a box of Milk Duds and a bag of popcorn.

He sighed, realizing he had to say what he dreaded saying. "Money's in the pot. Time to call the bet or fold."

She held him in her gaze. Her brown eyes doing a job on him.

"We talked about this." Her voice had a clinical sound to it. "We do what we have to do."

And you'll be listening.

He tried to not think about that, and said, "That was before reality stared me in the face."

She didn't talk for a moment. A deafening silence. Finally, "There is no room in this plan for dime-store morality shit. Turn her down when she comes on to you and walk away from her and what we're attempting to pull off, if that's what you want to do. We'll come up with some other plan to stop them."

Some other plan . . .

The lethal blow that brought to mind the men who had been lured to their death. And those who would die if Amanda and Corey weren't stopped now.

"You know I can't do that."

"I just needed to hear you say it."

"To sort of remind myself?"

"Perhaps it would be easier for you if you shrugged off that air of idealism you carry around and accept the fact that Man is basically despicable."

"Despicable me." He laughed.

CHAPTER 53

Jack found Amanda and Corey sitting in the Caribbean Lounge, the open-air bar located at the stern of the ship three decks up from his cabin.

The sun had already set, leaving only a hint of pale blue on the western horizon. Stars were out, and a crescent moon shone bright overhead. The air retained much of its balminess with only a slight breeze from the movement of the ship. A fine evening to be on a cruise, the travel brochures would say.

He sidled up to the bar and ordered a beer on draft. A Michelob Light he could nurse while maintaining his wits. Out of the corner of his eye, he saw Amanda look in his direction. Barely more than a glance, but enough for him to know she had watched him walk in. Had seen him scan the tables. And in spite of his attempt to not appear overly obvious, had noticed his gaze settle on her.

She looked gorgeous in the evening lights.

And she knew it.

Her superb beauty did not remove all his qualms, but those eyes, those full lips, that fabulous all-woman body made the potential of having to go to bed with her much less distasteful.

The word 'despicable' came to mind.

This time he carried his beer over to their table without invitation. She did not appear to mind.

"This is a surprise," he said. He glanced at Corey but clearly directed his comment at Amanda. "I didn't expect to run into you here."

She smiled. "Are you disappointed?"

Corey settled back in his chair. He paid attention, but kept quiet. Clearly, Amanda sat in the driver's seat.

"Not at all," Jack said. "Actually, I hoped I'd run into you."

"I'm glad you did. Please, have a seat."

He looked at Corey, then back at her. "I don't want to intrude."

"I don't mind at all. And he was just leaving."

Convenient.

Corey stood as if on cue. "You two enjoy the evening. I have a date waiting."

"Have fun," Jack said.

Corey's expression registered mild approval. He held it a second, looked at his sister, then strode away in a long limber stride.

Jack watched him leave, then slid a chair close to Amanda and sat down. "You're sure I didn't interrupt something?"

"Not at all."

"I take it his date isn't traveling with you. He moves fast."

"As you can imagine, Corey never lacks female companionship." She leaned in and kissed him on the corner of the mouth. "Let's talk about you."

"I've been thinking how it would be to kiss you," he said. "But I imagined more than a peck."

"That was for starters." She stood and offered her hand.

Jack rose and took her in his arms. She still wore her heels and had to lean down a couple of inches in order to fully embrace the kiss.

"Better?" she asked when they separated.

"Much," he said. "It's been a while since I've been kissed like that."

Of course what he said was a lie. The part about it having been a while, anyway. But the remark worked because she leaned into him a second time and covered his mouth with her rich, full lips. His hands found her hips. Then her butt. And this time the kiss went on forever.

She nibbled his lower lip as they unglued themselves from the embrace. With no desire to let go of her, he slid his hands to the small of her back. And, pressed tight against her mound of breast, he felt a tingle of arousal.

She had to feel it too.

"It must be the tropical air," he said, feigning embarrassment.

She smiled. "I'm sure it is."

Two drinks and a ton of playful talk later she had his back pressed to his cabin door. She kissed him so vigorously, he had to squirm to free himself long enough to work the card key and turn the latch.

She groped her way back into his arms and they stumbled inside.

With great effort, he eased her away from him. He had become suddenly aware his three friends, especially Cherise, could see and hear everything going on. She had cautioned him about that, and he kept her warning in mind while he stripped off the watch and dropped it in the dresser drawer.

When he turned his attention back on Amanda, she was naked. Her evening gown lay in a heap at her feet. No garter belt. No stockings. Only a nothing-pair of white lace panties lay on top of the dress. She stood looking at him, obviously pleased with herself.

And for good reason.

Her body had an even shade of all-over tan. Her breasts—more magnificent than he imagined—accentuated a firm, flat belly and narrow waist that broadened into smooth, powerful hips and superb roundness of butt before surrendering to a pair of long, athletic legs.

He tore his eyes away from her and set the dead bolt.

There'd be no distractions.

CHAPTER 54

The night passed in a haze of wild sex. No act seemed too outlandish or completely out of the question: standing, sitting, kneeling, on her belly and on her back with miles of leg drawing him deep into her. Liberal use of the mouth. All the expected sounds. And when they were both exhausted in the wee hours of the morning, she lay cuddled up next to him drawing lazy circles in his chest hair.

"I hope you don't think I'm this way with everyone I meet," she said. "I'm not. Really I'm not."

He hugged her tight against him, feigning affection, knowing all the time she was a murderer. Sex for the sake of the sex act alone, void of caring, no sincerity of any kind, had been a fragmenting experience that left him with an almost overwhelming feeling of self-disgust. But he had played the game. And for what it was worth, she was fantastic in bed.

"Honestly," he said. "I wasn't thinking anything other than how wonderful you are."

"So I was okay?"

"Are you kidding? You were fantastic." And she was.

She carefully slipped out of bed and pulled on her panties and dress. "I hate to do this to you, dear, but I need to go. We have a long day ahead of us."

He watched her slide her heels on and straighten her hair. She had called him *dear* so casually that it implied a degree of ownership. He wondered if this would be their last night in bed together. Would the lure of more sex become the carrot dangling from the string at the end of the pole?

The black widow spider came to mind. And what she did to her mate.

He could easily see how Amanda's web of deceit and lust could ensnare men and lure them to their death.

* * *

Jack managed to get two hours sleep before being awakened by a change in the motion of the ship. During the night, the *Caribbean Sensation* had made the run to Key West. The first port of call. He felt strange having traveled full circle.

A flurry of activity in the companionway outside his door, suggested passengers were hurrying to be among the first to disembark the ship.

He slid his legs off the edge of the mattress, buried his face in his hands, and did his best to rub away the fog. Feeling marginally better, he started to reach for the dresser and stopped, having remembered moving his watch to the bedside table after Amanda left his cabin. He picked up the Doxa, checked the time, and groaned. Seven fifteen felt way too early to be getting up.

His cell phone was vibrating on the counter when he stepped out of the shower. He wrapped a towel around his waist and answered the call.

"Do me a favor," he said to Robert. "Please spare me your usual repertoire of pointed comments. I had a rough night."

"So I gathered."

"Have you talked to the women?"

"Do you want to know what Cherise thinks about your tryst last night?"

"Well, yeah."

"Truth is, she didn't have much to say. I think she accepted it as something that had to be done."

Jack wondered.

Now he felt even more disgusted with himself. He would

rather have been told she had stomped and swore like a sailor. Had threatened to kick in the door and drag Amanda out by her hair. Toss her overboard.

Shark bait.

He sighed inwardly and asked, "Has she made plans for today?"

"She talked about staying aboard. With the three of you ashore, she doesn't want to chance being seen."

"With four thousand people crowding the sidewalks, I don't think there is much chance of that."

"Maybe she's afraid of what she'll do if she sees Amanda."

"Nice thought. But she'll have to wait. After all, this is her idea."

"I'm sure she hasn't forgotten."

"Why don't you drop by my cabin and pick up the keys to the *Adeona*. She'd probably love to see it. You can give her and Lindsey the nickel tour. Besides, you'll have a chance to open the boat up and dry her out a little. You can even pick up something tasty and have lunch aboard."

"That's a great idea. But don't you think it would be a good idea for me to hang close to you in case . . . you know?"

"There shouldn't be any problem. Not yet."

Silence.

After a moment, "Feels strange, doesn't it? Us being back in Key West."

"Déjà vu," Jack said. "Have you given any more thought to Hemingway's manuscript?"

"I can show Cherise the diary. Maybe there's a clue in there I missed. I'm sure her Italian is better than mine."

"Either way, she'll be interested to have a look at what we found."

"When are you supposed to meet up with Amanda and her brother?"

"Ten o'clock. At the Mel Fisher museum."

"What about Ned? You're not forgetting about him?"

"I couldn't very well tell Corey no. I'm thinking you can go ahead of me and make sure he isn't working."

"And if he is?"

"I'm confident you'll come up with something."

"You think they'll make their move?"

Jack considered what Cherise had said about Amanda having her tenterhooks in him.

She had called him *dear*.

"Can't say. But I'm sure curious about what Corey wants to show me."

CHAPTER 55

Jack left the ship feeling a little better about himself, having talked to Cherise on her cell and made all the necessary apologies and assurances.

She turned out to be far more understanding than he deserved.

He found Amanda and Corey standing next to a pair of sixteenth-century cannons sitting outside the entrance to the museum. She looked fabulous in her pleated white shorts and sleeveless pale-orange top opened to the second button allowing an ample amount of cleavage to show. Corey wore tan slacks and a white, short-sleeved knit shirt that made him look like a pro golfer.

Jack felt appropriately dressed in his aloha shirt, khaki shorts, and sneakers. Key West daywear.

He waved and walked toward them, relieved to have received a text from Robert letting him know Ned wasn't working.

She strode up to him when he was still ten feet away from where she had been standing, and wrapped her arm around his. "You're late."

He checked his watch. Straight up ten. "You said ten o'clock."

"I figured you for a man who is five minutes early everywhere he goes."

"Normally. But I had an excuse this morning."

"I can't imagine."

He'd play the game. "You're not mad, are you?"

"You can make it up to me."

He doubted she intended to give him the chance. "How about a kiss right now, for starters?"

"Later."

Exactly what he figured.

The carrot is in play.

She led him back to her brother and kept hold of the arm. "Shall we?"

To Jack, Corey said, "I believe you will find what I'm going to show you extremely interesting."

"I look forward to it." He motioned at the building. "After you."

"I haven't forgotten how you feel about gold," Corey said over his shoulder. "You're in for a treat."

Jack didn't reply. He followed Amanda and her brother inside the museum and paid his fifteen-dollar admission. To no surprise, Corey did not appear the least bit disturbed by his sister's late-night sex games. His focus was obviously on whatever lay inside.

Jack saw no reason to speculate. That time had come and gone.

He would find out shortly.

Though he had viewed the exhibit several times, as far as Corey and Amanda knew, this was his first visit to the museum. He needed to keep that in mind.

Or the game would end here.

With Corey leading the way, they entered the 1622 Treasure Fleet Exhibition and walked past the seventeenth-century cannon to an illuminated display case where a jewel-studded gold cross, at least ten inches tall, lay draped with gold chains. Several pieces of gold jewelry were included in the display. Among them, a familiar-looking idol. Gold. Three inches tall.

Small in comparison to the ones Sam King bought.

Sitting among the jewelry and especially the cross, the figurine appeared oddly out of place. He leaned close, aimed the camera in his watch, and stared at the crude little man. Strangely, he hadn't remembered seeing it during one of his prior visits. But then, he hadn't entered the museum looking for Mayan artifacts.

"Interesting, isn't it?" Corey said.

"Very." Jack straightened. "What did you want to show me?"

"You're looking at it."

Jack pointed at the idol. "That?"

"Amazing, right?"

"Is it Aztec?"

"Mayan, I believe. From the Yucatan."

Jack touched his fingertips to the glass, feigning a desire to caress the treasure. "Odd the Spaniards didn't melt it into one of those gold bars."

"Perhaps they believed it had some religious significance. Who can say? What's important is they didn't. Which brings me to why I brought—" He stopped talking and stepped back from a young couple who approached the display.

Jack made no attempt to probe.

When Corey motioned for him to follow, Amanda linked arms with him and they walked into the heat of the day. The Old Town Trolley slowed to a stop and let off a dozen people who sauntered toward the museum.

Jack looked at Corey. "You were saying?"

"It's hot out here in the sun," Amanda interrupted. And Jack watched her eyes focus on him. "You'll make me much happier if you take me somewhere and buy me a cool drink. Then you and my brother can talk."

Jack wondered about the maximum range of the microphone and camera inside his watch. Cherise, unfortunately, had failed to provide him with what had turned out to be vital need-to-know information. He would have to hope for the best.

He and Robert had spent too much time in Sloppy Joe's the prior week to chance being recognized by one of the staff. And the Pier House was out of the question for the same reason.

There weren't too many bars they hadn't spent at least some time in.

"Captain Tony's is only a couple of blocks from here," he said. "We can try that place if you don't mind walking."

CHAPTER 56

Jack walked into the bar, mildly surprised to see a few empty tables. He half expected to find the place hopping since the *Caribbean Sensation* had added a flood of cruise ship passengers to the usual flock of tourists already in town.

He scanned the room. Seeing no one he recognized, he led Amanda and Corey to the most remote table available.

Amanda patted him on the arm. "Do be a dear and order me a Rum Collins."

"But of course," he said, and ordered three.

Their waiter returned with their drinks and Amanda went to work on hers. Corey let his sit. Jack took a sip and waited.

More customers walked in and took seats at the empty tables. Business had picked up. So had the noise from the customers' chatter.

"It's interesting," Corey began. "Take that idol I showed you. What do you have? Three or four ounces of twenty-karat gold. Worth what? Even at today's prices, three thousand dollars . . . four thousand at the most. Sink it to the bottom of the ocean along with a King's fortune and it's worth ten times that much."

Jack rested his forearms on the table. "That's what makes us treasure hunters. I assume you're going somewhere with this?"

Corey took hold of his drink and leaned close. "As you probably know, there are collectors lining up to buy that stuff. And not just gold and silver from sunken galleons. The best part is they're willing to pay top dollar. I've made a few contacts over the years, particularly in Central and South America, and occasionally I'm given the opportunity to buy artifacts that, let's say . . . have been *found*. I don't normally invite someone in on the deal. But my sister begged me to make an exception with you. Which I'm doing now. I think it will make her *very* happy."

Amanda set down her Rum Collins and gripped Jack's arm with a cold hand. "Isn't that wonderful, dear? Just think . . ."

He *could* think. And he doubted she'd like the thoughts running through his mind.

"What kind of deal are we talking about?"

Corey glanced at the customers closest to them and lowered his voice. "Three idols similar to the one I showed you. Only larger. And worth considerably more money."

Three?

Jack began to get the picture.

"How much are we talking about?"

Corey grinned. "At least two hundred and fifty thousand to the right buyer."

Jack looked at Amanda and saw her smiling. He added his grin to the mix. "And you know who this buyer is?"

"Someone I've dealt with on numerous occasions."

"You got my interest. What's the buy-in?"

"Your part, a hundred grand."

"That's a lot of money."

"And you'll double it."

"The man selling the idols," Jack said, "he knows he's being cheated?"

"Does it really matter?"

"To me, no. You're sure the artifacts are genuine?"

"They are. Trust me."

Jack took a sip of his drink and returned the glass to the table. "Not that I don't appreciate your offer, but if this is such a sweet deal, how come you're letting me in on it when you could have all the money?"

"I told you my sister asked me to. And since the two of you are hitting it off so well, I agreed."

"There has to be more to it."

Corey stared at his drink. Jack watched him turn the glass with his fingers as though hesitant to speak his mind.

He knows how to play the game.

"You got me there." He glanced at Amanda, playing the role to the hilt. "My sister is part of the reason. Plus, I'm a little tapped out at the moment. I planned to try and negotiate a deal on one of the idols. Beat the price down. If you buy in, I won't have to. You'll end up with a tidy profit, which will make my sister happy. And I'll make fifteen percent for brokering the deal."

Her hand was back on his arm. She didn't have to say a word. He could imagine the thoughts swirling in her mind. And how she'd play the game right up to the moment Corey dumped him overboard.

The carrot.

He covered her hand with his and gave it a pat. They had made their move and he didn't intend to let them off easy. He said, "So you had a plan all worked out. Where are these idols?"

"In Cozumel. My contact is waiting for me there. That's why Amanda and I are on this cruise."

"You're sure you have a buyer?"

"Several. And they don't ask questions."

"What about customs? The feds frown on this sort of stuff."

"Not to worry."

Amanda watched, lips slightly parted, moist. Her brother made the deal sound too simple to turn down.

A perfect one-two punch.

Jack couldn't resist. "You've done this before?"

Corey cracked a smile.

Amanda eased her hand from his and protruded her bottom lip in an obvious pouty face. "You're going to do it, aren't you? For me?"

He let the questions hang for an appropriate few seconds to further the ruse.

His silence proved to be too much for her.

She leaned forward, offering maximum exposure of ample cleavage, and peered into his eyes. The final springing of the trap.

She asked, "You can get the money, right?"

He hesitated, only for effect. "I'll need to have it wired from my bank."

"Then we have a deal." Corey lifted his drink. "Take care of your business and we'll meet back aboard the ship."

"You've made me so happy, dear." That word again. She added, "You have no idea how happy. I promise, you won't regret this."

But you *will.*

He sucked down half of his drink, and stood up. Staring at her cleavage, he said, "I'll hold you to that."

CHAPTER 57

In preparation for contingencies, Jack had already made arrangements on both ends for a wire transfer up to a hundred and fifty thousand. He stopped by the bank and put in the request for a hundred. The money had been previously cleared and would be available for withdrawal in a couple of hours.

There had been no sign of Corey or Amanda. He took a chance and walked to the Pier House hoping to meet up with his friends. If they had been out of range and unable to listen in on his conversation, they'd be anxious to hear how it went.

When he got to the dock where he and Robert had left the Boston Whaler tied, he found the dinghy gone. Stolen or moved, or more likely Robert had used the tender to ferry the women out to the *Adeona*. Rather than talking into his wristwatch like Dick Tracy, he called his friend's cell.

"I'm at the dock," he said, when Robert answered.

"And I suppose you want me to pick you up?"

"I'd appreciate it. Did Cherise like the boat?"

"So did Lindsey."

"Did you order lunch?"

"We were just discussing that."

"Is there beer in the refrigerator or did you drink it all?"

"Don't be an asshole."

Jack laughed. "I'll order sandwiches. The food should be ready by the time you get here."

Robert motored up to the dock at the same time Jack arrived with a bag of takeout. He handed the paper sack to Robert. "Feels good being away from those two jerk-wads for a while."

"Get in. Cherise is anxious to see you."

"Really?" Jack smiled.

Robert kept the speed down, taking his time it seemed.

"We were lucky," he said. "Amanda and Corey were walking up to the museum as I was leaving."

"I'm just glad Ned wasn't working."

They didn't have far to go, and Jack took advantage of the couple extra minutes to savor the rich odor of the harbor at low tide. He would miss the quirky little town and its unique aroma when it came time to leave Key West behind and return to Oahu and new sea smells.

When they neared the boat he saw Cherise, wearing a short sundress, that silly blonde wig, and sunglasses, stand and wave from the sundeck. Lindsey, looking every bit as ridiculous in her blonde wig, sat waving from a deck chair.

"I see you rigged the sunshade," he said to Robert.

"Too hot otherwise. And the inside is still cooling off." Robert cut the engine and drifted the last few feet to the boarding ladder. Jack climbed up and Robert handed him the bag of food.

"It's nice up here," Cherise yelled down.

Jack looked up at the sound of her voice. She stood leaning over with both hands on the safety rail. He'd taken a chance joining them. Seeing her smiling down at him made him glad he did.

"I'll be right up with lunch," he said. "Either of you want a beer?"

Lindsey appeared at the rail. "Bring a couple, if you can manage."

Jack tied off the Boston Whaler and said to Robert, "Grab a cold one for you and Lindsey. I'll take Cherise one."

They all sat around the cocktail table up top and waded into the fish sandwiches and curly fries. A breeze off the Gulf helped keep the temperature under the canvas tarp comfortable.

Cherise asked, "Did your meeting with Corey and Amanda go the way we expected?"

Jack washed down a bite with a swig of Red Stripe. Robert and

Lindsey set their sandwiches on their plates and looked at him.

They hadn't heard.

He said, "I take it you weren't able to listen in on my conversation with those two?"

Cherise shook her head. "Not after you left the museum. Too much background noise."

"So you were close by?"

"Close enough to see you walk out with Amanda hanging onto your arm."

He chuckled at her jealousy. "For king and country, my dear. For king and country."

Cherise didn't laugh. "If you say so. What's the setup?"

"One hundred thousand in cash," he said. "For three gold idols. That's what it will cost me. Corey made up a phony excuse about being tapped out and inviting me in on the deal only because Amanda begged him to. Supposedly, he stands to make fifteen percent brokering the sale. Which is okay with him."

Cherise pursed her lips. "Three gold idols. Sounds familiar, doesn't it?"

Lindsey furrowed her brow. "You're not thinking—"

"Too much of a coincidence not to," Jack said.

"And you're putting up the cash?" Cherise asked.

Jack met her gaze. "Unless you have a hundred grand in your purse?"

"It's not right." Lindsey glanced back and forth at Cherise and Jack. "I should be the one putting up the money."

Cherise didn't blink. "Do you have that much cash at your disposal?"

Lindsey's gaze dropped. After a moment, she dabbed the corner of her eye with her napkin and took a second to answer. "I don't know what to say. You . . . all of you, have done so much for me. But that's too much money . . . "

"And let Amanda and Corey keep on killing?"

Lindsey sniffled. "But everything is getting too crazy."

"You and I have talked about this." Cherise's expression firmed with resolve. "It's Jack's decision whether he puts up the money or not. Personally, I plan on finishing what we started. Those two won't get away with murder again."

Lindsey looked at Jack. He saw the question in her eyes.

"I'll figure out a way to get the money back," he said. "And if not, you can pay me when you hit the lottery."

CHAPTER 58

The *Caribbean Sensation* was scheduled to leave port at four. At two-thirty, Jack helped Robert button up the *Adeona*. When they were done, all four of them overloaded the eleven foot Whaler by a couple hundred pounds and Jack motored them with care to the dock at the Pier House.

"I'm going to the bank to pick up the cash," he said. "You three board the ship and I'll be along in a few minutes."

"I know you told me you want to go alone," Robert said. "But are you sure you don't want me to tag along at a discrete distance to step in if some undesirable character tries to relieve you of your money?"

"I'll be okay." Jack waved and walked off in the direction of town.

On the way to the bank, he stopped at a dive shop and bought a small, red, nylon bag the size of a man's shaving kit. He knew the thickness of a ten-thousand-dollar packet of hundred dollar bills measured roughly half an inch. He'd have ten such bundles or five inches of currency that would never fit in his wallet.

The transaction at the bank went off without a hitch. But the manager, a friendly middle-aged woman, did not act at all happy to know he planned to walk out of the place with that much cash on him instead of a cashier's check. He assured her there wouldn't be a problem, and stepped into the heat of the afternoon with the bundles tucked into the bag.

It took him ten minutes to power walk the five blocks to the port. He boarded the ship with a crowd of other passengers. Got a raised brow from security when he ran his bag through the scanner, and blew it off with a smile. Once he made it into his cabin and had the door bolted, he relaxed.

He called Robert on his cell. "I'm in my stateroom. Meet me here."

"I was watching." Robert sounded relieved. "I'll pick us up a beer on the way. You're probably ready for one."

Jack ended the call and placed one to Cherise. "I'm aboard with the money."

She sighed. "Do you feel all right about leaving it in your cabin?"

"It'll only be for one night."

"What about Amanda?"

He knew what Cherise was hinting at. "If my guess is correct, she'll have a headache or some other excuse for not wanting a repeat of last night."

Silence.

And he knew why.

"So we wait and see," she said after a moment.

"Cherise . . . you know how I feel about you, right?"

"It's okay, Jack. Really it is. I just don't like that devious bitch."

"Meaning it's personal?"

"Damn right, it's personal. I can't wait to see that scum sucking bottom-feeder get what's coming to her."

Jack laughed into his phone. "Can I call you tonight, even if it's late?"

He heard her breathe in and out. "I'll be in my cabin."

* * *

After a chatty and rather uneventful dinner with Amanda and Corey, Jack again found himself sitting with them at the Caribbean Lounge. Amanda had changed into a pair of white, loose-fitting linen or cotton pants and a pull-over green blouse that showed just enough cleavage to keep men interested.

Him included.

He leaned back in his chair with his hands laced behind his head and soaked up the night air. The evening had retained much of the day's heat. Stars twinkled in a clear sky. The moon revealed more of itself. The bright arc no longer a narrow crescent in the darkness, the cool lunar light added a flavor of romance to the evening.

Not for Amanda.

Or so it seemed.

Since returning to the ship, he'd noticed a subtle change in her behavior toward him. She continued to schmooze with the occasional sexual innuendo thrown in, but she wasn't laying on the allure to the extent she had.

Not that he minded.

Still, he needed to keep them talking. And figured he'd help the conversation along.

"What's the plan when we get back to Miami?" His question was directed at no one in particular.

Amanda answered, "You worry too much, dear."

He cringed at the way *dear* rolled off her tongue. If he never heard her say that word again, it would be too soon.

"Maybe I do," he said. "I'd still like to know."

"Very well, if it will help you relax. I've got wonderful plans for us. To start, I have a beautiful place in Miami Beach close to the water. You and I can spend our days and nights doing absolutely nothing we don't want to do while Corey is away taking care of business. After that, let's just say you won't have a thing to worry about."

Enough dribble.

He turned to her brother. "She's, of course, referring to you selling the artifacts?"

"It should only take a couple of days," Corey said with indifference. "What you two do after that is up to you and her."

And the police. Jack couldn't help thinking.

And he couldn't ignore the fact that Corey still hadn't explained how the purchase of the relics would go down. Or how to get the artifacts through customs . . . or even onboard the ship without drawing undue attention to them. Important questions that required answers.

Especially when faced with the possibility of doing time in a Mexican prison.

He asked, "How is this going to work tomorrow?"

The question clearly got Corey's attention.

He straightened in his chair. "I'll tell you how it's going to work. The ship docks in Cozumel around nine in the morning. I'll be at the head of the line to get off. You wait half an hour. Then you get off. Across from the pier, on the opposite side of the street, is a t-shirt shop. Be out front."

"What will you be doing?"

"That's my business. I'll pick you up in a rental Jeep and drive us to San Gervasio, a Mayan ruin believed to have been the sanctuary of Ixchel, a goddess of fertility. My contact will be waiting for us next to Chichan Nah, a structure archeologists believe served as a refuge or chapel."

"A chapel?" Jack couldn't hide his surprise.

Corey chuckled. "Kind of fitting, since the idols represent gods of death and the underworld."

Jack didn't appreciate the morbid humor.

"And after I purchase the artifacts?" He was more than a little curious. "I just run the idols through the security scanner onboard the ship like they're worthless tourist trinkets?"

Corey nodded. "I have special packaging to put each one in. Security won't give them a second look."

"You've used this method before and it works?"

"You'll find out."

CHAPTER 59

Jack got in line with the other disembarking passengers. He had the money in the nylon bag clutched in the crook of his arm, much the way a star running back would carry a football.

He felt a certain satisfaction knowing he had guessed correctly about Amanda. In the Caribbean Lounge the night before, he had tried several times to coax her back to his cabin. A test. And each time had been unsuccessful.

Even so, that hadn't put her off her game. She had kissed him passionately and whispered enough steamy talk into his ear to get his motor revved. But when Corey bade him goodnight, she apologized for not staying, gave reassurances she'd more than make it up to him, and walked off with her brother.

The carrot had been put back in play.

Amanda had left him aroused, he couldn't deny that. Nor did he want to. It served as a reminder this was all a game to her.

Not him.

And he needed no reminder that his smoldering desire burned for Cherise.

No mistake.

He had been quite explicit with her on the cabin phone when he returned to his stateroom following his evening at the Caribbean Lounge. To his disappointment, she refused to join him in his bed for fear Amanda might yet show up. He agreed that was a chance they couldn't afford to take, and drew consolation from knowing they would soon pull the noose tight around Amanda and her brother.

The line moved quickly.

Jack scanned the crowd ahead of him, hoping to catch a glimpse of Cherise or Robert. They were somewhere among the initial swarm of passengers exiting the ship.

Or were supposed to be.

He didn't rush. But he kept a steady pace all the way to the t-shirt shop. The business filled with expectant shoppers while he stood idle out front with the money clamped tight in the crook of his arm.

He hated the waiting part, and spent ten minutes in the sun watching tourists come and go with their souvenirs. When Corey finally pulled up in front of him and stopped, he opened the passenger door, anxious to be on their way.

"Everything good to go?" Corey asked.

"Money's right here." Jack showed him the bag. "Let's get this done."

* * *

Cherise and Robert watched from a hundred feet away. They knew the location of the exchange.

"Get the Jeep and pick me up," she said. "I'll wait here."

More passengers crowded the port.

"Keep an eye out for Amanda," he said, looking around. "We don't want her showing up and spoiling everything."

Cherise hadn't forgotten.

When Robert stopped the Jeep next to her, she opened the driver's door and said, "You ride shotgun."

He didn't argue. "Hope I don't need one."

She caught up with Corey and Jack at the edge of town. A sunbaked car occupied the gap between their Jeep and hers. A local, most likely. Corey did not appear to be in a hurry. Neither did the car. She backed off on the gas and gave them room.

* * *

Jack paused in front of the map at the edge of the parking area and assessed the layout of what had once been an important Mayan community. The ruins comprised four different areas extending over several kilometers. But only the site they were about to enter was open to the public.

Corey seemed to know where they were going. He didn't wait. Instead, he kept walking, putting distance between them. Taken in by the centuries-old ruins, Jack hurried to catch up.

The stone structures of San Gervasio—though less impressive when compared to the huge step pyramid of Chichén Itzá on the Yucatan Peninsula that he'd read about in *National Geographic*— were fascinating in their own right.

Ahead, a gathering of visitors lingered around what appeared to be a stone altar of some ancient importance. Corey stopped in the middle of the path.

Jack stepped beside him. "What's wrong?"

"We'll wait for those people to move on to the central plaza."

Jack fought a surge of uneasiness that proved difficult. "Can't we go around them? I want to get this done."

"Patience, my friend."

Jack silently urged the tourists to leave the area. Standing amidst ancient stone ruins surrounded by foreboding jungle in a remote section of the island, a hundred thousand dollars in cash tucked in the crook of his arm, was not his idea of how to spend a morning.

Recalling the map on the edge of the parking area, he knew Chichan Nah lay off to the right of their location. He looked in that direction and noticed a rail-thin man about forty, with leather brown skin and thick, curly black hair, standing next to a small stone building on the edge of a forested area.

He asked Corey, "Isn't that your contact over there?"

Corey didn't look. He simply nodded in the direction of the people at the altar platform, and said, "After they leave. Now relax."

Relax . . .

Jack scanned the ruins, his nerves tight with anticipation.

He was in no mood for tricks.

CHAPTER 60

Cherise parked near the entrance to the ruins, a couple of car lengths from Corey's Jeep. She tossed her blonde wig on the floorboard behind her seat, removed the bobby pins, and shook out her dark hair. There was no need for the disguise here. She and Corey had never met.

"Take it slow," she said to Robert who stood next to the passenger door. "But keep them in sight."

He stepped around the front bumper and joined her. "So let me get this straight. We're only supposed to intervene if something goes wrong? You really think Corey will try something?"

"Guaranteed. The question is when and where?"

They walked slow and without sound.

About a hundred feet in, she stopped and pointed. On a trail leading off to their right, Jack walked a half step behind Corey. Thirty meters ahead of them, next to a stone structure, stood a thin, plainly dressed man with dark skin and black hair. And barely visible in the gloom beyond, in an entrance into what remained of the building, a much larger man holding a MAC-10 pointed toward Jack.

She realized they had to let the scene play out. An armed man didn't necessarily mean double-cross.

Until it was too late.

Motioning Robert forward, she continued along the pathway

to a stone altar and stooped on the far side of its massive base, as though marveling at the centuries-old stonework.

Robert hunched down next to her.

Twenty-five meters in front of them, Jack continued toward the structure and the dark-haired man.

The exchange would take place there.

When the accomplice holding the submachine pistol took a step forward, she drew in a breath and held it.

* * *

Jack kept step with Corey.

The heavy, moist air among the trees and vegetation made him sweat. A damp ring had already formed in the armpits and on the chest of his shirt.

Drops of perspiration streaked his side.

He noticed the silhouette of a large man holding a gun, watching from the shadows inside the stone structure. He kept his eyes on him. If there was trouble, it would come from there.

Corey didn't appear to be concerned.

When they neared the meeting spot, the big man stepped into view long enough to show himself and a submachine pistol easily recognized as a MAC-10, then slipped back into the gloom.

A bodyguard.

Jack refused to be intimidated by the gun.

Or Thin Man.

Corey raised his hand in greeting. "*Hola, amigo.*"

Jack watched through a veil of wariness. He'd been given no names. Only promises he knew would not be kept.

All lies.

Himself, included.

Thin Man stepped forward and embraced Corey in a hug. "You brought the money?"

"My friend did."

Time to conclude the deal.

And get the hell out of there.

Expecting the worst, Jack showed the man the nylon bag while keeping a tight grip on the bundle inside. "It's right here."

Corey gave him a nothing-to-worry-about slap on the back. "This is Juan Perez. You'll be doing business with him."

Jack tucked the money into the crook of his left arm and offered his right hand in a pretense of politeness. He trusted no one. "Nice to meet you, Mr. Perez. I'm Jack."

"I also am pleased to meet you." Juan gripped Jack's hand with surprising strength. "Now let us get on with our business."

"The artifacts," Jack said. "You brought them?"

Juan nodded to his bodyguard who stepped from the shadows and handed him a small wood box—nothing fancy—and a piece of heavy, white cloth. "I believe you will be pleased when you see what I've brought."

Jack took a calming breath. "I'm sure I will."

He watched Juan spread the cloth on the surface of a low stone wall next to him, remove and unwrap three idols, at least four inches tall, clearly gold, and lay them out on the fabric so they could be viewed.

Jack stepped closer.

Each relic looked identical and yet different. Bloated looking round-bellied deities adorned with ornaments. Clearly male. Quite ugly in his opinion.

And unmistakably, the same three idols shown in picture on Cherise's phone.

He picked one up and examined it. Then the other two.

"Are they not what I promised, *amigo*?"

Corey asked, "What do you think, Jack?"

"I'm speechless." He looked at Corey. "That idol you showed me in the museum is nothing compared to these. I have to have them."

Juan collected the artifacts, rewrapped them, and returned them to the box.

"Well . . ." Corey motioned at Juan.

Jack exchanged the money for the box. His breath caught. He tightened his grip and turned to Corey. "Let's get out of here."

Corey pointed toward the trees. "This way. It's shorter."

Jack didn't debate the point. He hurried into the foliage, anxious to be away from there.

They were almost back to the parking area when Corey stopped him with a hand on his arm. An uncomfortable feeling made him scan the pathway behind them.

"What is it?" he asked.

"Probably nothing," Corey said. "Go back to the Jeep and wait. I'm just going to backtrack and make sure we aren't being followed."

"The hell with it. We need to get back to the ship."

"In a minute. Wait for me at the Jeep."

* * *

Cherise remained crouched, her monitor in her hand.

The transaction had taken less than a minute. Jack exchanged the bag of money for the box containing the idols, and he and Corey walked into the trees on a direct route back to the parking area.

The deal had gone down without a problem.

She decided to wait and see if they were followed.

A double-cross after all.

From her vantage point, she could see the parked vehicles and the two men who remained at the structure.

She gave it some time.

Not more than two minutes later, she drew in a breath when Corey walked back into the ruins and straight up to the man Jack had just done business with.

"Isn't that—"

She raised her hand to quiet Robert.

When he looked at her, she saw worry in his eyes.

"Stay down," she whispered.

She watched Corey take the red nylon bag from the thin man, remove a banded stack of hundred dollar bills and hand the money to him. Only the one packet. Corey removed the remaining cash and tucked the stacks into a money belt he had concealed under his shirt. He and the thin man then shook hands, and he walked back toward the parking lot as though nothing had transpired between them.

A move she failed to anticipate.

She needed to talk to Jack.

CHAPTER 61

Cherise waited for the men's attention to be averted elsewhere before she stood up.

Robert rose with her.

"This way," she said, and started walking toward a gathering of tourists studying a cluster of stone structures at the end of a path to her left.

Robert followed.

Fighting an urge to check behind her, she thought about what Corey said. He had introduced the thin man as Juan Perez.

Friendly . . .

A man he knew well.

When they reached the group of sightseers, she heard a woman speaking in French. A tour guide. And others in the group asking questions about the structures. She needed no translation.

She turned and looked.

Juan and the other man were gone.

"We need to leave, now," Robert said.

He shoved his receiver at her. The interior of Jack's rental Jeep visible on the screen. Corey at the wheel, driving he and Jack away from there. The only sound, the roar of the engine.

"Go." She swept her hand toward the lot. "We need to catch them before they get too far ahead of us."

Robert hurried along the path at a fast trot, in need of no further urging.

She kept up with him, her receiver on in her hand.

And only one thought.

Don't let something happen to Jack.

She raced past Robert and reached their rental. Skidding to a stop on the gravel, she pressed the door lock release on the fob and jerked open the driver's door.

The clock in her head ticked another few seconds.

They were cutting it close.

She scrambled behind the wheel, shoved the key into the ignition, and turned it. Robert jumped in on the passenger side at the same moment the engine roared to life. The seatbelt warning buzzed.

The least of her worries.

Corey had the money. Why not take the idols.

With only Jack to stop him.

She put the transmission in gear and stepped on the gas.

* * *

Jack sat in silence until they were out of the parking lot and on the road to town. He could only wonder why Corey thought it necessary to go back and make sure they weren't followed. By who? What he did know was the man was an antiquities thief and, in all likelihood, a killer.

That meant anything was possible.

He opened the box and stared at the relics swaddled in cloth. Three neatly wrapped idols. One hundred thousand dollars spent.

"You mentioned having some special packaging to get these through security. Now might be a good time to talk about it."

"Inside the sack in back." Corey motioned his head toward the rear of the Jeep. "We'll make the switch before we board the ship."

Jack twisted and peered at the white paper shopping bag sitting on the seat behind him. The cruise line logo clearly visible on it. "Let's have a look at what you brought."

"Not just yet."

"Why not?" Jack couldn't help raising his voice.

That brought a sly smile from Corey. "Patience, Jack."

Easy for him to say.

Jack settled into his seat, unconvinced. "You'll have to excuse me. I can't help being a little concerned. A lot is riding on this. A hundred thousand dollars, to be exact."

"There's nothing to worry about. Ship security's not a problem. They're interested in weapons and explosives. And I suppose drugs."

"What about your friends back there?" Jack couldn't resist.

Corey looked at him. "What about them?"

Jack detected a flicker of irritation in Corey's eyes that betrayed the man's attempt to appear unconcerned. "Were they still there when you went back to check on them?"

"They must have left by another route." Corey faced the windshield, letting the subject die.

Jack smiled with self-satisfaction. Corey had lied.

But about what?

"It bothers me," he said, prodding. "That you'll only get fifteen percent from the sale of these relics. I realize I put up all the money, but you deserve more. Juan's your contact. And this was originally your deal."

Corey laughed as though it were a big joke. "Don't worry about me."

Now that's funny.

Only Jack didn't feel like laughing.

He wasn't concerned about Corey.

Not in the least.

He worried about himself.

* * *

Cherise raced out of the lot and onto the roadway leading to town. She had no reason to believe Corey drove Jack somewhere other than back to the ship. Still, she couldn't relax until she had their Jeep in sight.

And reasonable assurance Jack would make it to the port alive.

CHAPTER 62

Cherise eased her grip on the steering wheel, allowing color to return to her knuckles. With Jack's Jeep in view ahead, she backed off on the gas. The low jungle that covered the island, bordered the roadway on both sides.

"What's happening?" she asked Robert, her focus on the Jeep in front of them.

He directed the screen of his receiver toward her. "They're talking about getting the idols onboard the ship without alerting security. Jack's asking Corey about the special packaging he talked about."

"I don't think ship security is cause for any real concern."

"Corey told Jack the same thing."

She glanced at the receiver, trying to think positive. "At least if they're talking about returning to the ship, we know everything's okay."

"Except for that stunt Corey pulled back there. There's no telling what the guy is up to."

The same thought had crossed her mind.

And there was no denying it.

She started to tell Robert not to worry, and stopped when she saw brake lights come on.

What the . . .?

She took her foot off the gas and gently braked to match the speed of the Jeep ahead of her. "Appears they're stopping."

Robert looked. "That can't be good."

She kept her foot poised on the brake pedal and watched the Jeep continue to slow. "I was afraid something like this would happen."

"Off to the left." Robert pointed. "Isn't that a road leading into the jungle?"

"I see it."

Shit.

Out of the corner of her eye, she noticed Robert straighten in his seat. He gripped the dash with one hand and balled the other into a fist.

He asked, "If Corey makes the turn, how do we handle it?"

She didn't have to think about her answer. "We stay on his tail like a couple of nosy tourists. And if we stop and it calls for pictures, be ready to snap a few with your phone. He won't make a move with witnesses around."

"And if he does?"

"We stop him."

* * *

Jack felt the Jeep slow and saw Corey's foot pressing on the brake for no apparent reason.

Corey was up to something.

What?

He asked, "We're stopping?"

"Taking that road up ahead," Corey said. "There's something I want to show you. I think you'll find it quite interesting."

I bet.

Jack knew exactly what Corey had in store for him.

And it sure didn't involve sightseeing.

He turned in his seat and peered through the rear window. Cherise and Robert stared back at him through the windshield of their Jeep. He felt relieved knowing his friends were close, but remained alert. Sitting next to Corey reminded him of a tiger shark circling a seal pup. The strike could come at any moment.

245

He'd be ready.

"More ruins?" he asked.

"Something like that. A sinkhole, actually."

Jack noticed Corey look toward the rearview mirror mounted on the inside of the windshield, and then toward the one on his door. From the expression that formed, the man wasn't happy.

"Something wrong?" Jack asked.

Corey kept glancing toward one mirror, then the other. Jack didn't have to look to know what had the guy so pissed. Cherise had followed him onto the gravel road. And had closed the distance between them.

Witnesses.

"Someone's in a Jeep behind us," Corey finally answered.

Jack couldn't help thinking Cherise had inserted a knife into the man's plan that surely included murder and a long goodbye down a sinkhole. He wanted to twist the blade a bit.

"Your friends?" He held back a grin.

"Juan, again?" Corey gave him a hard look. "Seriously?"

He glanced innocently behind them, and shrugged. "If you don't know who they are, they're probably a couple from the cruise ship interested in seeing that sinkhole you want to show me."

"Dammit," Corey said. "That's all I need. A couple of nosy tourists."

Jack settled into his seat, relishing the man's frustration.

He permitted himself a chuckle. "Isn't it ironic how things work out that way?"

"Isn't it, though?" Corey wasn't laughing.

Jack glanced at his watch. "Maybe we should just turn around and head back to the ship."

CHAPTER 63

Jack closed the door to his cabin and bolted it. For a moment, he stood there, shoulders slumped, catching his breath. A slow, satisfied smile spread his lips. If someone were to ask him if he felt lucky, he'd tell them that was an understatement.

This wasn't the first time.

Cherise and Robert were to thank for that. With their unanticipated arrival at the sinkhole, Corey had little choice but to return to the *Caribbean Sensation*. No doubt the constant presence of her Jeep in his rearview mirror kept the man to the main road with no more side trips.

And, Jack thanked God, no more attempts on his life.

For now.

As much as it pained him, he had to give Corey credit for the method he devised to smuggle the idols through security.

Quite simple, really.

And it worked perfectly.

He dumped the packages onto his bed with little concern for their value and stared at the relics. They could just as well have been worthless junk.

Souvenirs brought home from Uncle Jack's relaxing Caribbean cruise.

Cheap trinkets for the kids.

Corey claimed he came up with the idea while in a tourist shop on one of his prior visits to the Yucatan. Each package a plastic rectangle as wide and a little taller than a paperback book, with a red plastic bottom and a clear plastic top that slid over the base so the ten-dollar, pot-metal imitation of the Mayan god Hunab Ku stared ominously at the buyer.

Though the weight of each inexpensive casting was lighter in comparison, when swapped with one of the gold idols, each relic fit the indentation in the base of its respective packaging almost perfectly. And with the name of the deity, an explanation of its role in Mayan life, and a price printed on the package in Spanish, ship security didn't give them a second look when they passed through the scanner.

Jack, antiquities smuggler.

The name didn't resonate.

And now he faced a new problem.

If he guessed right, and Corey *had* intended to hit him over the head and dump his body down the sinkhole, he would have seen his last sunrise—eaten his last breakfast. Corey would have the idols and a nice profit with no official investigation and no one to complain how he got them.

Quick and sweet. The whole enchilada.

But the scenario didn't work out that way.

And since the initial scheme had failed, thanks to Cherise and Robert throwing a monkey wrench into the mix, Corey and Amanda would surely not stop after only one try. They'd have a backup plan. The challenge would be foiling it without knowing how or in what form their next attempt would come.

Only how it would end if he failed.

Perhaps the better plan would have been for him and Cherise to dump Corey and Amanda down a sinkhole and be done with them. Go back to Key West with the knowledge the killers had ensnared their last victim in their web of deceit. Murdered their last unsuspecting mark. Load the *Adeona* full of provisions, top off the tanks, and take a long boat ride back to Oahu.

Sure.

And never discover the truth behind what happened to Lindsey's father?

Or if the mother was involved?

Veronica Kelly.

What part did she play in this family of black widow spiders?

Would the killing continue?

He couldn't fool himself.

No way would he want to spend years of his life, or even one minute fighting off nightmares every time a passenger on a cruise ship went missing. Wondering if he should have done more.

If he could have saved a life.

He pulled his cell phone from his pocket and placed a call to Cherise. The one person he wanted to talk to most.

"You're aboard?" he asked when she answered.

"We're in my cabin," she said.

"Robert, too."

"The three of us."

He looked at the idols on the bed. "I'll be right down."

CHAPTER 64

Jack knocked on Cherise's door. Till now he had avoided her and Lindsey's cabin to not chance spoiling their ruse. At the moment, though, he did not feel particularly worried. He figured Corey and Amanda were busy plotting their next move. Which would likely come later in the night, after they had dinner and drinks together.

He wanted to be ready.

The door cracked open, Cherise's face appeared, and she pulled it open without bothering to invite him in.

He hurried past her and set the shopping bag on the end of one of the two beds. The dead bolt clicked closed. Lindsey stood at the foot of the bed next to him. Robert sat on the chair at the desk looking amused.

Not much room to move around.

He placed the idols on the spread where they could be seen. "It amazes me what people are willing to kill for."

"I'm sure that's what Corey had in mind out there," Cherise said from across the room.

"But we saved your ass." Robert was quick to point out. He stepped to the bed, picked up one of the packages, and studied the idol through the clear plastic cover.

Lindsey joined him, staring over his shoulder. Her hand on his arm.

Jack stepped away from the bed, giving them room.

Robert asked. "Were you worried?"

"About you and Cherise finding me? No. Not with a GPS transmitter in my watch."

"I meant us finding you alive."

Corey had size and slabs of muscle. And the man moved far more nimbly than expected. Jack said, "I'd be a liar if I didn't say I was a little concerned. It was a relief when Corey noticed you in his rearview mirror."

"You're not the only one." Cherise picked up one of the packages and studied the relic inside. "An interesting way to get them through customs. It's possible we may have underestimated just how clever he and his sister are."

"The real test will be in Miami."

She removed the idol, examined it, and laid the relic on the spread. She removed the other two and laid them next to it. All three in a row. Then she compared them to the photo on her phone. "As alike as two peas in a pod. These are the same ones Lindsey's father bought. No doubt about it."

Robert crowded in and picked one up. He turned it over in his hand. "Heavy suckers."

Lindsey said over his shoulder, "Can I see that? I want to have a look at what got my dad killed."

Robert handed the idol to her and she swiped a tear from her cheek.

"I can't believe Dad was murdered for something like this." She looked at Cherise. "All of a sudden, it feels surreal to have gotten this far."

"It's what you wanted," Cherise said.

Lindsey swiped away another tear. "Honestly, I can't thank you . . . all of you enough."

Cherise smiled. "We're not done yet. And Jack, there's something you need to know. It confirms what we suspected. After you concluded your business and walked into the trees, Robert and I stayed. I wanted to make sure you weren't followed. What I saw was Corey stride back into the ruins and straight up to the man you had just done business with."

"Juan," Jack said.

"Exactly."

"Let me guess. Corey didn't walk back there to say thank you?"

"I couldn't hear their conversation, but I watched him take the bag from Juan, remove a banded stack of hundred dollar bills, and hand the money to him. Only the one packet. Ten thousand dollars. His cut. Corey removed the remaining ninety thousand and tucked the cash into a money belt he had concealed under his shirt. The bag, he tossed aside. He and Juan then shook hands, and he walked back toward the parking lot as though nothing had transpired between them."

Jack nodded. "So that's their scam."

Robert made a sucking sound with his cheek. "Do that a dozen times a year, and you gross a million bucks or more."

"And think about it," Cherise said. "This way, Corey cuts a ten percent deal with the middleman in a scheme to resell the idols over and over so he doesn't have to rely on a steady flow of valuable artifacts coming on the market."

Jack saw the logic in the plan.

And the fallacies.

"There's risk," he said. "There always are risks. But they'd be minimal as long as Corey and Amanda worked it right. Sam King could have been the first pigeon in their scheme and me the second, with a slight variation. Truth is, we don't know how long this has been going on. Or how Amanda got involved. Maybe she had her own hustle in the beginning. Lure a married man back to her cabin and then put the squeeze on him for big bucks to keep the affair quiet. Fortunately, we don't have to sort it out."

Cherise asked, "Any ideas?"

Jack scanned his friends' faces. "It's a given Corey and Amanda have a backup plan. They'd be fools not to. The challenge for us is figuring out how to foil that plan without knowing what it is."

Lindsey spoke up. "That'll be some trick if we can do that."

"Maybe not," Jack said. "We know Corey intended to dump my body down that sinkhole so he could have the idols and a nice profit with no official investigation and no one alive to complain how he got it. No one they're aware of, anyway. Why would they change tactics in mid-stream?"

"They wouldn't," Robert said. "I'm all ears."

They were all looking at him. He nodded. "If you have an animal coming around at night to eat your dog's food, what do you do?"

Cherise answered. "Take the food away."

"Exactly."

Lindsey sniffled. "We could throw the damn things overboard, for all I care."

"I'm inclined to agree," Jack said. "Unfortunately, we need to hold onto them a little longer. But we can remove the temptation. "

"How do we do that?" she asked.

He smiled. "I'm going to ask the purser to lock them inside his safe until we dock in Miami."

"Could work," Cherise said. "Better yet, we'll keep them here. Just tell Corey and Amanda you had the idols locked away for safe keeping. It will have the same effect and you won't have to draw attention to the damned things or fight the crowd to get them back when we dock in Miami."

"I hadn't thought about that."

"Believe me, we want to be ready to go when it's time to disembark."

He had a good feeling about her idea. "I'll break the news to Corey and Amanda at dinner tonight."

CHAPTER 65

As it turned out, Amanda and Corey had been no shows for dinner the night before.

And again at breakfast.

But he had seen them at the pool. About one in the afternoon. On the far side of the deck. Corey first. Then Amanda. He'd melted into a shadow and watched. Corey, looking like a Mister Universe contestant, wore a Speedo that left little to a woman's imagination. The three women who'd tried to put the make on he and Robert at the bar, were hovering like kids at a candy counter.

Corey flexed his muscles, bringing smiles of delight to their faces. The four of them flirted and joked and laughed in a game of grab-ass.

Twenty feet away from her brother's antics, Amanda—in an orange, painted-on, two-piece bathing suit—lay on a chaise lounge. One long leg stretched out before her. The other bent at the knee. Designer sunglasses. A large-brimmed, white sun hat. Her head moved in slow motion as though scanning the sunbathers around her.

A lioness surveying the African savanna.

At one point her head paused, facing in his direction. He figured she had noticed him watching, and maybe she had, but her attention was drawn to the diving board where Corey bounced and jackknifed into the water. She remained a moment longer, stood, and left the deck. Corey surfaced on that end of the pool, heaved himself out, and followed after her.

The three women stood watching, clearly disappointed.

He'd spent the afternoon trying not to think about what Corey and Amanda had cooked up for him.

Now he was about to find out.

* * *

Jack took the stairs down to deck six and walked half the length of the ship to the main dining room located in the stern. He wore the suit and tie Cherise had picked out for him—not a tux—though he felt no compulsion to dress up for Amanda, and certainly not for Corey.

But he wanted to appear as though he'd dressed to impress them.

A night of celebration.

In more ways than one.

When he walked in, he found her and her brother already seated at a table. He thought he had overdressed for the occasion. Quite the opposite. Amanda looked stunning in her sequin-studded, pale blue evening dress. Corey wore a light blue suit with sleeves stretched tight over his biceps. No tie. The collar of his yellow shirt open one button.

He ambled over and said to Amanda, "You look positively stunning. So how was *your* day?"

She took a sip of her martini and said, "In a word. Disappointing."

I bet.

He took a seat and scooted close. "That's unfortunate. You should have joined me at the pool."

"We weren't in the mood," Corey said.

Liar.

Their server stopped at the table and Jack ordered a Knob Creek. When the attendant stepped away to get him the drink, he said to Corey, "I have to admit, this cruise was certainly not boring."

"You look nice all dressed up," Amanda said, as though she had suddenly warmed to his presence. "I thought you outdoorsmen only wore khaki bush pants and shirts with oversized pockets."

He smiled. "Actually, I spend a lot of time in ratty cutoffs and tennis shoes. I bought this hoping to wear it in the company of a lady as lovely as you."

"I must say, you're full of compliments tonight."

"Because I feel good."

"I'm sorry we had to skip last night; I wasn't feeling well."

"But now you're all right?"

She smiled. "And looking forward to the evening with you."

His drink arrived. He took a large sip, and said, "I can't think of anything better than spending it together. Speaking for myself, I feel like the luckiest man on the entire ship."

"I suppose we should order." Her gaze shifted about as if she was embarrassed.

Jack wasn't fooled. "We should. I'm starved."

They placed their dinner orders and Jack went back to his drink. To her brother, he said, "I meant to compliment you on your scheme to get those idols through security. A stroke of genius, really."

Corey grinned. Maybe for the first time. "I think it's one of my better ones."

"You've had others?" Jack gave his full attention. "If they are half as ingenious as this one, I'd love to hear some of them."

"You know about the reality program I had on television. A fishing show like that has its perks. The first gold trinket that I smuggled home, I carried through customs inside a mounted roosterfish. The poor dumb bastards never checked it."

"Inside a stuffed fish?" Jack shook his head. "Chancy."

"Not really." Corey flashed him a smug look. "I had my cameraman and all of our equipment with us. The customs agents were more interested in looking through our suitcases than anything else. When I gave each of them a DVD with my first six episodes on it that pretty much ended that."

Jack had the man talking and he wanted to keep him talking. "How many times have you done this?"

"A couple—"

"Corey," Amanda cut him off. "Let's not bore Jack with any more of this talk. I'd love to hear more about him."

"I think I've told you the interesting parts." He swigged his bourbon, hoping to change the subject.

"Really?" She winked. "Then we'll have to come up with something else to talk about."

Their food arrived and they ate silently for a couple of minutes. Amanda spoke first. She pointed at Jack's glass. "Drink up and I'll order you a fresh one. I'm going to indulge in another martini."

"Why not," he said. "I think a celebration is called for."

She laid a cool hand on his arm. "If you'll excuse me, I'll be right back."

He downed his bourbon and let her place the order.

She returned to the table a couple of minutes later. "I asked him to bring you a double." She smiled. "Since we're celebrating."

"My thoughts, exactly." He'd been playing along with her but he hadn't forgotten about Corey.

Her brother sat, quietly devouring his steak. He appeared more interested in his meal than the conversation. But his eyes betrayed the skullduggery festering inside his brain. There was a little too much shiftiness to them. A slight narrowing. What a person would see in an old gangster movie.

Jack didn't let the man's actions bother him.

He knew exactly what vile intentions Corey had in mind.

Amanda as well.

The drinks arrived and he took a sip. Less ice, more Knob Creek.

She let her glass sit. He watched her remove the two-olive garnish from her glass. When her gaze rose and met his, she parted her lips in a seductive gesture and spent an hour pulling one of the olives off the pick with her perfect white teeth.

All quite sexy, had she not been an ice cold killer.

He forked a slice of filet mignon, along with half a green bean, into his mouth. She could be drinking water for all he knew.

He excused himself to the restroom and carried his glass with him.

Robert stood with his back to the wall outside the men's room. His arms were crossed against his chest. "You rang?"

"Perfect timing," Jack said.

"I figured you were hoping I'd show up. Cherise, Lindsey, and I are in the diner eating cheeseburgers. You're still planning to break the news to Corey and Amanda, right?"

"I'll wait until they bring up the subject." Jack handed Robert the glass of Knob Creek. "You can have that. Get me another, in a tumbler just like this. Only make it iced tea."

Robert held the glass up to the light. "That should work. One double iced tea coming up."

When Jack stepped out of the restroom, Robert had his drink ready.

"Thanks," he said. "I probably should get back."

Robert grinned. "We don't want Amanda getting lonely, do we?"

"Something like that."

"She's one smooth cookie, I'll give her that much. Just so you know, I tipped your waiter fifty bucks to make sure you get tea if she insists on ordering you another drink. I'm thinking she will."

"Good call."

Jack returned to the table and retook his seat. Amanda's martini had gone down maybe a quarter of an inch. Corey had finished his steak and his beer. A snifter of what appeared to be brandy or cognac sat in front of him. "I apologize for taking so long. Did you miss me?"

"I had our waiter bring me a brandy," Corey said. "I would have had him bring you one, only you weren't here."

Jack drained half his tea and held up his glass. "No worries. Tonight, I'm sticking with bourbon."

"Speaking of which." Amanda nodded in his direction. "Looks like you're in need of another."

He pointed. "And you've barely touched your martini."

"I'm pacing myself," she said. "There's a beautiful moon out tonight. I'd like to enjoy it."

"And I got the impression you were trying to get me drunk so you can take advantage of my body."

"The thought did cross my mind." She gave him a sly smile.

He smiled back, then lifted his tumbler and tossed back the tea.

"I see you like my idea." She sipped her martini down another quarter inch.

He figured he might get a look at the moon a second or two before Corey hit him over the head with something hard.

Won't they *be disappointed.*

"Which idea are you referring to?" he asked. "The moon, or taking advantage of my body?"

"Can't a pretty woman have both?"

He smiled. "Perhaps it's time we take our celebration to the Caribbean Lounge?"

CHAPTER 66

Jack got up and slid the chair out for Amanda.

"Shall we?" he said.

She stood and laced her arm around his. "By all means."

He looked at her brother.

"You two go ahead," Corey said. "I'll catch up."

I bet you will.

Jack escorted Amanda to the elevator and rode it up five decks. They stepped off and he asked, "Do you mind if I take off this tie?" He began undoing the knot. "I feel a bit overdressed out here. And it is a beautiful night."

She arched a brow. "As long as you don't mind if I leave my dress on."

He peered into her eyes. "On or off. The choice is yours."

She hugged his arm. "I'll leave it on for now."

"Good choice."

He liked the feel of her on his arm and couldn't imagine so much woman locked away in a prison cell. A shame, really. A total waste of someone so gorgeous. But then, she had made her choice. And being dumped over the railing was no more appealing than being dropped into a sinkhole.

The sliver of moon had grown to near half. They seated themselves so they could watch it and a sky full of stars. She ordered herself a white wine and him a double Knob Creek. He gave up thinking about the take-advantage-of-his-body part of their earlier conversation.

"Is Corey all right?" he asked, as if concerned.

"Sure. What makes you think something's wrong?"

He shrugged. "Nothing really. I just thought . . ."

"It's okay, Jack." She gave him a placatory pat on his hand. "Knowing him, he went to the cabin to change. He's having a drink with Elena and doesn't like to dress up any more than you do."

"Since you're so observant, maybe I should excuse myself and make a quick trip to *my* cabin?"

"Then I'd have to change."

"That wouldn't be bad. You could wear the dress you wore at the bar the evening we met."

She stood and smoothed the sequin-studded fabric over her curves. "But I love this dress. It makes me feel glamorous."

"Stunning is the word I'd use." He got out of his chair, thinking she looked like she had been called to the stage to receive an Academy Award for best actress.

An award she deserved.

He hadn't done badly either.

"I have an idea," she said.

"I have one, too."

"Mine first." She put her arms around his neck and devoured him with a kiss on the mouth.

He didn't resist. And gave full into it until he had to stop and take a breath.

"Walk with me, Jack." She linked her arm around his and led him toward the starboard rail.

Against his better judgement, he allowed her to string him along. "Can I ask you a question?"

"Only one, providing you don't mind if I refuse to answer."

"Do you enjoy taking cruises with your brother? There's no man in your life?"

"That's two questions."

"Well?"

She hugged his arm. "Who says I don't have a man in my life? I'm holding onto one now."

He couldn't help but smile. "Yes, you are."

She put her arms around him and met his gaze. "You haven't had too much to drink, have you?"

He played along. "I'm a little wobbly. What did you have in mind?"

She eased his back against the railing and pressed her breasts against his chest. He felt her nipples harden beneath the fabric and pictured her breasts in his mind. Her hands slid up his arms to his shoulders as her mouth found his.

It would have been easy to give into the kiss as he had done minutes before. But at that moment, his sense of preservation kicked in.

Finally.

He worked his hands under her arms and gently turned her in a sort of dreamy slow dance until they had switched places. Only when her back pressed against the rail did he kiss her long and passionately.

"Pardon me for interrupting." Corey's voice broke the spell.

Jack eased himself away from Amanda. "Thought you were having a drink with your lady friend."

Corey glared at his sister. "I got delayed. Let's sit."

Jack led Amanda back to their chairs. Corey pulled one over. He'd changed into khaki shorts and a t-shirt with a tagline: "Fisherman Catch More Bass." A line ran through the 'B.'

"You worried about tomorrow?" Jack asked.

"I thought we might go to your cabin and take a look at the idols."

"Tonight?"

"Of course. I want to make sure everything is set for tomorrow."

"I'd like to oblige you, but unfortunately I can't. They're locked in the purser's safe. I figured it would be prudent to keep them locked up until I disembark in the morning."

Corey's jaw visibly tightened.

Jack saw the veins stick out on the man's neck. "Sorry if I upset you."

"Fine," Corey said. "That's just fine."

Of course it wasn't.

"Should we order drinks?" Jack asked.

Corey stood. "I'm going to bed. You and my sister do what you like."

Amanda got up from her chair, leaned down, and gave Jack a dismissive peck on the cheek. "I'm sorry to bring the evening to an end, but I want to be packed and ready to leave the ship when it docks in the morning."

"The celebration's over?" He reached for her as though he intended to pull her into his lap. "What about a few minutes ago? You certainly weren't talking about packing, then."

She pulled away. "I was caught up in the moment."

"You had me in the moment as well. I still am, in case you haven't noticed."

"So I see," she said.

He enjoyed what had developed into a game for him and motioned her down with his hands. "You could hike that dress up on your lovely thighs and sit right here. Show me those garters you wear. I'm guessing you're not wearing panties."

"I could, but forget it."

Jack suppressed a laugh. The change in her demeanor couldn't have been more abrupt. He'd have thought he dumped a bucket of cold water on her.

And wished he could.

He grinned. "See you in the morning, then."

CHAPTER 67

Jack sipped the remainder of his Knob Creek while he walked back to his cabin. Along the way, he noticed passengers had begun setting their bags outside their staterooms, tagged and locked, ready for crewmembers to pick up.

He needed to focus. Disembarking a cruise ship, he found out, is not like checking out of a hotel.

Group assignments, colored baggage tags, a final reconciliation of your charges, a clearing of the ship by immigration officials, long lines at the front desk to consider. All can make for a chaotic debarkation.

In the morning, when a voice over the passenger address system announced that his group was clear to disembark, he wanted to already be in line with his carry-on in hand, waiting to show his cruise card one last time. With a little luck, he would then breeze through customs, join up with his friends, and be collecting their baggage at the terminal before Corey and Amanda showed up.

When he arrived at the door to his cabin, he paused and made a small wager with himself before going in. A bet he couldn't lose. Fifty bucks said Corey had been inside searching for the idols.

He swiped his card and pushed the door open. Immediately, the hackles on his neck bristled with the spine-tingling awareness a person gets when they enter a closed room and sense someone has been there. His cabin had been rifled. A search that would have gone un-noticed had it not been for the not-so-subtle nuances left by the hasty intruder. His suitcase and carry-on left only partially re-zipped. Drawers pulled out and not pushed completely closed. Bedding left ruffled where the pillows and mattress had been lifted and put back in place.

Sloppiness contrary to habits second nature to him.

It was clear to Jack, Corey did not expect him to return to the cabin.

Amanda had made a point of ordering him doubles—hundred proof Kentucky bourbon whiskey—and used her womanly wiles to maneuver him to the railing. Had he been consumed by her kiss, unaware of his vulnerability, had her brother not shown up and interrupted the embrace, he would have been sleeping with the fish.

A watery grave in Davy Jones' locker.

Just like Sam King.

He tossed his jacket on his bed and placed a call to Cherise.

"I'm in my cabin. Corey searched it, like we figured he would."

"Then your idea worked."

"Have you seen Robert?"

"He and Lindsey are up on deck somewhere. After Amanda and Corey bailed, they decided to take a stroll in the night air."

Jack still hadn't adjusted to Robert's attraction to Lindsey. He hoped they were getting their priorities straight.

"Children," he said. "What can you say?"

"She'll miss him when this is over."

"And he'll miss her, I'm sure. Are you packed and ready for morning?"

"We have our bags set out. Robert said his are out as well. All that remains is for you to pick up the idols."

"I'll get my suitcase in order, set it out for the crew to pick up, and be right down. If Robert returns, have him wait there."

"Glad to. But I don't think that will be an issue."

He changed into the bush pants and t-shirt he'd wear off the boat, put his suit into its garment bag, and folded it into his suitcase. At least Corey hadn't emptied the contents of his luggage onto the floor. And it was still tagged. He zipped and locked it, and set it in the passageway outside his door.

There were passengers crowded in the elevator when he stepped on. From their conversations, they were hurrying to their cabins to get their baggage in order. The activity of the evening, it seemed. Three stops later, he got off on deck four and followed the companionway to Cherise's cabin. Her and Lindsey's bags, with the same orange colored tags as his, were sitting next to the door. Cherise answered his knock without making him wait.

Black compressive running tights, a short-sleeved black T, and running shoes. Not the first time he'd seen her dressed this way.

"Like your outfit," he said, stepping inside.

"I didn't dress to impress." She closed and bolted the door.

He flashed a grin. "Impresses me."

"You're easy, though. And speaking of easy, you let yourself get a little carried away with Amanda, didn't you?"

"You talking about the fun I had with her tonight when she wanted to leave?"

"Actually, every time the two of you were together. But that's the incident I referred to."

"Couldn't help myself. The bitch deserved to be screwed with after what she tried to pull."

"Robert told me. He was there watching and thought for sure you were going over the side."

"There at the lounge, huh? He's getting good at shadow lurking."

"You realize neither Corey nor Amanda admitted to killing anyone."

"Not like we didn't try."

"It's not enough, Jack. There's no case against them."

"By that, you mean no murder case. What about antiquities smuggling? They can at least go down for that."

"And Corey might even skate on that one. Amanda probably won't even be charged."

"In addition to the photos and texts, don't you have a recording of him admitting to bringing black market antiquities into the country?"

"Every conversation you had with them."

"Including the ones when Amanda and I were alone?" A stupid question, he realized.

"Everything."

He chuckled. "Some detective is really going to get an ear full."

"But like I said, there's no murder case. We're screwed."

"Before you ask me, once was enough. I'm done playing the part of helpless victim."

"I would never ask you to. We gave it a try and came up short."

He stepped to the window and stared into the night. The moonlight glistened on the ocean swells. "So we went through all of this for nothing. A hundred thousand dollars and a shitload of expenses down the drain."

"You have a right to be upset."

"Upset is not a strong enough word. Pissed is more like it."

"You're not alone. I want you to know that when we get off this ship, I'm sending Lindsey home and going after them."

He turned and looked at her. "The way you did Yang Li?"

She stared as though his question had taken her back. "I doubt I'll stuff a baggie full of Fentanyl down their throats. But in a manner of speaking, yes."

"With the same outcome?"

"For them." She moved to the end of the bed where the white paper gift bag containing the idols sat. "I tried playing by the rules for Lindsey's benefit and it didn't work. So, game over. I won't let one more person die by their hands."

"An angel of vengeance?"

"Don't worry. I'm not asking you to go with me."

"You know I will."

"Not this time. What needs to be done, I'll do alone."

CHAPTER 68

At nine the following morning when the faceless voice announced his group designation over the speaker, Jack stepped into the chaotic atmosphere of cruise ship debarkation. A frenzied dash for the elevators and staircases leading to the gangway.

He didn't bother with an overcrowded elevator and used the stairs to descend the five levels to the crew quarters on deck three where the line of disembarking passengers formed. To his disappointment, he had grossly misjudged the flood of people waiting for their turn to leave the ship.

If Cherise hadn't already joined the throng, she soon would. Robert and Lindsey, too. Robert insisted on being the gentleman and help the women with their carry-on luggage. Which worked for Jack. The plan was for him to join up with them in the baggage area since his friends had nothing to declare and would likely breeze through customs.

The crowd continued to grow. So did his concern. He stepped to the side, stood on his tip-toes, and felt relieved to see his friends a couple of dozen people ahead of him. One thing about a cheap blonde wig, it stands out in a crowd, especially when there are two such atrocities close together, and one is on the head of a six-foot-tall, one hundred and thirty-pound exotic beauty.

He didn't see Corey or Amanda anywhere.

Which unnerved him more than he imagined it would. He

had a very vivid recollection of dives when he encountered really big sharks in murky water. Knowing the killers cruised the gloom beyond his field of vision, but not knowing from what direction they might strike.

At last, the line in front of him began to dwindle. He finally got his turn to show his cruise card for the last time and descend the gangway. The two dozen people who had been ahead of him were moving through customs. His friends were already on their way to collect their bags.

As it worked out, the customs agent did not give him any trouble. He thanked the woman and started walking to where his bag and his friends were waiting. He had gone about fifteen feet before all three of them began waving and shouting something that got lost in the noise of the crowd.

Given the number of departing passengers swarming the baggage area, he figured they were letting him know where they were standing.

He tried to wave back and was stopped by a big hand gripping his bicep from behind. It became suddenly clear why they were trying to get his attention.

He twisted out of Corey's grasp and pasted on a plastic smile.

"There you are," he said. "Where's Amanda? I was afraid I'd lost you guys."

"Not hardly, buddy boy. Amanda and I were one of the first ones off. She's waiting at the car."

Whether Jack wanted to or not, he was back to playing the helpless victim. He looked at his friends and saw them watching. Cherise stood in the shade of her white sunhat, hiding behind her Burberry sunglasses, shaking her head from side to side as though saying *don't do it*. He mentally shrugged off the warning.

"Has something changed?" he asked. "She had plans for us."

"She still does." His smile wasn't a nice one. "We have unfinished business to take care of first."

"You're referring to finding a buyer for these?" He held up the paper bag. "If you remember right, you were supposed to take care of that."

"And I will. Come on." He motioned his head. Then he placed

a beefy hand on Jack's shoulder, and dug his fingers in. "This way."

Jack tensed. "Give me a minute to grab my suitcase."

"Leave it for now." Corey urged Jack forward with a push. "We'll come back for it. Trust me."

Jack knew he needed to stall.

"Hold on." He stopped and started to turn around. "It'll only take me a second to grab—"

Corey tightened his grip. "I said we'll come back for it. Now let's go. Amanda's waiting."

What the fuck?

Jack still had his watch. He recalled Cherise shaking her head at him in a silent warning. His instinct had been to tell the man to keep his fucking paws to himself, to slap the guy's hand away and bring an end to this sick game. But then he remembered her having pointed out that they had no case against Corey or his sister. To play along with these two now, might yet get Cherise the murder confession she wanted.

And save her from herself.

"You can take your hand off me, Corey. I certainly don't intend to keep Amanda waiting."

CHAPTER 69

Jack followed alongside Corey. The beefy hand gone from his shoulder. He saw Amanda standing next to a silver Range Rover parked in a loading and unloading zone. Her brother's car, most likely. She didn't look happy.

Not even when she cast them a pasted-on smile.

He glanced at Corey and said, "Nice Range Rover."

Corey gave him a not-so-gentle slap on the back. "A man in your line of work should own one."

That hand again.

"I own a Jeep," he said.

Corey lengthened his stride. "Get in the front seat. We're going for a ride."

Jack stopped, stalling for more time. "You're not forgetting about my luggage, are you?"

"Trust me."

"You said that already."

"Then don't worry."

Jack glanced behind him and caught a glimpse of Cherise. Robert and Lindsey were nowhere in sight.

"Hard not to," he said.

He kept his fear in check and walked up to Amanda who had yet to say anything or even acknowledge his presence beyond her fake smile. The new woman. No longer the anxious lover.

Not her usual role.

He said, "Good morning, dear. You look lovely." He leaned in for a kiss on the lips and got a turned cheek instead.

"You made me wait. Get in."

"How can you say that?" He feigned indignation, buying him a few more seconds. "I came right over when your brother found me looking for you guys."

Her expression didn't crack. "You were supposed to get off the ship with us."

Where had that *come from?*

He took a calming breath. "Be nice if you had told me."

She huffed. "I thought you were smart enough to figure that out."

The conversation was undoubtedly going nowhere. Swallowing the comment he wanted to make, he opened the front passenger door and stood for a moment watching her slide in back. The spider had revealed her red underbelly.

Not that she needed to.

He climbed in and buckled his seatbelt.

Corey slid behind the steering wheel, started the engine, and drove away. "Ignore her," he said. "She's been cranky all morning."

Jack turned and looked out the rear window in time to see Cherise run to the curb where they had been parked a moment before. He realized now he should never have gotten into the SUV under any circumstance. The only hope he had was that his friends figured out a way to stay with him.

He heard the automatic door locks engage. In the silence, there had been a finality in the way they snapped closed, not unlike that of a dead bolt turning.

Or a cell door.

They'll soon know that sound.

I hope.

He asked, "Where are we going?"

Corey glanced at him as though the question sounded ridiculous. "Taking care of business. I already told you that."

"Doesn't tell me where we're going."

"You'll find that out soon enough."

Jack knew what that meant.

Corey faced the windshield, his attention back on the road. Traffic jockeyed for position. Departing cruise ship passengers added to the congestion. He stayed in the center lane of one-way traffic.

"I'm not playing this game." Jack fumbled for the button to release his door lock. "Pull over right now and let me out."

Corey ignored the order.

"You're a fool, Jack." Amanda chuckled behind him. "You have been from the day we met at the bar."

"You can't be serious." He started to turn and face her. Cold steel pressed into the back of his neck, stopped him.

"Just relax and enjoy the ride."

"How do you expect me to do that with a pistol to my head?" He didn't have to look to know the feel of a gun barrel. Round. No slide. A revolver.

"Because you don't have a choice. Be a good little boy and hand the idols back to me."

He didn't argue, and tossed the bag into the back seat.

"That crappy little duffle, too. You won't be needing it."

"Take it." He tossed his carry-on back as well. And as if he didn't already know, he asked, "Now tell me what the hell is going on?"

A lame question but he wanted to keep her occupied.

"Change of plans," she said.

The gun barrel no longer drilled a hole in his neck. He didn't know exactly what he expected when he climbed into the car, but this wasn't it.

Not even close.

He didn't know how much longer he could play dumb. But he needed answers he wasn't getting. Answers Cherise wasn't getting, provided she could hear him. For the time being, he had little choice but to play along.

"We're not going to your place?"

"Did you really think I meant any of the stuff I said? All playacting, darling. Even the sex."

His turn to laugh. "If you were playacting, don't wait for the reviews to come out. You weren't that good."

"That's not what you said the other night."

"Trust me, I've had better."

"Impossible. I'm the best. No one makes love the way I do."

"You're nothing more than a pathetic narcissistic bitch. You're lucky I could get it up."

Again, he felt the cold steel of the barrel.

He drew in a breath.

"You dumb bastard," she said, when it appeared she had puffed up her ego enough to answer. "You're forgetting, I'm holding a gun."

Obviously.

She dug the bore into the flesh at the base of his skull.

He cringed.

"Careful with that thing," he managed. "You might hurt yourself."

"The only person who's going to be hurt, is you."

"Is that what gets you off?" he asked. "Or is hurting someone simply not enough? It's killing that you enjoy."

Corey turned with anger flaring in his eyes. "Both of you, give it a rest."

"I'll give it a rest, all right," Amanda said with a tone of contempt.

Jack sighed. The barrel gone from his head.

He didn't need her to voice her thoughts. He could picture the disdainful smile on her lips. She wanted to shoot him in the back. Couldn't wait.

Only a matter of time.

He looked at the face of his watch, not for the time. Rather for the transmitter inside.

His only hope.

CHAPTER 70

Cherise turned at the sound of a vehicle and saw a taxi slow to a stop at the curb. Robert and Lindsey sat in back.

She slid in next to her friends who moved over to give her room, slammed the door, and yelled, "The Intercontinental. And step on it."

The driver drove away from the curb and into traffic. Getting them to the hotel, but not fast enough. She doubted 'fast enough' existed.

Fucking traffic.

Death, it seemed, claimed the people she loved. When she was six, her mother, a French foreign intelligence agent. When she was twenty-eight, her father, who held a key position in US Naval Intelligence and laid the foundation for the person she'd become.

He brought her to the US from France and immersed her in the life of a military brat. At eighteen, she'd enlisted in the Navy, hoping to follow in his footsteps. It was during her military service that, because of his position in Naval Intelligence along with influence from Admiral Casey, she had been permitted to attend SEAL training where she learned to fight and shoot.

Had he not died, her life would have been much different.

It was when her tour ended a few months later, that she left the Navy and went to work for Blackwater–since renamed, Xe Services. Being female and pretty and highly trained had its advantages. But after five years of private military work, she went into business for herself. And when she wasn't devoting her life to the needs of others, she searched for the truth behind her father's death.

A quest that continued to haunt her.

Maybe it was time to think beyond that.

Beyond the desires of others.

For once—instead of ignoring her needs while pursuing those of others—she may have finally found something for herself.

Something she wanted.

And couldn't imagine losing.

She dug a hundred dollar bill out of her purse and jammed it into the fare slot on the screen separating them from the driver. "Here's a hundred. I said step on it."

The c-note seemed to provide sufficient encouragement. The driver pressed on the gas and fought his way through traffic. Cars slammed on brakes and honked horns. Cherise had only one thought on her mind.

Save Jack.

She had been too busy trying to catch up with him at the terminal to monitor her receiver. At the time, keeping him in sight seemed more important.

She asked, "Have you been monitoring him?"

"He and Amanda have been arguing," Robert said. "She pulled a gun on him when he demanded they let him out of the car."

"A gun?"

"A pistol of some kind."

"And Corey?"

"Driving. And I don't think he's armed. The strange thing is, I got the feeling he and Amanda weren't getting along."

"I got the same feeling," Lindsey said. "When he got into the SUV, I heard him tell Jack she had been cranky all morning."

"They haven't seen cranky." She leaned forward and said, "Can't this thing go any faster?"

"Take it easy, lady." She noticed the driver's eyes flick to the rearview mirror. But only for a second. "I'm doing the best I can."

She leaned back and sighed.

A fucking gun.

The cabby screeched to a halt in the portico of the hotel five minutes later. The three of them exited the rear seat, and Cherise yelled, "Take care of the bags."

"I'm on it," Robert answered.

She raced inside the lobby to pay the parking fee for her rental, leaving Robert and Lindsey at the taxi.

They were all aware of the urgency.

She returned to the portico a few minutes later and saw a bellman loading the last bag onto a cart. Robert had his wallet in his hand.

She said, "They're bringing the car around now."

He removed a fifty and handed the bill to the bellman. "My name is Robert Foster. Hold our bags here at the hotel. We'll be back for them."

The bellman wheeled the bags away. Lindsey, who was holding Robert's monitor, said, "GPS shows Jack traveling southbound on 95."

Cherise asked, "Any indication where they're headed?"

"None."

The Charger arrived and Cherise urged the driver out with a twenty dollar bill. She slapped the Jackson into the guy's hand and slid behind the wheel. Lindsey had already seated herself in back. Robert had one leg in on the passenger's side hurrying to get into the car.

"Let Lindsey out," she said. "She's not going with us."

Lindsey leaned forward and gripped the edge of Cherise's seat. "What do you mean I'm not going with you?"

Cherise felt it important that her friend see the sincerity in her eyes. She pulled off her sunglasses, tucked them above the sun visor, and faced Lindsey. "You're a dear friend. Please understand. You have to stay here. You can't be involved in what I have in mind."

"Robert's going. Why can't I?"

"I don't have time to argue. Call the cops and tell them everything. I'll come back for you when it's over."

Lindsey got out and shoved the monitor at Robert. Cherise peered at him over the passenger seat. "It's up to you. Going or staying?"

"You kidding?" He started to slide onto the seat.

"Hold on a sec." She hit the trunk release button. "Grab the gun case out of the back before you get in."

Robert didn't question her and returned with a soft-sided, black satchel. "Is this it?"

"That's the one. Can you shoot a Glock?"

"Of course I can." He climbed in and slammed his door.

"Good." She mashed the gas pedal to the floor.

The tires screeched on the concrete and the Charger roared away from the portico amid a cloud of burned rubber.

"Directions?" she yelled.

"Take a right and then a left on First Street." Robert studied the receiver in his hand. "First will take us straight to the 95. Enter on the southbound on-ramp and we should merge into traffic not too far behind them."

She pulled off her wig and shook out her hair.

Pray to God we do.

CHAPTER 71

Jack concentrated on the road ahead. He'd gotten nowhere pushing Amanda's buttons. But he did feel better.

Small consolation.

And he had learned two things about his captors. Amanda's narcissistic ego far exceeded her common sense. Any contradiction to her exceedingly high opinion of herself caused an outburst of irrational behavior. And Corey, every bit as self-absorbed as his sister, apparently didn't like her all that much. Or he had grown tired of her.

All good information.

His thoughts turned to those of his friends. What were they thinking? How much had they heard? Had they been able to hear him at all? They'd surely track his movements via GPS. Notify police. Do their best to race to wherever Amanda and Corey were taking him.

But would they arrive in time?

Would anyone?

He couldn't count on that.

He weighed the odds of survival if he jumped clear of the Range Rover. At sixty miles per hour, slim to none. In traffic, practically zero.

And with a gun aimed at his back . . .

He had to assume Amanda knew how to shoot.

Even if by some stroke of luck he could manage to unbuckle his seatbelt, climb over the seat, and wrestle the gun away from her, he had her brother to contend with. With his height, weight, and slabs of muscle, the man appeared more than capable of inflicting great bodily injury or death.

And had.

Jack gave up on trying anything foolhardy until he had at least a chance of making a successful escape and coming out of it in one piece. That chance, he figured, would come when they got to wherever they were taking him.

Far into the Glades, he guessed.

Until then, he would play the obedient kidnap victim. He didn't want bullets punching holes through any of his vital and irreplaceable organs.

"I know what you're thinking," Corey said. "Forget it."

"What's that?"

"Opening the door and jumping out. Try it, and I'll snap your arm like a twig."

Jack grinned back his concern and kept his hands in his lap. "The thought never entered my mind."

"Don't hand me that shit." Corey motioned with his fingers. "Give me your phone."

Jack held out his cell. "You must have been surprised when you didn't find the idols in my room."

Corey grabbed it. "You were lucky, that's all."

"Meaning you or Amanda would have dumped me overboard if you'd gotten your sticky fingers on them?"

Corey ran his window down and tossed the phone. "You've been a pain in the ass from the start. Too bad I didn't get rid of you earlier."

"You're of course referring to the sinkhole."

Corey kept his eyes on the road. "So you've figured it all out, huh?"

Jack laughed. "Anyone could see what you two were up to. I do have to admit, Amanda is a nice touch. Most men would have been all weak-kneed by then."

"You weren't?"

"I played along. She was entertaining, if nothing else."

Amanda smacked him on the side of the head with the gun barrel. "That's more than I can say for you."

He rubbed his scalp and checked his fingers, surprised not to see blood. "Tell me Amanda, is that sinkhole where you disposed of the others?"

"I guess it doesn't matter now. You'll be dead in a few minutes. First off, you have no idea how much I wanted to laugh every time you called me Amanda. My name's Jessica. Amanda's my twin sister."

"Your twin?"

"My identical twin."

Suddenly, the truth fell into place. Jessica worked at Dream World Travel with her mother. He'd seen her that day he dropped in, not Amanda.

"Why the deception?"

"Amanda was the first born," she said with a haughty tone. "And, I'm afraid, a little too virtuous for me. When we were kids in school, we had fun switching places. All those games identical twins like to play in school. One time in particular, when we were seventeen, I made a date to go water skiing with a really cute guy, forgetting I already had a date for that night. I didn't want to miss out, so I went to the lake with him and had Amanda go out with my other date. No one ever knew. Not even Corey. Not until little Miss Goodie Two Shoes shot her mouth off to everybody. Daddy's Little Girl, that's what our father called her. What pet name did he have for me? None. Only for Amanda. The good twin while I was the bad seed."

She paused. And he had a feeling she wasn't finished. He furrowed his brow in a struggle to understand the depth of the anger that would cause her to want to set up her own twin to take a fall for murder.

After a moment, she added, "I'll never forget the day Amanda accidentally scratched our dad's new truck. We were ten when it happened. Corey was off with his friends. When our dad saw the damage to the paint, he turned and, without a word, slapped me right across my face. Hard. The bastard just assumed I did it. And Miss Priss stood there watching. Not a word in my defense. She told me afterward that she was too scared to say anything to him. The gutless bitch. I told her to go fuck herself. Harsh words for a ten-year-old, but our dad was a good teacher. And that wasn't the only time the drunken asshole slapped me around for something Amanda did. I'll never forgive him for all the times he hit me. Or my spineless sister for letting me be the scapegoat. I learned quickly, and have screwed her every chance I get. And if anything goes wrong, she'll be the one who's screwed, not me."

What a cold-hearted bitch.

He cringed at what she had said. "And you'd let your sister take a murder rap for you?"

"What do you think?"

Corey laughed. "Seems fair to me."

Jack looked at him. "Don't you live next door to her?"

Corey shrugged, his hands gripping the wheel. "So what? Amanda likes me. And I let her take care of my condo when I'm away."

Jessica added, "My brother and I were always in trouble. Blamed for every little thing. Never Amanda. He loves her about as much as I do."

"Meaning as far as the two of you are concerned, Goodie Two Shoes gets what she deserves?"

"Something like that."

Jack shook his head in disgust. "You've been at this a while. What about the other men you lured into your web and killed?"

"One, Corey threw overboard because the man became suspicious and threatened to notify the captain. Which we wouldn't have had to do if my idiot brother had rented a Jeep that was worth a shit."

"Screw you," Corey said. "I can't help it if the damned thing broke down. And don't forget, I'm the one who convinced that dumpy chick in security to falsify the ship's records to show that guy got off in Miami with everyone else."

"Only because you screwed that fat pig when no one else would."

"It worked, didn't it? How about some of the men you fucked?"

"Because it was necessary. You're forgetting, I'm the one who made our scheme work. Try to remember that."

"Yeah, like this one?"

"We both made mistakes." She softened her words. "But we're making it right, aren't we?"

"Yes, we are." Corey went back to concentrating on his driving.

"Since you're telling all," Jack said, turning his head to Jessica, "and since I'm a dead man, anyway. How many men are we talking about? Or were there some women, too?"

"You don't miss much."

"Well . . .?"

"Over a dozen. Eighteen, actually." She tapped the gun barrel against his sore spot. "Not counting you."

The confession Cherise needs.

Finally.

CHAPTER 72

Cherise maneuvered the Charger onto Interstate 95 southbound. Traffic moved in an orderly fashion for a Monday, but not fast enough. "Holy shit. I can't believe what we're hearing."

Keep them talking, Jack.

He was finishing what they started . . . and what she failed to get done.

"Eighteen people. Identical twins. The whole enchilada," Robert said.

She waited for a gap between the vehicles and moved into the center lane behind a fast-moving BMW.

"You hear him okay?" she asked. "You're recording, I hope?"

"Every word."

She glanced at the receiver in his hand. "How are we doing?"

"They're up ahead about a mile, approaching Highway 41."

"Where does that lead?"

He turned the screen toward her. "The Everglades."

"Alligators," she said.

He nodded. "And really big snakes."

She punched the gas and got around the Beamer. "Are we gaining on them?"

"You need to drive faster."

She roared around another car.

"I guess I was right about her."

"About who?"

"Amanda. The feeling I got after I met her at her condo. She's innocent."

"Maybe," Robert said. "I hope Lindsey isn't having a problem with the cops."

"I should have thought to leave her one of our monitors."

"Nothing we can do about that now," he said. "Get ready to exit. They're heading west on Highway 41."

"Try Lindsey on her cell."

He reached for his hip. "Dammit. My phone's clipped to my duffle back at the hotel. Where's yours?"

"In my purse." She tossed it to him.

He dug out her cell. "I can't believe this shit. Your battery's dead. We can forget about 911, as well."

"You're kidding me." She grabbed the phone from his hand, tried it, and tossed it into the tray on the center console. "We'll just have to hope the police department does their job."

* * *

Jack settled into his seat. All he could do at the moment was feed Cherise intel over the microphone in his watch. And hope she recorded every word.

Especially the confession.

"This road takes us into the Everglades, doesn't it?"

Corey grinned. "Ever heard of Alligator Alley?"

"Can't say I have," Jack lied.

"You have now."

"So that's your plan? You're going to feed me to the gators."

"I have a friend in the glades. Billie Cypress. A full-blooded Miccosukee Indian. He has an eighteen-foot boat with a bottom flat as a pancake, and a 175 horse Mercury outboard with a short shaft able to negotiate shallow water. He lets me use it whenever I want to."

"Without calling ahead?"

"Anytime."

"Be a shame if the motor's down for repairs."

"I wouldn't count on that if I were you."

"You don't mind if I do?"

"Won't do any good, but suit yourself."

"Tell me, Jessica. How do you feel about swimming with a bunch of gators?"

"She won't be swimming with them," Corey answered for her. "You will. I know a hole with two or three really big ones in it. I watched ol' Billie throw a guy in there once. The dumb-shit owed the Indian some money and refused to pay up. Gators took him right down."

Jack had seen sharks do the same thing.

Not pretty.

He joked, "I heard rubbing their bellies paralyzes them."

Corey laughed. "Go ahead and try."

CHAPTER 73

Jack could see the edge of the Everglades in the distance. A seemingly endless line of green prairie extending from north to south for as far as the eye could see.

The river of grass.

A million and a half acres of sawgrass marshes, cypress swamps, mangrove forests, and thousands of islands and tropical hardwood hammocks. Home to panthers, alligators, snakes, and over a million insects.

Most of which bite.

He thought about the tough scrapes he had been in and how they compared to this one. He'd always found a way out of them.

Many times with Robert's help.

Cherise had said it. *Let's hope your luck holds a little longer.*

So far, it had.

He asked, "What would it take to buy my way out of this?"

"More than you have," Jessica said.

"Don't be so sure."

"Okay," Corey said. "How does ten million sound?"

"It'll take a couple of days, but I'll go along with that."

"You pompous ass." Jessica tapped him on the side of the head with the gun barrel. "You don't have that kind of money. And even if you do, you can't expect us to believe you won't run to the cops the first chance you get."

"Did you ever stop to think the cops are probably after you right now?"

"Don't be so sure."

"But I *am* sure. I had friends with me at the terminal. They witnessed everything. By now every police officer, deputy sheriff, and game warden within a hundred miles is on the lookout for this Range Rover. Even if you kill me, how far do you think you'll get?"

"The desperate words of a doomed man," Corey said. "Who's to say we didn't just drop you off in town somewhere?"

Jack didn't want them to know they were being recorded.

He said, "If you think you can lie your way out of a murder rap, forget it. The authorities will shove a needle in your arm and inject enough shit into you to make your blood boil. The only chance you have is to pull over and let me out."

"Wrong," Corey said. "Once those gators get done with you there won't be any evidence to prove a thing against us."

Jack stifled a nervous laugh. *If they only knew.*

"Don't you watch TV?" he asked. "Ten different law enforcement agencies will crawl up your ass with a microscope and expose every dirty little secret. Jessica, they'll start on you, first. And they'll tell you in no uncertain terms, and in very graphic detail, how it will be for a beautiful woman like you in prison. Then they will go to work on you, pretty boy. When you go down, you'll be some MS-13 drug lord's queen within a week. And you'll never shit right again. I guarantee it will come down to making a deal, and one of you will crack."

"Don't listen to him," Jessica said. "And if he doesn't stop talking trash, I'm going to shoot him and put a stop to his big mouth."

"You fucking know she'll do it," Corey said. "So shut up. I don't want your brains splattered all over the interior of my car."

* * *

Cherise still couldn't see the silver Range Rover. She steered the Charger into oncoming traffic to pass a slow-moving, rusted-out Ford pickup and had to swerve back into her lane to avoid a head-on collision.

Dammit.

She asked, "Where are they?"

"Entering the glades," Robert said. "They've sped up."

"How far ahead of us are they?"

"Maybe a couple of miles. It's hard to be exact. But you need to speed up if you're going to catch them."

"Piece-of-shit truck won't get out of my way."

She honked her horn and tried to pass a second time. And was again forced back into the lane behind the slow-moving pickup.

"Do something, dammit."

"Hold on," she said. "I'm going for it."

He gripped the shoulder strap and pulled his seatbelt tight. "Just don't kill us in the process."

A car passed in the opposite direction and she floored it.

CHAPTER 74

Jack knew what Jessica was capable of. The woman could pull the trigger in a heartbeat, regardless of what her brother had said. No qualms or remorse. He'd take his chances when they stopped.

Within minutes, he began seeing billboards advertising airboat rides, Gator Park, Everglades Safari Park, and the Miccosukee Indian Village. The end of the line. And the boat ride into the swamp.

He was running out of time.

And options.

"Get ready to kiss your ass goodbye," Corey said.

Jack watched the man's lips narrow in a self-satisfied smile. He was sick of looking at that smug expression.

"Go fuck yourself, asshole."

That brought a mild chuckle from Corey.

Jack bit his tongue.

Grabbing for the revolver and making a mad dash for safety seemed a pitiful choice. The desperate act of a doomed man whose luck had run out.

And a horrifying way to spend the last seconds of his life.

One chance remained.

Cherise.

* * *

Cherise saw the Everglades loom ahead of them.

A single thought occupied her mind.

The same one that had been there from the moment Corey drove away with Jack in the seat next to him.

Save Jack.

She mashed the accelerator.

I can't let you die.

She focused on the ribbon of asphalt. "Where are they now?"

"Still a couple of miles ahead."

"Not for long."

A minute later, miles of grassy marshland appeared beside them. Ahead, trees lined both sides of the roadway. She maneuvered around a minivan and had to slow for another pickup while a couple of cars in the eastbound lane passed by. Once again, she accelerated around the vehicle and onto a stretch of open road.

"No cops around," she said. "Guess it's up to us."

"Lindsey must have had a difficult time relaying the information."

"All they could do is put out a broadcast on the Range Rover and keep their eyes open. Doesn't really matter now. Open the gun case."

He retrieved the bag from the floorboard and slid the zippers aside. Balancing the case on his lap, he said, "Where'd you get this, anyway? Didn't you fly here?"

"Checked it though on the flight, along with my luggage. I have a carry permit and a letter of authorization from The White House."

"We can be thankful for that. You want me to load this thing, right?"

She glanced at the pistol, spare magazines, and the six-inch stiletto. "The gun's not going to do us any good if you don't."

He picked up the semi-automatic and slid a magazine into the butt.

"It's a Glock 21," she said, ".45 caliber. Thirteen rounds in a double-stack magazine."

"That ought to do it."

He set the case flat on the floorboard at his feet and laid the Glock and two extra magazines on top of it. Raising the receiver in front of him, he said, "Looks like they're slowing down."

She scanned the swamp to the side of her. "Slowing or stopping?"

He turned a worried look at her. "They've stopped."

* * *

Jack tensed when Corey rolled to a stop behind a small house. Ancient, by the look of the place. The white paint on the wood siding had chipped and faded from years of neglect in the fierce Florida sun. Sparse, untrimmed grass and broken shell littered the slope leading to the water where a flat-bottomed boat sat tied to a wooden dock that looked as though it had been there since before Noah and the flood. Nobody appeared to be home.

The nearest house sat on the other side of a stand of trees a hundred yards away. An airboat bobbed next to a small dock. Somewhere beyond that lay the Miccosukee Indian Village. And all around him, a broad expanse of swamp wilderness where a man could die a hundred different ways.

His body never found.

Corey switched off the engine and Jack heard the automatic door locks disengage with a loud click.

His opportunity.

"Put your arm under you lap belt," Corey ordered. "Jessica, if he tries anything, shoot him dead. I don't give a shit about the interior of the car."

Jack heard the edginess in the man's voice and complied.

"Didn't your father ever teach you any manners?"

"The only thing that asshole taught us before he ran out on Mom, was to hate his fucking guts."

"Okay. So now what?" he asked.

Corey opened his door. "Sit there and don't move."

Jack scowled. "Can't very well do much else."

"I'm making sure of that." Corey grasped the shoulder strap where it crossed Jack's chest, and pulled the lap belt even tighter. "Hand me the gun, Jessica."

Jack cringed, but tried not to let his grimace show as the polyester webbing bit into his flesh until it felt as though his bones would snap. Unable to move, he watched Jessica hand her brother the revolver. A Smith and Wesson, .38 or .357 caliber. Four-inch barrel. He could see the hollow-point bullets in the cylinder holes when Corey pointed the gun at him.

Six shots.

That's all he had.

"Jessica," Corey said. "Reach up and grab his shoulder harness. When I let go of it, pull on it hard. And Jack, if you move, I'll kill you."

Jack knew he'd never get his arms out from under the webbing fast enough to make a grab for the gun. Even if he thought he could get his hands on the revolver and somehow overpower the bigger and stronger man.

In a matter of seconds, his plan had been dashed.

A feeling of helplessness threatened to drag him down.

But he didn't let it get the best of him.

Cherise was out there. So were the cops.

He still had a chance.

"Where's your friend Billie?" He glanced at the house. "Won't he have something to say about what you're doing?"

"Not home. And he couldn't care less what I do." Corey backed out of the Range Rover, gun hand extended, and aimed the revolver. Jack tensed at the thought of getting a bullet in the skull.

"You sure?" he asked.

"Shut up." Corey kept the barrel trained. "Jessica, you can get out. Take the idols with you. Jack, stay where you are."

She opened her door. "I'll get some rope or wire or something to tie him up with."

The moment she released her grip on the shoulder strap, the seatbelt loosened across his chest and lap. He breathed with relief when circulation returned to his arms. The least of his worries.

He peered into the tangle of mangrove swamp.

The end of the line for him.

"Be smart," he said, looking at Corey. "There's still time for you and Jessica to walk away from this."

"Talk all you want, but you're wasting your breath." Corey steadied the gun in his hand. "Won't change a thing. You're a dead man."

Jack had to stall.

And think.

He said, "I wouldn't be so sure."

Corey cocked the hammer on the Smith. "Don't make me laugh. Now, nice and slow, crawl across the console head-first. I don't care how you do it. Slither like a snake if you have to, but keep your hands out in front of you. Then slide to the ground on your belly, face in the dirt."

Jack knew he was on borrowed time and shouldn't push his luck, but couldn't help himself.

"I assure you, I'll have the last laugh."

"Stop stalling and move."

Jack knew he couldn't argue with a cocked gun.

He unbuckled his seatbelt and worked his way out the driver's side and onto the ground. The oppressiveness of the swamp seemed to press him deeper into the soil with a bad smell to it. The air, too. Slimy muck and rotting organic matter.

"This is all I could find," he heard Jessica say.

"Good enough." Her brother sounded anxious. "Get your hands behind you, Jack. And keep them there."

He complied, but took his time.

His only ally at the moment.

"Now get up," Corey said, when she had him tied. "And walk to the boat."

Jack worked his legs under him and rose to his feet. "Don't do this. Drive away from here while you still can."

Corey extended his arms, both hands gripping the butt of the Smith, the muzzle aimed for a headshot. Jack didn't flinch. The expression on Corey's face hardened. The Ken-doll look gone.

"Move it," he said. "Now."

Jack weighed the odds. He didn't have a choice.

"You're a big man with a gun," he said, and started walking.

"Without it, too." Corey fell in step.

Jack could hear the soles of the man's shoes crunch the broken shell. Close, but not carelessly close. The man obviously knew his business.

Where's the cavalry?

CHAPTER 75

Cherise slowed behind a car with Alabama plates, and accelerated around it.

"Where is he?"

"Up ahead on the right." Robert motioned with his head. "On the other side of the canal."

She saw the access road. A narrow one-lane strip of asphalt.

The only way in.

"Hold on," she said.

She slowed and put the Charger into a four-wheel drift through the turn. Gaining control, she studied the white house to the left of them. "Is that it?"

A second passed.

Two.

"There." He jabbed a finger at the windshield. "I can just make out the Range Rover."

"Movement?" She couldn't see any from her seat.

"None."

"Grab the gun."

He had the Glock in his hand, the command unnecessary. Picking up the stiletto, he asked, "What about this pig-sticker?"

"Give it to me."

He did, and she slid the sheath beneath her thigh. An easy grab on the way out of the car.

"Here we go," she said.

She pulled into the dirt drive and skidded to a stop on the crushed shell.

Dammit.

Twenty yards from shore, Corey throttled the boat deeper into the swamp while Jessica held the revolver on Jack.

"What do we do now?" he asked.

She spied an airboat sitting at a dock a hundred yards away and pointed at it. "We borrow that."

"As in, ask permission?"

"As in, take."

She backed out of the drive and raced down the road. Taking no notice of anyone. Or caring.

He asked, "Can you drive that thing?"

"Maybe. Can you?"

"I can fly a plane. Yeah, I think so. You do the shooting and I'll operate the boat."

"Let's go." She slammed on the brakes

* * *

Lying belly down on the flat deck at the bow of the boat, Jack had a view of the murky water and the moss-dappled trees and vines. It seemed there was no solid ground in a mangrove swamp, only an impenetrable barrier of snarled roots and muck.

He had placed most of his hope in Cherise arriving in time to put an end to this madness. That hadn't happened. Getting his hands and feet free and taking his chances with the alligators and snakes seemed to be the only hope he had left.

But what then?

Even if he survived, which way would he go?

And how would he get there?

No one walks through a mangrove forest.

Corey didn't spare the throttle.

Jack heard the roar of the outboard. Felt the spray on his skin. Having his face close to the water made it feel like they were skimming along at a hundred miles per hour. Probably closer to twenty or thirty. Even so, had the surface been wind-whipped to a chop, he would have been bounced to death.

Corey shouted something that got lost in the wind and the sustained drone of the motor.

Jack couldn't imagine anything the man had to say would be good.

He continued to work on his bindings. The rope Jessica had used wouldn't break. But the cord stretched a little more with each flex of his wrist, each tug of his ankle. A minute, perhaps two or three, and he would be able to free himself.

Providing he didn't get a bullet in the back for his efforts.

A gamble, but he had to try.

* * *

Cherise ran straight for the airboat. No stopping to ask permission. The one thought in mind.

Save Jack.

She held the Glock in her right hand and used her left to untie the mooring lines while Robert climbed into the cockpit. Jack's chance for survival hinged on being able to start the engine.

To her surprise, the airboat roared to life.

Forget trying to talk.

She climbed onto a seat, strapped herself in, and motioned her hand toward the neighboring house where they had seen Corey and his sister speed away in the boat with Jack on board.

Robert eased the airboat around the end of the dock and raced into the mangrove forest.

She pointed at the channel Jack disappeared into. In the labyrinth of waterways, the GPS did them little good. The best choice they had was to stick to the passages where the water had been noticeably disturbed when the big outboard churned a trail.

And catch up to the other boat as quickly as possible.

Or risk losing them.

Robert nosed the airboat into the gap in the mangroves and increased speed. The wind whipped her hair and watered her eyes causing her to squint. Overhead, a canopy of limbs turned the passage into a forest tunnel. Cursing herself for leaving her sunglasses wedged above the sun visor of the Charger, she turned and waved him forward as though he needed encouragement.

He didn't.

The airboat skimmed the surface, sending a ripple of waves into the rubbery roots.

She thought she caught a glimpse of the boat.

Then saw nothing.

* * *

Jack turned his head and twisted onto his shoulder to peer into the sky behind them. But saw only a leafy tree-limb canopy. He could have sworn he heard a high-pitched roar different from that of the four-stroke Mercury. Unmistakable. A sound that compared to a single-engine airplane bearing down on him.

One he had heard many times when flying with Robert in his floatplane.

A prop biting the air.

Corey must have heard it also, because he shoved the throttle lever forward to gain speed.

Too fast at first.

In the next turn, the big outboard provided more power than the antiquated flat-bottomed hull could handle in the narrow alley between the mangroves. The port side skidded into a mass of exposed roots sending down a snowstorm of leaves and organic debris from above.

A snake hit the water next to them and swam away.

A python. A small one.

Corey eased off on the power.

But only as long as it took to gain control of the craft.

Jack, having regained his balance after the collision, twisted his body and saw a tight-faced Corey stooped over the steering wheel with his hand on the throttle, working the lever forward and backward in an obvious attempt to weave through the labyrinth at the fastest speed possible. Jessica appeared equally worried. She kept looking behind her while at the same time trying to keep the revolver aimed at him.

The first sign that brother and sister were on the edge of losing control.

Cherise.

It had to be.

CHAPTER 76

Cherise saw the boat in the waterway ahead. Sure of it, this time.

She didn't bother pointing.

The increase in the high-pitched roar of the engine indicated Robert had added power, intent on catching up to the fleeing boat.

Nothing would happen to Jack.

Corey and his sister were not getting away.

The gap narrowed.

With Robert's deft touch on the controls, the airboat skimmed the surface of the water, perfectly suited for the narrow passage. Cherise figured, at this rate, they would catch the other boat in the next turn or two.

When they did, what then?

She had no plan, other than saving Jack.

A matter of playing the deadly game by ear as they went.

Her eyes continued to tear from the wind in her face. More so now that Robert pushed the machine to its limits.

They raced through a series of turns and gained some water.

By now Jack had to know they were behind him.

She swiped her eyes dry with her fingertips and tightened her grip on the Glock, unsure if she would have the clear shot she needed.

A decision she hated having to make.

If she did get a chance to shoot without endangering Jack, she had to make the shot count.

She might not get a second opportunity.

* * *

Jack caught sight of the airboat coming out of a turn, and immediately recognized Cherise and Robert. Her wig and sunglasses gone.

The charade over.

Ahead of him, the lane between the trees opened into a sawgrass marsh.

He would make his move then.

Again, he went to work stretching his bindings. Ankles and wrists. Until he could almost slide his hands free. One good tug would do it.

His ankles would come next.

After he swam clear of the boat.

He had no way of knowing the depth of the marsh. But he wanted to be prepared to tread water when he rolled over the side. At the very least, he needed to be able to claw and pull himself away from the spinning prop.

He waited and watched.

Corey jammed the throttle lever forward, sending them racing into the flooded sawgrass prairie. Speed no longer appeared to be an issue.

Not at the moment, anyway.

With the dense wall of mangroves and the leafy canopy behind them, Jack scooted to the side of the boat, ready to roll over the side.

Corey juked the flat-bottomed hull through a serpentine of grassy channels. Robert kept up, maneuvering to within thirty yards. Cherise sat poised to shoot. That she had armed herself, came as no surprise.

Now or never.

Jack made his move.

Not the quick roll over the side he intended.

Each time he made a move in one direction, the boat swerved and centrifugal force rolled him in the opposite direction.

He concentrated on his timing and glimpsed Jessica facing

aft, the revolver no longer pointed at him. The greater threat now coming from behind.

His chance.

Only Cherise made the decision for him. A shot from her semi-automatic tore through the cowling on the outboard. A second bullet must have severed the steering cable because the boat veered, first one way then the other.

Corey fought a steering wheel that no longer worked.

Jessica swayed and tumbled over the side.

Jack pulled his hands and feet free of the rope and gripped the narrow gunnel, ready to take his chances in the marsh.

The next instant, the side of the hull pushed a wake ahead of it, caught the water, and flipped.

A violent motion that tossed him airborne a second before he splashed down ten feet from Corey.

They came up facing each other.

Jack swiped the muck from his eyes while the big man opposite him did the same.

Off to the side, fifteen feet or so, the boat drifted in the river of grass half submerged, keel up, the prop dead in the air.

His mind began to clear, and he searched out the airboat that had fallen quiet. Robert had beached the nose on a gentle rise fifty yards away and was climbing down from his seat. Cherise pounded after Jessica who made a desperate run for it on a patch of dry land. A distant vacillating, high-pitched buzz signaled the presence of airboats racing through the Everglades.

Tours, perhaps.

A mile or more away. Not here.

He and his friends were on their own.

And he had Corey to deal with.

CHAPTER 77

Jack faced the big man wading toward him in grassy, thigh-deep water. Corey's ape-like arms hung at his sides, moving forward and backward with each stride, fingers curled, his sun-bleached brown hair streaked black with muck. The man looked every bit like a swamp monster.

"It's over, Corey," he said.

"Wrong, buddy boy."

Jack could see anger flare in the man's eyes.

He took a step sideways and the crust under his foot broke, letting him sink into muck halfway to his knee. He followed up with the opposite foot and the same thing happened. Corey had to be having similar difficulty.

They lunged at each other.

Jack ducked under a round-house right and hammered an ineffective uppercut to a gut as hard as a frozen side of beef.

He caught a left fist on the back of the head that drove him into the murky water.

It felt like his skull had split.

He managed an uppercut to the ape's groin. A solid punch that brought a howling scream from the big man, his eyes pinched against the pain. A wide strip of tan fabric, probably heavy canvas, came loose from around Corey's waist when he staggered back a step.

Jack recognized the money belt for what it was.

He shook feeling back into his hand and grabbed the trailing end as it began to sink. Corey blindly groped the water to the front and sides of him.

Jack held the belt up like a trophy fish. "Looking for this?"

Corey groaned, his left hand holding his crotch. "I'm going to kill you."

Jack seized the moment. He tossed the money aside and drove his shoulder into the guy's chest, propelling the stronger man onto his back.

Everything happened in a blur.

Jack landed on Corey and rolled off. Gaining his feet, he straightened with his fists raised. Ready to finish the fight. Through a haze of water clouding his eyes, he saw the blades of grass part ten yards to his right.

An alligator, he thought at first. But the creature swimming toward them sailed too smoothly through the weeds. A slithering, undulating body. The head, large as a dog's, held high out of the water, tongue flicking, searching.

A giant snake.

One of the Burmese pythons he'd heard about. Its body broader than his thigh and twenty feet long.

Corey screeched. He had managed to get onto his hands and knees, but no farther. He and the snake were eye to eye.

Jack watched the big man's expression go slack, his face drained of color. His body frozen in place as though unable to move. Two feet away, the serpent's tongue flicked, searching for body heat.

Jack knew he couldn't stop the inevitable.

Not that he wanted to.

The snake struck with split-second speed and sunk its fangs into Corey's thick neck. In a heartbeat, the length of reptile wound around him—a writhing, coiling mass that churned the water and silenced the scream that never had a chance to escape the man's open mouth.

Jack had no desire to stick around. He grabbed the money belt and mucked his way toward Robert and the airboat as fast as possible, leaving the snake to its feast. He got no more than a couple of steps when he heard a gunshot.

The fight wasn't over.

He looked and saw Cherise and Jessica engaged in a struggle on the ground. Cherise held on to Jessica's wrists, the barrel of the revolver pointed in the air. In the next instant, Cherise hammered an elbow into the woman's face.

A blow that he figured would do the trick. But Jessica managed to squeeze off another wild shot.

Cherise put an end to the fight with a punch to Jessica's throat.

He wondered why Cherise hadn't shot her. Too easy, perhaps. Maybe she wanted the pleasure of personally kicking the woman's ass. He even imagined a bit of female jealousy could be involved. Getting even. He liked thinking that was the case.

The thrashing in the water behind him stopped.

He knew what that meant.

He turned and saw the enormous python dragging the crushed body onto a mound of dry land where the reptile would begin to swallow him whole.

Oddly enough, he felt a tinge of regret that the man had suffered such a horrible death. But the feeling was fleeting when he recalled Corey and his sister having trussed him up like a Christmas goose and bringing him into the swamp at gunpoint with the intention of tossing him into a watery hole full of hungry alligators.

Better him than me.

He heard Robert yell his name.

Surely his long-time buddy could see he was okay.

He took one more look at the capsized boat, turned, and saw the white gift bag submerged a few feet away from where he stood. He scooped up the sodden mess, cradled it under his arm, and sloshed off in the direction of his friends.

* * *

Cherise jerked Jessica up by her muddy hair, not caring if she ripped some out in the process.

"Let me go," Jessica croaked, her hands gripping Cherise's arm. "You win."

"Damn right I win." She tightened her grip on the woman's scalp to add emphasis. "Try anything else and I'll break your arm."

"Okay. Okay. I told you. I give up."

"Fuck giving up." Cherise shoved the woman toward the airboat, and warmed when she saw Jack walking toward them. "You tried to kill my friend. You're lucky I didn't put a bullet in you."

"I got her gun," Robert said.

"Corey made me help him." Jessica's voice was gravelly. "All of this . . . it's his idea. He killed those men. Not me."

Cherise looked the woman up and down as she stumbled toward the water. Body caked with mud. Once blonde hair now stringy and stained black with muck. A whimpering pathetic mockery of her former self.

"And Sam King, the man you and your brother pushed overboard a few weeks ago, you had nothing to do with that?"

Jessica stumbled and fell to her hands and knees. She struggled to her feet and glared at Cherise. "How do you know about him?"

"You dumb, fucking, psycho bitch. Do you think we're all here by accident? Sam King was my friend's father. This whole romance on the high seas bit these past few days was a setup. Only, you and your brother had to get cute."

Jessica stared toward the overturned boat as though suddenly concerned about Corey. Her gaze appeared to fix on Jack.

Cherise enjoyed watching shock and reality widen the woman's eyes.

"What . . . ? Where . . . ?" Jessica turned her attention back on Cherise. Anger flashed in her expression. "My brother. You killed him."

Cherise smiled. "I suspect Jack had something to do with that."

CHAPTER 78

Late that evening, Jack sat on the steps of the police station, his elbows on his knees. The sun had set on the Gulf side of the peninsula, bathing the sky in front of him in shades of crimson.

He had told a not-so-simple story, and retold it a dozen times. He tolerated being called stupid and thanked the detectives when they let him go.

There are some things you admit to, he silently told himself. *And some you don't.*

He felt he'd chosen correctly.

Cherise sat down beside him, a cold pack on the knuckles of her right hand.

"Hurt much?" he asked.

She turned a smile on him and gave a slight shake of her head.

He knew better.

She said, "I guess you heard that Park Rangers killed the snake and recovered Corey's body."

He huffed. "Poor snake."

"Did the detectives give you a hard time?"

"Hard enough," he admitted. "You?"

"They tried. Until their captain got a call from Admiral Casey. Then they backed off."

"The admiral called?"

"I called him first. Figured we could use some backup."

He flashed on his prior dealings with the admiral. "That's some backup."

"I heard the detectives talking among themselves. Apparently, Jessica is singing like a canary."

"Blaming everything on Corey, I suppose."

"Most likely. Did you notice they hauled in Amanda and their mother? Amanda sure didn't look happy when she saw me."

"Probably about as happy as their mother was when I waved to her."

"Not our problem."

"Unless this goes to court."

"Which is doubtful," she said. "By the way, how's *your* hand?"

He flexed his fingers. "I'll live. But I sure could use a shower. Where are Robert and Lindsey?"

"He's in the restroom. Washing up, I imagine. Linds is waiting for him."

"She know he's married?"

"You're worried. Don't be. They've become good friends, but she swears nothing has happened and nothing will."

"I'm glad to hear that. She's lucky to have you in her corner."

"You were in that corner as well."

"Because you asked me." He peered into Cherise's dark eyes. The woman he couldn't imagine not seeing again. "Out there, I—"

She pressed two fingers to his lips, silencing him. "I know. Me, too."

And she kissed him.

* * *

Later that night, when they sat around a table in the restaurant at the Intercontinental Hotel, Jack quietly nursed his Knob Creek over ice while the others sipped their drinks and chatted in a festive mood.

"Why so quiet, Jack?" Robert sat looking at him from across the table. "You're acting like you had a bad day or something."

"I'm fine." He spotted their server approaching with a bottle of Dom Perignon. "Fantastic, actually."

The server presented the champagne to Jack and he nodded

approval.

"What's this about?" asked Cherise. "When did you order that?"

"On the way in." Jack grinned, and looked at his friends. "I thought we deserved a celebratory toast."

She said, "Surely that's not the bottle I—"

He winked at her. "Fresh from the hotel wine cellar. Chilled to perfection. Our bottle is waiting for us in an ice bucket up in the room."

"I'm surprised it survived the cruise."

"A special bottle like that?" He shook his head. "I wasn't about to let anything happen to it."

Robert chuckled. "It's a good thing we were able to rescue your bag from the port or some baggage agent would be drinking it by now."

"Seriously," Lindsey said. She scanned the group, her gaze settling on Jack. "I can't thank you guys enough for all you've done. And Jack, words aren't enough to express my gratitude for what *you* went through."

"One thing is for sure," Robert added. "That snake came close to having him for its lunch."

"He did," Jack agreed. "But he chose Corey, instead."

"That's something worth toasting to," Cherise said.

Jack raised his glass. "To a great big snake and a whole lot of luck."

"And to two beautiful women," Robert added.

"Absolutely," Jack said.

They clinked glasses.

Robert said, "I suppose we ought to be thankful we weren't arrested for antiquities smuggling."

"Speaking of antiquities." Jack searched each of his friends' faces for a hint of their thoughts. "What should we do with them?"

They exchanged looks.

Cherise said, "Are you referring to those ugly gold idols the cops are searching for out there in the swamp?"

"It's a shame they flew overboard when the boat flipped," Robert added.

"Sure is," Jack said. "So what do you think?"

Robert said, "I'll let you and Cherise decide."

Jack looked at Lindsey, the remaining vote.

She shrugged. "I couldn't care less what happens to those things."

Jack turned to Cherise. "This is your caper. I'll leave it up to you."

She asked, "Why me?"

Jack sipped his champagne and returned his flute to the table. "Because you have the connections. And because I trust you to do what's right. *Ho'oponopono*. We can't forget that."

Lindsey's knitted brow morphed her stoic expression into one of confusion. "What does *Ho'oponopono* mean?"

"It's Hawaiian. Doing what's right. Correctness. Or simply *Pono*. Incidentally, the name I gave my old boat."

"Correctness. Now that's something the world could use more of."

He lifted his glass in honor of his friends. "Speaking of *Ho'oponopono*, I'd like to thank everyone for not telling the police that I recovered the idols or the money belt after that boat flipped. They'd have seized both for evidence. And likely as not, that's the last I'd have seen of my ninety thousand."

"Here, here." Robert raised his glass. "Unfortunately, you're still out ten grand."

"Perhaps I can do something about that," Cherise said.

And they clinked glasses one more time.

CHAPTER 79

The following morning, Jack sat next to Cherise at a table in the Blue Water Café overlooking the pool. Robert and Lindsey sat across from them. Their server had removed the breakfast dishes and left them to finish their coffee.

"Place is starting to fill up," he said.

"The breakfast crowd getting a jump on the day," Robert answered.

"Speaking of jumping, we should get on the road."

Cherise said, "I think you made a good choice driving down rather than flying."

Jack thought about the Cooper they had left at the airport in Key West. "It'll be relaxing, providing Robert didn't rent us a sub-compact."

"Got a yellow Camaro convertible waiting for us out front," Robert said. "I thought you looked a little peaked, like you could use some sun on your face."

Jack ignored the comment and turned to Cherise. "Wish you were coming with me. I've kind of gotten used to having you around."

"You're sweet, Jack. But Lindsey and I are flying to New York this afternoon. She'll be flying on to D.C. in the morning. She has work to get back to and I have important business to take care of in the City."

"Yeah . . . well . . . I guess we'll say our goodbyes then." He slid back his chair, continuing to look at her. She held his gaze as though she felt the same sense of loss. One night together, alone in each other's arms with no interruptions, hadn't been enough.

He asked, "You ready, Robert?"

They all stood, and Jack peered into Cherise's eyes. "Walk me out?"

She smiled. "Of course."

They were a quiet group during their stroll to the porte-cochère. The parking attendant brought the rental up and loaded their bags into the trunk. Jack tipped the guy a twenty and he and Robert climbed in.

Cherise leaned on the driver's door and smiled. "Drive careful, sailor."

"Piece of cake," he said.

She leaned in and kissed him.

* * *

Four hours later, Jack parked the Camaro at the Pier House. A cruise ship sat in port. Tourists flocked in Mallory Square. Normally he wouldn't have given the boat or the crowd of people a second thought. That had changed, and he supposed it would be some time before he could look at either and not think about the past few days.

A brush with death has a way of doing that.

Or so he thought.

"I'm ready for a beer," he said. "Let's load the bags in the dinghy and take them out to the boat."

"We're out of beer."

"I'm sure Sloppy Joe's has plenty."

"Some lunch, too," Robert said.

They motored out to the *Adeona* and carried their bags aboard. Below decks she was hot and stale and damp. Jack fired up the generator, turned on the air conditioner, and set the thermostat to sixty-five.

He stood underneath the vents on the ceiling assembly and let the cold breeze hit his face. The air would have to run a while.

Robert stepped into the salon and asked, "Are you going to stand there all day or are we going?"

"Feels pretty good to me right here."

"Well, I'm hungry."

"And let's not forget thirsty," Jack added. "We'll let the air run while we're having lunch. Give her a chance to cool down and dry out a little."

"She'll need to if you expect me to sleep aboard tonight."

"Quit bellyaching and let's go."

They motored the dinghy back to the Pier House and tied her to the wharf. The Camaro sat where they had left it. But they had walked to Sloppy Joe's enough times that Jack thought it ridiculous to drive the two blocks, even in the hottest part of the day.

"Let's walk," he said.

"I'm with you."

CHAPTER 80

Jack and Robert stepped inside Sloppy Joe's and scanned the crowd.

"Packed," Robert said.

"About the same as it was the day Officer Zackary and his partner kicked us out of the place."

"At least no one's fighting."

Jack clapped Robert on the back. "There're two places at the counter. And we're in luck. Vicky's tending bar."

"Those are the same stools we sat on before," Robert pointed out. "Do you think she saved them for us?"

"Without a doubt."

They stepped to the bar with smiles on their faces.

Vicky swiped a damp towel across the counter, and said, "You're back. I thought you had taken off for good."

Jack said, "You know what they say about a bad penny, or two pennies in this case."

She chuckled. "You made my day. What can I get you?"

"A beer and something deep fried and tasty."

He and Robert slid onto the stools and ordered pints of Island Ale. She stepped away, and Jack pointed at a framed photo on the wall below the menu. "This year's Hemingway lookalike."

"Looks just like him," Robert said. "I forgot the Hemingway Days celebration was last week. Almost sorry we missed the party."

"I'm afraid we had a more pressing engagement."

"Didn't we, though."

Vicky set their beers in front of them, a question showing in her expression. "Did you guys ever find those documents you were looking for?"

Jack shook his head. "We kind of got sidetracked."

"There's still time," she said.

Jack noticed his friend staring into his beer. "What's the long face about? You were the one who couldn't wait to get something to eat."

"I'm sorry. It's that I can't help thinking how much I enjoyed spending time with Lindsey. She's really a nice person. That deep down sincere kind of nice where you know it's genuine. I'm glad she got to bring closure to her father's death."

"You two did get awfully friendly."

"I could tell you were concerned." Robert smiled into his glass. "I felt good just being around her."

"What you do is your business. Far be it from me to preach morality."

"But you cared. And I appreciate that. We both love Kazuko—have for a long time—and that's a fact."

"Maybe so." Jack sat thinking, *what if*? Not about Kazuko. About Cherise. After a few long seconds, he gulped down a couple of swallows and said, "Let's eat. Then I need to get busy and make arrangements to get the *Adeona* home. It's high time you and I were out of here."

For the next hour, they chatted, ate crab cake sandwiches, and drank beer. And during that time, Jack kept glancing up at the marlin on the wall. He read and reread the engraving on the brass plaque: *In Memory of Papa.*

He raised his glass to his lips for a sip and squinted at the tiny engraving below the dedication: *Rafael Fuentes, 1963.*

The first time he had taken particular notice of it.

On the edge of his memory, something Corey said to him materialized out of a fog.

He leaned close to Robert and asked, "Remember what Corey said about the mounted roosterfish?"

"Had something to do with smuggling in a gold relic, didn't it?"

"That's right. Concealed it inside the fish."

"I assume you're going somewhere with this?"

"Take a look at that marlin on the wall. And check out the name at the bottom of that brass plaque."

Robert squinted the same way Jack had to. "You're not thinking—"

"I am," Jack said. "Think about what Rafael wrote in the note concealed behind that photograph I knocked off the wall."

Again, Robert stared into his beer. Only this time Jack knew what his friend was thinking.

"I can picture the note in my mind," Robert said.

"And what did he write?"

"He said it's only right that the photo belongs in the bar Hemingway spent so much time in."

"And the last line?"

Robert peered up at the marlin. Jack saw resolve in his friend's eyes.

As does so much more.

CHAPTER 81

That evening, back aboard the *Adeona*, Jack sipped a Red Stripe and watched the sun sink into the Gulf. Robert sat in a deck chair a few feet away, talking to Kazuko on the phone. His bottle of beer sat next to him on the deck.

Jack stepped to the railing and scanned the broad expanse of ocean. He listened to the music from town and saw a fish swirl the surface of the water twenty feet away from the boat. He felt the air under the topside awning stir with a breeze blowing inland, bringing with it a strong scent of the sea. He embraced a sky filled with an artist's palette of color.

Another glorious Key West sunset.

His favorite time of day. That and sunrise.

Here, or on Oahu, or on the open ocean.

One signals the end of what was; the other, a fresh beginning.

Each new day, the first day of the rest of his life. Free of mistakes. Only those that have been made and those that are yet to be made.

Each cycle the same.

A time of reflection.

This sunset was no different. And he'd had a long drive and all afternoon to reflect on it.

To think about Cherise and validate the decision he had already made.

He was tired of shallow women, superficial love affairs, and meaningless deaths. His own damned empty life included.

Robert and Kazuko were every bit as much his family as his brother in California. And it saddened him to know he had readily come to rely on them to enrich his salty existence with what he didn't have on his own.

Some things in a person's life need changing. The status quo no longer good enough.

The trick, he realized, is being able to recognize that special moment when it comes.

And embracing it, even with no guarantees.

The way he was now.

He heard Robert say goodbye to Kazuko and end the call. With his back to his friend, he asked, "All good on the home front?"

Robert joined him at the rail and stood at his side, beer in hand. "She misses me."

"That's a good thing, I think."

"I miss her, too."

"Love does that."

"Speaking of love, do you feel like you've maneuvered yourself into a corner with Cherise?"

"Not at all. And the more I think about it, the better I like it."

"Welcome to the club. Have you figured out how we're going to get Hemingway's manuscript out of that marlin?"

"I've come to a conclusion. Who are we to question Rafael Fuentes' motive?"

"Meaning?"

"The man was right. Those manuscript notes belong here."

"So we leave them where they are?"

"That's what I'm saying."

"And never know if we guessed correctly or not?"

Jack turned to his long-time friend and hoisted his bottle. "Some questions are better left unanswered."

EPILOGUE

On a warm Oahu Wednesday afternoon in late October, Jack stood next to Robert and Kazuko on the dock at their home on Kaneohe Bay. Freshly painted and renamed *Pono II*, the *Adeona* tugged at her mooring lines, the hull no longer bearing the name the boat had been christened with.

"She's beautiful," Robert said. "Appears her freighter ride across the Pacific didn't do her any harm."

"Not a bit. Course the paint job helps." Jack pointed at the large scrawling green letters with gold shadow. "Personally, I think the name does her justice."

Robert clapped him on the back. "Ol' buddy, I do believe you're right."

Jack continued to admire his boat. Imagining the modifications he had in mind to convert it into a floating lab. The name change had only been the beginning.

He asked, "Think Cherise will like it?"

"Of course. And that reminds me." Robert dug an envelope from his pocket and held it out. "I almost forgot to give you this. The letter arrived yesterday when you were gone. It's from her. Too bad she isn't here to take part in this."

Jack took the sealed envelope and looked at it.

He'd read it later.

"She wanted to join us," he said. "But she's off on some supersecret assignment she couldn't talk about."

"And she didn't invite you to join her?"

Jack laughed. "Not this time. Did I tell you I received a reply from Salvatore Vincente? Ms. Faggini wants us to keep the novella, but she would like to have the journal. I'll send it to her, of course."

"And the book?"

"That's going in my collection."

Kazuko joined them. "What's going in your collection?"

"The book I showed you. Ms. Faggini wants me to keep it."

"That's extremely nice of her." Concern pinched her brow. "You're sure Kimo and his uncle are going to make it over?"

"They'll make it," Jack assured her. "Our friend was extremely pleased I asked Keoni to perform the blessing. And thankful when I told him I'd arrange to have them flown over."

"I hope so. The luau is all planned."

He hugged her. "Relax, you've done a wonderful job putting everything together."

The distinctive *wop, wop, wop* drew their eyes skyward. The black dot, like a single gnat bearing down on them, approached from the south.

Jack eased away from her and pointed. "Perfect timing."

They followed the dock back to the slope of grass leading up to the house, the sound growing louder overhead.

Rebel abandoned her patch of shade beneath the flowering ginger plants and trotted over to join them. Jack bent and gave the Basset's head and ears a pat for luck, before watching the helicopter land on the sprawling expanse of lawn.

The rear door of the cabin opened and Jack spotted his old friend. He ducked under the spinning blades and stepped to the chopper to greet him.

Kimo climbed out, a little grayer on top, a few more wrinkles around the eyes. His smile broad as ever.

They clasped hands.

"How's Maui?" Jack asked.

"Rainy. Nice here, though."

"That's the islands for you. I trust Keoni is feeling well?"

Kimo turned and held the cabin door open. "See for yourself."

Jack stood back, giving Kimo's uncle ample room to step out onto the grass. It appeared the priest had dressed for the occasion.

The elderly *kahuna* wore a multi-colored *tapa*-cloth *kihei* slung over his left shoulder and tied at the right side of his waist. And a bright red sash. A lei of feathers—most of them red, a few yellow—crowned his head. The Hawaiian had aged dramatically since they'd last seen each other, but not so much that Jack didn't recognize Keoni immediately.

The people of Maui and other islands held the *kahuna* in high regard. Jack shared the native people's sentiment. So did Robert and Kazuko.

He grasped Keoni's hand, leaned close and touched foreheads in the ancient custom of the islands. "It's good to see you, my friend. Thank you for coming."

Keoni tightened his grip. "I'm happy you asked me."

They stepped clear of the blades, and Robert and Kazuko joined in the greeting. Smiles were exchanged. As were hugs and handshakes. Kazuko gave Kimo and Keoni a kiss on the cheek. And at last, they wandered onto the dock, Keoni in the lead.

Jack paused and glanced around, half expecting to see Cherise running to catch up to them. Of course, she was nowhere to be seen.

He swallowed his disappointment.

At least he had the letter.

Stealing a moment longer, he tore open the flap on the envelope and removed the contents. A cashier's check and a two-page handwritten note. He scanned enough of the first page to learn she had sold two of the idols to a dealer in New York and divided the money accordingly to cover everyone's out-of-pocket expenses, with an extra ten grand to him. The third idol, she turned over to Pacal Balam, the professor of Central American History she met at the museum.

Professor Balam promised her the artifact would be returned to the Mayan people.

A noble gesture.

The amount of the check would replenish the remaining ten thousand of the money he had withdrawn from his bank account. The remainder would come close to covering the cost of having the

Adeona shipped to Honolulu.

He refolded the note and returned it and the check to the envelope.

You'll get no complaint from me.

Robert called his name and waved for him to join them. Kimo had his arms raised, ready to begin the blessing.

He tucked the envelope into his pocket and walked toward his friends.

Some letters are meant to be read over a drink at sunset.

* * *

From the side of the road a hundred yards away, Cherise gazed over the roof of the dark blue sedan at the helicopter perched on the grass. She'd seen Jack duck under the spinning rotors and greet the Hawaiian's he'd told her would be performing the blessing. Robert and Kazuko were there, too. And she'd watched them all walk onto the dock. Except Jack. He'd paused and read a letter he pulled from an envelope. Possibly the one she'd sent.

It comforted her to think so.

She wished she could hear her friends' voices, and peer into Jack's beguiling blue eyes. But drew a degree of comfort being able to see them admire his boat.

She would have been there as well, had it been possible for her to join them.

Pono II . . . to put things right.

Perfect.

"I'm sorry we can't stay here longer, Ms. Venetta," the driver of the car said. "I got a text from Susan. We need to get back to the base."

"One second, Sergeant." She cast a long-distance smile at Jack. *Soon.*

With that, she climbed back into the car. "We definitely don't want to keep the admiral waiting."

*

ABOUT THE AUTHOR

William Nikkel is the author of nine *Jack Ferrell* novels and two steampunk, westerns featuring his latest hero Max Traver. A former homicide detective and S.W.A.T. team member for the Kern County Sheriff's Department in Bakersfield, California, William is an amateur scuba enthusiast, gold prospector, and wildlife artist who can be found just about anywhere. He and his wife Karen divide their time between Northern California and Maui, Hawaii.

GLIMMER OF GOLD
A JACK FERRELL ADVENTURE

**The Discovery of WWII West Point Class Ring
Leads to Sex, Murder** and Revenge

Jack Ferrell is engaged to a rich drop-dead gorgeous blonde Ellery Seaport and living rent-free in the guest cottage at her parent's house on Maui. Most men would consider him one of the luckiest guys alive.

But is he?

Free diving on a reef off the south coast of Maui, Jack spies something small and round—like a golden eye gleaming at him from the coral—and makes a grab for it. Back aboard his Zodiac, he discovers he's found a 1941 West Point class ring with the initials C. W. M. inscribed on inside of the band.

While struggling with his failing relationship and his new job working for his fiancée's father, an unscrupulous developer, Jack sets out to find the soldier who lost the ring—a quest that leads him to Charles William McIntyre. But it's not until he gets a phone call from McIntyre's twenty-seven-year-old granddaughter Katie that he learns the ring's secret.

"This proves my dad was telling the truth," she says. "He didn't kill my mother."

The ring is evidence needed to support her father's alibi, and Jack's statement is crucial. To help secure her father's release from prison, he joins Katie in Henderson, Nevada where she lives. But it's not that easy. Someone is willing to kill to keep her father behind bars. As Jack and Katie race to stay a step ahead of the killer, they put their lives on the line to discover the identity of the man responsible for her mother's murder and the truth behind her death.

"Great story, great adventure, great new writer!"
—James Rollins, *New York Times* Bestselling Author of "Blood Line"

NIGHT MARCHERS
A JACK FERRELL ADVENTURE

A Dying Old Man's Request Leads to Treachery, Death, and Lost Treasure

Kealakekua Bay, the Big Island of Hawaii, February 1779
Enraged warriors attack. Ten minutes later, Captain Cook lay dead on the beach, his body hacked to pieces. His attempt to ransom King Kalaniopuu for the return of a boat stolen by the natives for its iron has cost the renowned explorer his life. One week later, Cook's remains are buried at sea. His spinal column, ribs, sword, and uniform were never recovered.

South of Necker Island, Northwestern Hawaiian Islands, Present day
A tiger shark attacks. Marine biologist Jack Ferrell plunges his dive knife into a coal-black eye. That afternoon, a floatplane lands next to the NOAA research vessel Albatross. Jack's friend Robert Foster has come at the desperate request of Jack's former girlfriend, Katie McIntyre. Her grandfather is dying, and it's imperative he talks to Jack.

Katie's grandfather Charles tells Jack an incredible tale about Hawaiian antiquities—including the bones of King Kalaniopuu and the final remains of Captain Cook—stolen by a soldier during WW II and lost inside a lava tube on the island of Kahoolawe. A story Charles McIntyre dismissed until Coleman Treadway—a ruthless antiquities dealer claiming to be the soldier's grandson—showed up asking questions.

Now Katie's grandfather wants Jack to find the relics and return them to the Hawaiian people before Treadway can get his hands on them.

Jack's promise to fulfill the old man's dying request propels him, Katie, and Robert into a deadly race for the treasure, but it's no easy task. Not only is Treadway willing to kill to satisfy his insatiable greed, but Kahoolawe is a restricted island littered with unexploded ordnance and home to Jack's most dreaded foe of all, the legendary ghost marcher of the night.

CAVE DWELLER
A JACK FERRELL ADVENTURE

Two civilizations collide in a subterranean world
December 7, 1941, Pearl Harbor: Five Japanese two-man mini-subs speed toward the mouth of the harbor. Four mini-subs are sunk or captured. The fate of the fifth sub, *I-16*, is unknown.

Late at night, nearly three quarters of a century later: Marine biologist Jack Ferrell sails into a mysterious fog off of Kauai's Na Pali coast.

Dense fog banks don't form in Hawaii . . . or so he thought. They certainly don't glow in the dark.

Concealed within the mist is the sloop *Julie Ann* floundering in a rogue remnant of drift net. A young woman's scream pierces the damp air, and he rushes to her rescue.

The next morning, Jack dives to check the damage done to the reef by the net and discovers a sunken WWII Japanese mini-sub and the answer to a Pearl Harbor enigma: the fate of I-16. But in a depression in the coral, lies a greater mystery: a human skull the size of a grapefruit.

Through a colleague, he learns the skull is from an extinct species of child-sized human being that lived 12,000 years ago on the remote Indonesian island of Flores. But this skull is no 12,000-year-old fossil

In search of answers, Jack, the woman from the *Julie Ann*, two close friends, and a select team of scientists plunge into a subterranean world deep within the rugged mountains of the mystical Na Pali coast. And what should have been a routine scientific excursion becomes a deadly encounter with the unknown and a race against time when the expedition battles the elements, personal fears, and even one of their own to unearth the key to the origin of the skull and the surprising truth behind one of Hawaii's famous legends: *The Menehune.*

MURRIETA GOLD
A JACK FERRELL ADVENTURE

A Century-old Tale Leads to a Fortune in Bandit Gold
Jack Ferrell clutches a cryptic e-mail his brother Deacon sent days earlier when he wrote of treasure hunting and buried gold. Now Deacon's missing. And the authorities won't get involved. For Jack, a single objective remains.

Find his brother.

Deacon's trail leads Jack to the Historical California gold-rush town of Angels Camp. There he talks to Al Brink, a local drunk Deacon mentioned in his notes. Al tells Jack a story he told Deacon—a wild-west tale about a stagecoach robbery committed on the road outside of town in 1862 in which the legendary bandit Joaquin Murrieta and his gang of killers made off with three hundred pounds of gold bars destined for the San Francisco mint. Gold that Murrieta allegedly hid in the nearby mountains during his getaway.

An interesting wild-west yarn and one Jack would've believed if not for the historical fact Joaquin Murrieta was killed in 1853 by Captain Love of the California Rangers, his head placed in a jar of brandy and put on display in San Francisco. But Al swears history got it wrong—Murrieta was alive to commit the robbery in 1862, and that Deacon believed it as well.

Find the gold, find Deacon.

Jack sets out to retrace the fabled bandit's footsteps. Then he meets Theresa Montero, Murrieta's great, great, great granddaughter. The two of them join forces, and with the aid of valuable clues provided by Ms. Montero's family bible, they embark on a quest for the gold.

For Jack, it's to find his brother. For Theresa, it's to set history straight.

BLOOD GOLD
A JACK FERRELL ADVENTURE

Death, Murder, and Greed in the Guyanese Jungle
Marine biologist Jack Ferrell is in Guyana, South America conducting research into an increase in shark attacks when he witnesses a man violently assault a beautiful woman. He rushes to her rescue and afterwards discovers the woman is a part of an international research team analyzing water samples at the request of the government.

The only explanation for the woman's attempted murder is that the person behind the attack doesn't want the research team to expose the source of the deadly toxins killing the Mazaruni River.

Jack is quick to discover the shark attacks and the water pollution are connected. And when his two close friends join him expecting a leisure holiday, the three of them are immediately drawn into a deadly cat-and-mouse game as they race against time to stop the man behind the poisonous tide. A pursuit that takes them deep into the Guyanese jungle where a modern-day gold rush is destroying the rainforest and men kill for the riches buried there.

"Brings plenty of wild action to an exotic setting."
—Thomas Perry, *New York Times* Bestselling Author of "A String of Beads"

TIBETAN GOLD
A JACK FERRELL NOVELLA

Deception and Resolve Lead to the Recovery of a Golden Idol
Marine biologist Jack Ferrell is on the beach on Maui loading supplies in his Zodiac in preparation to drive his friend's new boat to Oahu. He hears a woman scream and sees two rough-looking men chasing her on the beach.

It only takes him a second to decide these are not good men.

He waves her into his waiting Zodiac and takes her to his friend's boat. Safely on board, she tells him the two men chasing her had stolen a golden idol from a collection of antiquities that belonged to her father who died suspiciously. And that she traced the thieves to Maui and stole it back from them. The problem is, she tossed it into the sea to prevent them from reclaiming it.

There's a chance the precious statue can be recovered and he agrees to go after the idol. A relatively routine task until he finds himself fighting for his life when the thieves come after the girl. And he's the only person standing between her and certain death.

"William Nikkel definitely knows how to kick butt and take names. He's a gifted storyteller."
—Steve Berry, *New York Times* Bestselling Author of "The 14th Colony"

SHIPWRECK
A JACK FERRELL ADVENTURE

Death and Vengeance in Paradise

Jack Ferrell never expected to hook a body. When he embarks on a mission to catch and tag a great white plaguing Hawaiian fisherman, he is put to the test, physically and emotionally, in his most challenging adventure yet as he plunges into the treacherous water off the coast of Lanai in an area known as Shipwreck Beach.

A mission that reunites him with a former lover, Dana Mores.

As they head toward disaster, an unfortunate turn of events leaves Jack and his friends marked for death with "Shipwreck" exploding into one of the most dangerous and suspenseful adventures of his career. One that marks a major turning point in his life and leaves him a different kind of man.

" 'Shipwreck' is the perfect blend of mystery and adventure. An engaging, fast-paced thriller with a fascinating and fun hero."
—Allison Brennan, *New York Times* Bestselling Author of "Poisonous"

SAILOR TAKE WARNING
A JACK FERRELL ADVENTURE

Coin Fraud, Blackmail, and Lost Treasure

Jack Ferrell is spending time at Lake Tahoe. All he wants is a break from Hawaii to put Dana Mores death behind him. But a twenty-dollar gold piece, thrust into his hand by a dying man draws him into the enigma surrounding the coin.

But he's not prepared to stick around. Then his brother Deacon asks him to help a lady friend out of a jam. A brief interlude of indiscretion has left pretty, dark-haired, Melissa Martinelli the victim of blackmail.

He's ready to turn the fake coin over to law enforcement, bring about a quick end to the blackmail scheme, and return to Hawaii when he discovers a clue leading to a century-and-a-half old cache of stolen gold. A trail that entangles him in a web of violence and death in the seedy world of coin fraud, blackmail, and lost treasure. Making him the target of a vengeance-driven man named Ryan Chambers who wants the gold, and Jack's head on a platter. But nobody wants that more than Chambers' nephew, Paul Davidson.

"A mysterious gold coin . . . a murderous inferno . . . and a story that roars like an F-16. Nikkel is a true master of the thriller, so crack open 'Sailor Take Warning' and be prepared to stay wide awake till the very last word. Yes, it *IS* that good."
—Bestselling Author Shane Gericke, "The Fury"

SEA OF HEARTBREAK
A JACK FERRELL ADVENTURE

Murder, Drug Violence, and Lost Treasure

In 1945, a B-17 bomber takes off from Manilla carrying a gift to General Douglas MacArthur from the Philippine president. The plane disappears.

Until now. Jack Ferrell rescues Allison Hunter who'd been pushed overboard by her husband and left to drown. He takes her ashore in Waikiki, reluctant to get involved. She's not his problem to fix. Or is she? When his boat explodes under suspicious circumstances and she's killed, the situation turns personal.

He sets out to settle the score, and is reunited with the beguiling and mysterious Cherise Venetta. Through her, he learns the surprising truth behind her reason for being on Oahu. And the possible location of a gold-plated sub-machine gun that disappeared on a flight to Pearl Harbor nearly seventy-five years earlier. Working together, they become embroiled in a plot to bring down a major drug trafficker. A deadly trail that re-enforces what he already knows. When he's on the edge, he's completely alive.

"The much-appreciated return of Jack Ferrell serves up a smorgasbord of deceit and duplicitousness across a landscape steeped in classic crime noir. William Nikkel seems to be channeling his inner Don Winslow in crafting a book that is equal parts Raymond Chandler, Elmore Leonard, and John D. McDonald. Travis Magee has nothing on Jack Ferrell and Nikkel is every bit the equal of the genre greats 'Sailor Take Warning' emulates. Be warned: You won't be able to put it down!"

—Jon Land, *USA Today* Bestselling Author

www.ingramcontent.com/pod-product-compliance
Lightning Source LLC
Chambersburg PA
CBHW070058120726
47909CB00002B/424